Praise for Orrin Grey's *How to See Ghosts & Other Figments*

"*How to See Ghosts & Other Figments* by Orrin Grey conjures forth more monsters, ghouls and ghosts than any midnight horror show in memory, but with real emotional depths to back them up. It's like peering through the eye holes of a cheap Halloween monster mask to see the tangible and very human sadness lurking just beneath."

—Trevor Henderson, Illustrator

Praise for Orrin Grey's *Guignol & Other Sardonic Tales*

"In this career-spanning collection, Grey assembles 14 peculiar tales of horror into a veritable smorgasbord of horrific thrills and chills. [...] This collection is a must-read for hardcore fans of horror..."

—*Publishers Weekly*

"In his third and arguably best collection, Orrin Grey spreads his black wings and takes us on a thrill ride into his limitless imagination. Through musty attics and mist-shrouded crypts, down soot-choked chimneys and into mysterious portals to faraway planets we ride, emerging at the end buzzing, a little dizzy, and most certainly changed. Cinematic, dark, and daring, *Guignol* is a book that will bring out the monster in you...and let it feed."

—Matthew M. Bartlett, author of *Gateways to Abomination* and *Of Doomful Portent*

"To say that Orrin Grey is a phenomenal writer is like saying the Phantom of the Opera knew his way around a pipe organ. Nobody evokes classic terrors while simultaneously offering a melancholy, beautifully macabre world as brilliantly as Grey."

—Christopher Slatsky, author of *Alectryomancer and Other Weird Tales*

Praise for Orrin Grey's *Painted Monsters & Other Strange Beasts*

"*Painted Monsters & Other Strange Beasts* is a fantastic follow-up to Grey's first collection, *Never Bet the Devil.* This is the kind of writing that shows what can still be done with the classical weird."
—Laird Barron, author of *The Beautiful Thing That Awaits Us All*

"This is an outstanding collection, one to which you will return again and again long after the house lights have come up."
—Daniel Mills, author of *The Lord Came at Twilight*

"The horror genre is a many-splintered thing. Grey collects those splinters, mixes and matches them, concocting a beast of a collection that is as fun as it is scary, as charming as it is chilling."
—Philip Gelatt, director of *They Remain*

"In his latest collection, Orrin Grey not only pays homage to the classic horror films of yesteryear, he tears down the silver screen to reveal the true horrors that lurk on the other side. Fans of H. P. Lovecraft, Vincent Price, and the Hammer horror films will feel right at home."
—Ian Rogers, author of *Every House Is Haunted*

"If you're looking for something between Ray Bradbury's headlong genre-bending fabulist glee and the *Insidious* movie franchise's unapologetic vaudeville creep, then Grey's your man."
—Gemma Files, author of *Experimental Film*

"Orrin Grey's roots (or should I say tentacles?) run deep, squeezing the best from horrors both classic and obscure, twisting them in his own particular way. He's a fine storyteller who'll pull you in, and so will *Painted Monsters*. Don't miss it!"
—Norman Partridge, author of *Dark Harvest*

HOW TO SEE GHOSTS
& OTHER FIGMENTS

Other books by Orrin Grey

Anthologies:

Fungi (with Silvia Moreno-Garcia)

Chapbooks:

Gardinel's Real Estate (with M. S. Corley)
The Mysterious Flame

Collections:

Never Bet the Devil & Other Warnings
Painted Monsters & Other Strange Beasts
Guignol & Other Sardonic Tales

HOW TO SEE GHOSTS
& OTHER FIGMENTS

ORRIN GREY

WORD HORDE
PETALUMA, CA

Cover design by Scott R. Jones

Edited by Ross E. Lockhart

First Edition

ISBN: 978-1-956252-05-7

A Word Horde Book
www.wordhorde.com

TABLE OF CONTENTS

For every single old-timey stage magician
who had one of those posters where they
claimed they talked with spirits or whatever.

"If you wish to see strange things
I have the power to show them to you."

—*The Magician* (1926)

INTRODUCTION: FATHER OF MONSTERS

BY SILVIA MORENO-GARCIA

A mix of nostalgia and grotesquerie imbues the fiction of Orrin Grey who is, in true vintage tradition, one of those rare birds: a short storyteller. It's not that authors don't write short stories these days, but that most look forward to swiftly making the jump to novels. Grey, however, seems delighted to bounce from anthology to anthology, magazine to magazine. The result is an incredibly prolific writer who has penned not one, but three collections already: *Guignol & Other Sardonic Tales*, *Painted Monsters & Other Strange Beasts* and *Never Bet the Devil & Other Warnings*.

Had he been around in the glory days of the pulps, Grey would have made it into *Weird Tales* and shared a table of contents with the stars of the 1930s: Lovecraft, Howard, C.L. Moore, etc. One can picture stories such as "The Big, Dark House by the Sea" or "Prehistoric Animals" printed with lurid black-and-white illustrations by Virgil Finlay.

However, move the dial a little more, place him in the 1950s or the 1960s, in the era of the double feature and B movies, and Grey would have probably cobbled together a considerable filmography as a screenwriter for Roger Corman. Now we must imagine him as a name on a movie poster, with the words "Amicus Productions" or "Hammer Films" at the bottom. Now we must see the bright yellow letters and garish screaming faces on the lobby cards for "The Cult and the Canary."

Movies and the entertainment industry, after all, are one of the threads that keep reappearing in his fiction. His protagonists often include old movie actors, special effects experts who have been replaced with computers, and the like. They are two steps from the silver screen, from the limelight, whether they work in the entertainment industry, or merely consume it.

Nostalgia is another characteristic of Grey's stories. With VHS tapes or references to Full Moon Video and stop-motion effects, Grey often looks at the past. His characters wander through penny arcades and amusement parks. In a time and age in which people are more likely to take selfies on Instagram, dance on TikTok or stream TV shows on Netflix, his characters seemed removed from our world and out of time. Tied to this nostalgia is a sense of loss and sadness, and a certain tenderness which extends to monsters and creatures of the night.

That is the third characteristic of Grey's tales: the monsters and the monstrous, which are sometimes not the same. It is perhaps not surprising that a man who can be recognizable by his online, perpetual icon of a skeleton should be comfortable in the presence of ghouls and lake monsters.

This doesn't mean there isn't horror in Grey's tales, that the monstrous is perpetually embraced, like a beloved teddy bear. But the grotesque and the beautiful sometimes entwine, and the sublime might drive you mad, whether it comes in the form of an album or a game.

Horror has, since the 1990s, been something of an underground space. The demise of large imprints gave way to a vast ecosystem of mini-presses, print-on-demand anthologies, zines and oddball chapbooks. Money is scarce in horror, and perhaps that gives it a bit of its punk aesthetic.

Had Orrin Grey made his debut in the late 1970s or the 1980s, he might have been another Clive Barker, basking in the horror boom of the era, producing an iconic medley of short fiction, and would have been snapped up by one of the big imprints.

But Grey popped up in the horror scene in the 2000s, when the horror boom had been exhausted, and as a result has lurked in shadows and hidden spaces, as have most horror writers. It is only in the last handful of years that large imprints have turned their eyes to this often-maligned genre and began looking at it again with interest.

It is fitting that a man so dedicated to looking for the alien, who writes about the ones who lurk in the darkness, should appear on the scene in the era when horror was the realm of the outsider.

The future cannot be predicted. Tomorrow, we might get a second horror boom and Orrin Grey might be picked up by one of the Big Five presses. He might end up writing story treatments for streaming services. He could continue to dedicate his time and effort to the production of dozens of more short stories and assemble even more collections. Whatever happens, though, we are lucky to have an Orrin Grey, a graceful unique, distinctive father of monsters. It is a special alchemy that allowed for his appearance, like a wild mushroom upon a wilted landscape, and which may never come again.

Silvia Moreno-Garcia

HOW TO SEE GHOSTS

(or Surely Bring Them to You)

Outside, the haunted houses are loud, garish, crowded. The night air smells like kettle corn and cotton candy and the reek of stale smoke. A werewolf stalks by, ten feet tall on hydraulic stilts as Lily squeaks and points, grabbing Gavin's arm. I'm not looking at the werewolf, though. I'm looking to Gavin, as always, watching to see how he reacts.

The line shifts forward and everyone jostles ahead a step. The dark is made light by the sodium glow of streetlamps and the bare bulbs of trailers selling funnel cakes and hot dogs.

Every Halloween, we do this, or something like it. Me and Trent and Gavin and whatever girl Gavin is dating; Lily this time. We've done it since high school. Sometimes Trent brings a girl, sometimes not. I've never brought a guy, though, and if Gavin or Trent have ever wondered why, they've never asked.

Inside, the haunted houses are all smoke machines and blasts of sudden air and animatronic puppets lunging out of dark nooks. We go to them almost every year, and they're a little bit different every time.

We shuffle around in dark labyrinths, laughing, coughing, reaching out to grasp one another by the sleeve or a fistful of material from the back of a shirt. Even when the lights are up, the smoke is so thick that visibility is limited to a few hazy feet. Weird shapes

In every telling, the ghost's appearance was the same: a rough and indistinct figure, its head smothered in some pale cloth with uneven holes or smudges for eyes and mouth, bound all over in chains that can sometimes be heard dragging along the halls at night. Much more Dickensian than any of the comparatively prosaic murdered gangsters or spectral newlyweds on offer at the other establishments.

The best part, though? It has no history. No tale of specific woe or pain. No name. Though everyone agrees on the ghost itself—on its appearance and manners—no one has any idea who or what it is the ghost *of*.

Inside the hotel, our room has been renovated into a suite arrangement, with two bedrooms extending off a central sitting room that looks considerably more modern than the halls or the foyer. One bedroom is for Lily and Gavin, one for Trent and myself. Nothing but sleeping will happen in the bed I share with Trent. He's straight and, even if he wasn't, he's not the one I want.

There's a minibar and I offer to go get ice. Gavin stands up to come with me and I don't stammer, I don't even think I blush, but I can't stop myself from wondering *why*. Is there something he wants to tell me in private, away from the others?

As we let ourselves out, I hope for a quiet aside about how annoying Lily is being tonight, but I don't get anything except a breezy comment about the quality of the haunted houses. As we're walking down the hall, over the red-and-green carpet, I imagine seeing the ghost. My ears strain for the distant clanking of chains as I picture that shuddering form slipping around the next corner.

I wonder, if it did appear, would it change anything? Would Gavin touch me? Grab me? Would he be angry if I grabbed him?

Too soon, we're back at the door of the room, the ice bucket full. Trent is pouring drinks as I get out the stereo we brought along, the CD I burned for the occasion. It's mostly spooky ambient music, but the first track is something else. Something I found just for this.

It crackles, like an old record played on a phonograph and then the unmistakable voice of Vincent Price comes on. "How to see ghosts or surely bring them to you," he says, followed by some ominous music. "This part of the book is for children who were born in the morning or around lunchtime. If you were born at midnight—some say just at twilight—you were probably born with the gift of being able to see ghosts and other spirits and don't have to be told how."

The track is taken from an audiobook that Price released in 1976, its title borrowed from an Arkham House book of weird poetry by Leah Bodine Drake. *A Hornbook for Witches*. I know these things because that's my role in the group.

Everyone is quiet as Uncle Vinnie speaks. Lily starts to giggle, but Gavin moves and she stops. I'm hovering near the stereo and everyone's eyes are on me but, for the moment, I don't care. For the moment there is only Vincent Price's perfect voice, coiling out of the speakers like narcotic smoke. This is what I planned everything else around, the moment I've been waiting for all night, and I let myself treasure it, closing my own eyes to let those words curl up around me in the dark.

"Just say you aren't scared," that famous voice finishes, after a few minutes. "Just say how brave and nonchalant you'd be if you ever saw a ghost, and see what happens."

Once the track is over, I bring out the Ouija board. Lily is actually the one who brought it. She turned out to be the only one of us who already owned one. It's not a real Ouija board. It's a "talking board," off-brand, one of the *Buffy the Vampire Slayer* ones they put out when the show was still popular. It's not optimal—the YES and NO are at the bottom of the board, and I had to glue felt onto the legs of the planchette so that it would slide—but it should do.

We all pull the chairs closer together and sit with the board across our knees. Gavin's knee brushes against mine, and the touch burns through my jeans. The lights are dim, the music is playing quietly now, barely there. We place our hands on the planchette, draw in our breath, and wait. Nothing happens.

"Maybe we need to prime the pump," Trent says, and I nod, knowing he's right.

"If there are any spirits present in the room," I say, "we reach out to you now. We are open to you, receptive. We are here for any messages that you may wish to impart from the other side."

There's a quiet, nervous titter from Lily, a deep breath from Trent. Nothing. Then, a sound? Was that breathing one of the others, or something else? Did they hear it? Was that distant dragging in the hall outside, or only on the CD? I wish, now, that I hadn't included the music, but I had thought that it would help make the others more inclined to sit the séance out.

"Aren't we supposed to, like, ask it a question or something?" Lily asks, after a few more heartbeats, and the planchette shudders, moves. "Are you guys doing that?"

Of course, I know how Ouija boards work. Combined suggestion, subtle muscle movements, expectation, all working together in the service of simulating intelligence where there is only a hopeful longing. But I forget all that as the planchette shifts, stutters across the board, reaches a letter and stops.

"I," Lily reads aloud.

The planchette jerks, jumps again, slides along, moves to another letter, stops. Have the lights gotten dimmer?

"M," Trent says.

"I'm," I proffer faintly, half-afraid that to speak any louder will be to break the spell.

The planchette doesn't rest there, though. It continues its jittering dance across the board. H-O-R. Did the room just get colder? Is there a smell in the air now that wasn't there before, like the inside of a freezer? I hold my breath.

The planchette moves to N, but never reaches Y before Lily

starts giggling and everyone else realizes what's happening. Her giggling turns to laughter, and she falls back in her chair, the board slipping off our knees and the planchette from beneath our fingers to bounce across the carpet.

I want to hit her. To split her lip so she tastes blood. Much more than that, though, I want Gavin to be pissed, to stand up in disgust. Instead, he just shrugs. He looks at me, and I don't know what the look in his eyes is until he puts a hand on my shoulder. "It was a good idea," he says, and suddenly I know that the look is pity.

There was a time when I would have treasured just about any look that turned his eyes my way, but not tonight. Tonight, I can't handle pity, so I resolve not to be pitiable. "It was a dumb idea," I say back, "but it seemed Halloween-y."

From there, the night goes the only way it can—to drinking and bullshitting and, inexorably, to Gavin and Lily making out on the couch and then from the couch to their bedroom. Trent and I sit for a while longer, drinking and turning up the music so we can't hear the sounds that are coming from behind the closed door.

I think about kissing Trent, about trying. He might be drunk enough. Not because I want to, but because I want *anything*, anything at all except for this. I want to be kissing *someone*, rather than staring like a puppy after Gavin. I'm disgusted at myself. For my longing, for thinking these thoughts. I take another drink, and Trent mutters something about crashing for the night as he disappears into the other bedroom.

I turn off most of the lights and sit in the near-dark, looking out the window at the city below. Eventually, the CD reaches the end and it's quiet. The sounds from behind Gavin and Lily's door have stopped, and I hope that means they'll stay stopped for the rest of the night. I haven't had enough to drink, or maybe I've had too much.

Rising, I drift across the window and into the bathroom. A pale apparition stares back at me from the mirror, weighed down in chains that he's forged himself, link by link.

I run water into my cupped hands and splash it on my face, but it does little to clarify my thoughts or feelings. I go back out to the window and stand behind the curtains, staring out into the night.

Somewhere, I know, a few straggling kids are maybe trailing home in store-bought masks and bedsheets with holes cut for eyes. Somewhere, kids too old for treats are shrieking their way through the haunted houses or making out in the back seats of cars. And somewhere, I imagine, *real* magic is happening. Real ghosts are haunting real houses. But I don't see them. Because, for all the methods that Mr. Price enumerated for seeing ghosts, wanting to so badly that you feel hollowed out from longing wasn't one of them.

Author's Notes:

There's a quote, from Joey Comeau's review of *The Innkeepers*—a movie that had a big impact on writing this story—where he's talking about playing Bloody Mary. "There's something really satisfying about the desire to terrorize yourself," he writes, "because it also feels like it will be worth it if those bloody fingers come through the mirror and wrap around your throat. The world will be so much more magical and interesting, and so you kind of hope that it does work."

Even long before I read those words, that was essentially the operating principle behind much of my own writing, and much of why I watch horror movies and read scary stories in the first place. And there are few places where that ache for there to be something truly supernatural in the world—even, maybe especially, if it is also terrifying—comes to the fore more than in this, one of the only stories I've ever written without any speculative elements.

More than a few times, I've considered revising this one to add in more of a concrete haunting, but I actually think that would ruin the story. The horror here is that there isn't any horror—and maybe that's worse.

THE BIG, DARK HOUSE BY THE SEA

Muriel Linscomb was a fake mermaid in Cooper's Traveling Menagerie. She spent her nights sitting in a bathtub, topless, a rubber fish tail stuck over her legs with spirit gum and tape. For five hours a night she sat there, her skin puckering from the water, waving at the people who passed by, people she couldn't see because of a sheet of plexiglass and the bright lights that dazzled her eyes.

She didn't see Albert Winslow on the night he came to the show, but he saw her. No one knows what made him go, and no one knows how much he offered Mr. Cooper that night in his trailer, but everyone knows that the next morning, Albert Winslow owned Cooper's Traveling Menagerie, and it never traveled again.

That was the last night Muriel ever spent in the bathtub and the rubber tail. Within a month, she was Muriel Winslow. The rest of the show was dismantled, the performers given their severance and sent on their way.

No one in town was surprised to see Albert Winslow take a young, pretty wife, and those few who saw her didn't deny that Muriel *was* very pretty. Why she consented to the union was anyone's guess, but most guesses involved Albert's considerable fortune. Still, everyone agreed that the state of matrimony did him much more good than her.

He was seen in town more often, and those who saw him said that he looked younger and in better health than he ever had in their memory. Perhaps once a week he was seen to stop into one of the local taverns and buy a round for everyone in the place. His old miserliness seemed to have departed, and his famous temper was reserved now for his intense, jealous possessiveness of his beautiful young wife. Any man who made the mistake of so much as mentioning her was sure to feel, at the very least, the full effect of Albert Winslow's withering gaze.

As for Muriel herself, few people in town ever saw her. After the wedding, she moved into his big, dark house by the sea and seldom left again, though people walking along the beach sometimes claimed to see her standing with her hand pressed against the glass of the big front window, staring longingly out across the water. They said that the years had taken their toll on her, that her once-shining hair was now wispy and white, and her face looked prematurely drawn and old.

Time passed, and Muriel was seen less and less, until after a while no one ever saw her again, and even Albert Winslow's newfound vivaciousness began to desert him. He was seen to walk first with a cane, and then later it was reported that he was using a wheelchair to get around. Finally, he stopped coming to town at all. The mail piled up on his porch and, eventually, the sheriff went down and broke open the big, dark house by the sea.

They discovered Albert's body in his wheelchair, sitting in the parlor, facing out the big window toward the ocean. Of Muriel there was no sign at all, but in the basement of the house they found a big glass tank full of seawater, and a polished black coffin containing the carefully arranged bones of an enormous fish.

Author's Notes:

Not quite the shortest published piece I've ever written—that plum goes to the title story of my first collection, at only around 150 words—this one has a weird history. For a long time, the only place it existed was on an episode of the podcast *Professor Gruntsplatter's Spookatorium*, where I read it aloud during an interview. Years later, I dusted it off for the program guide for the Outer Dark Symposium on the Greater Weird, where it received a teeny illustration by my esteemed cover illustrator, Nick Gucker.

Aside from that, though, this is its first time in print. It's an odd little thing—probably inspired, not for the first or last time, by flicks like *Night Tide* and *The She Creature*—but I like it.

THE CULT AND THE CANARY

They all came out to hear the Canary sing. The men in their tall hats and the women in their diamonds and furs. They arrived in long, black cars at the front doors of that house on the bayou and there, in the parlor, they waited in the half-dark until she appeared, in that yellow dress trimmed in black lace.

The lights were bright where she sang, even while the rest of the room was choked in shadow. When she appeared, the room went quiet, no matter what had been transpiring before. The hush seemed to spread out from her, like a ripple through the water.

Sometimes, there were those who were new to the big, old house, and they would continue talking, or even laughing at the silence, especially if they had imbibed perhaps a bit more than their limit. These would then be hushed by their neighbors and friends, or else bundled out of the place by one of the big men, their knotted fists belying the crispness of their tuxedos.

"Get some air," the men would say, pushing the offender out into the dark of the swamp, beyond the light that spilled from those other rooms of the house, where cooks and servers still went about their work.

When the Canary sang, then, the room was still. It always began the same way. Just her voice, a capella, a single note that seemed to thrum in the air. There were those later who said that they could *see* it, burning above her. Then it was joined by another, and another, her voice seeming to layer over the top of itself, one voice becoming many.

Finally, her song was joined by the piano that sat in the twilight to one side, by the man on the upright bass, by the soft piping of a clarinet. Later, those who came to listen would try, in vain, to remember the words of the Canary's songs. "They were sad," one woman would say to her man. "She was longing for someone, something … no, some *place*, far away, maybe long ago. Maybe all three," another would say.

"There were names," one man opined, smoking his pipe in the back seat of the car on the road back to the city. "Familiar and yet foreign."

"She was calling out to the Hyades to bring rain," said one.

"No, it was the hydra," claimed another.

At times, these disputes would come to blows. Blood would be shed. At least one man died. Yet, this violence was never within the house. Those who came to hear the Canary sing left there always in a kind of quiet daze, however irreverent their attitudes had been before.

Of course, there were some who played at such irreverence still. "She was good, I'll admit," said one critic from the city, who had come to listen to the underground sensation, "but I wouldn't go back." Within three weeks, he was dead in a gutter, his kidney punctured, his wallet gone. "A robbery," said the police, but "the Sign," said some who had been to the house.

Once, a man, overcome, tried to mount the makeshift stage in the midst of the Canary's performance. There was, after all, little enough to separate her from the guests. She stood in a sort of solarium off the parlor; only three short steps up from where the guests lounged on divans or crowded around small tables. When she arrived to sing, she came through a door that led out to the gardens. None who listened knew where she had been before that.

This man who rushed the stage, he was sitting at one of the tables nearest her. His tuxedo jacket was off, the cuffs of his stiff shirt undone. He was young, his hair dark and slicked back. He had been lolling indolently in his seat, but when the Canary began to sing, he sat up straighter, then straighter still, until he was so rigid that he seemed to be almost levitating from his chair.

Finally, he said a single word—witnesses later disputed its exact nature, claiming that he spoke in Spanish or possibly French, that he said "carissimus" or that the word he spoke was, in fact, a name—and rose to his feet, climbing the steps without looking at them, his eyes never wavering from the Canary; or possibly from a point just above her head.

No one came to intercede with him. Though the big men with their knotted fists seemed always to appear from nowhere whenever there was trouble, now there was not one near enough. The man made it up to the top step. His shoe was there. The Canary did not stop singing, but those who were sitting closest later said that there was fear in her dark eyes.

"She thought he was going to attack her," said one of the women to her friend later, "yet she never faltered. Like that band on the boat that sank, you know the one."

With his foot on the top step, however, so close that he could have reached out and touched the Canary, put his hands on her slender arms, cupped his palm against her dark cheek, he stopped. He wavered there, that's how those who saw it later described his movements. "It was like a ripple passed through him," said one man in the club the following afternoon, "my hand to God."

Then he lurched, not forward but to one side, like a ship that scrapes against the rocks. That foot slipped from the top step, he went down onto one knee there, his hands reaching out, not to the Canary's slender arms, but to his own face, where they came away red with blood. Then he collapsed at her feet.

Two of the big men came and gathered him up. Some say that

they took him outside for air, as they did the drunks and those who were too rowdy. Others claim that his body is sunk somewhere in the swamp, food for the gators.

Regardless of his fate, the Canary sang on, and not one person in the crowd stood to leave until she had finished. Later, some would claim that they saw another woman, standing in the doorway to the garden. The one through which the big men carried the fallen man; the one through which the Canary always entered.

"She was standing in the shadows, so it was hard to see," one reported to her girlfriend later, her voice a confidential whisper. "She was dressed real fine, with a beaded black shawl across her shoulders. But it looked like maybe she was wearing a mask."

Among those who came to listen to the Canary, there were some who later received anonymous letters. Never in the post, the letters were always delivered by hand, though the final recipient never saw the deliverer. Always, a spouse, a housemate, a friend, a valet would tell them, "This came for you today," and hand them a piece of parchment paper, folded into thirds and marked with a strange symbol, rather like three *punctus interrogativus* sharing the same period.

"What could it mean?" the recipient would ask, but the person handing them the unknown missive could never offer even a guess.

If asked to describe the individual who had hand-delivered the letter, they would find themselves equally at loose ends. "Nothing much to say," they would reply. "He was here and then he was gone."

When the recipient read the letter—which they always felt compelled to do while alone, even though the paper was simply folded, with nothing to stop prying eyes—they staggered back against the wall, dropped the letter to the floor, let their reading glasses fall to their laps. Then, inevitably, when they had recovered from their indisposition, they would burn the paper, and watch the strange purple-yellow flame that resulted.

These individuals would then always drive back to the old house back in the bayou, where they would walk up to the door and let the knocker rise and fall not once, not twice, but three times. This they would do in the middle of the day, not during the dark of night, when they came to hear the Canary sing. A big man would open the door and they would disappear inside.

Some sent their drivers on back to town, with word that they would call when they needed a ride. Others bid their drivers wait there, and those who pulled their cars to the graveled lot along one side of the house found that there were others there, waiting too. When this had happened on several different days, those drivers took the opportunity to strike up games of poker or faro on the hoods of their waiting vehicles.

Inside the house, the returning visitors would be shown, not to the parlor where the Canary sang, but to a much smaller room, though equally dim. More so, perhaps. Its only illumination a bulb buried under thick red glass, painting everything in a chiaroscuro of scarlet and shadow. There they would be told to take a seat, and the door closed firmly behind them.

In the small room was a table, draped with black lace over a white cloth. On the nearer side was sometimes only a single wooden chair, sometimes two or even three. At times, those who were shown into the room were the first to arrive, while at others they were joining those already there—strangers, perhaps, or people they knew from their regular, daytime lives. Always so dimly-illuminated that their features were all but impossible to make out.

Once everyone had taken their seat, a woman would appear on the far side of the table. None could later say whether a door had opened to provide her entrance, or whether she had always been there, invisible somehow in the shadows. Most were reluctant to speak of it at all.

"I think she was in a wheelchair," one later said, in the madhouse. "I think she must have been. She came forward so quietly, so soft. But her face … oh God forgive me …."

Her face must have been a mask, they all told themselves later, and whether they could believe it or not determined whether they should ever sleep soundly again. It looked, in the dim glow, like it was made of chewed paper, the eyes and the mouth simply black smudges, holes from which some glittering darkness peered.

Of what was said to them in that dark room, none would ever speak. Not those who were thrown into cells and given the third degree, not those who later died raving. That the woman spoke, though, there is no doubt, and she also brought from one voluminous black sleeve a deck of cards, painted on some heavy vellum and older than the fledgling nation in which they all met.

These she would turn over, one at a time, laying each one down in front of the intended recipient. "They were like the Tarot," one wrote in his diary, found after his mysterious death in far-off Africa, "yet the symbols were unknown to me." A gilded globe, half-swallowed by the sea, with two dark, red suns setting on a horizon of jagged peaks. A woman in white, her dress sewn with stars, reaching up one pale hand toward the crescent moon. Three supplicants in yellow robes, the backs of their shorn heads painted with an inverted triangle, kneeling before a vacant throne.

As she revealed each card, she laid it before one of the visitors, who would take it and place it in a breast pocket, a purse, or somewhere else out of sight. Then, they would rise and depart from the room. The drivers who carried them back to their manors and penthouses later reported having seen them in the rear mirror, holding some card and staring at it all the way back to the city, yet the cards were never found upon their person, not even those who perished soon after.

Sometimes, those who received a card would later return to the big, antebellum house and receive another, and another, time and again. Others returned to their homes and carried out some task that left them behind bars, exiled to foreign shores, or dead by violence.

All this the detective was able to discover before he ever visited the house in the bayou a second time.

The detective had come to hear the Canary sing once. He was a member of the local constabulary, to be certain, but he was also a minor celebrity, ever since he solved the disappearance of the Lavigne siblings in the midst of those jazz murders.

This celebrity meant that he never again had to sit at a desk in the crowded, hot station house nor walk a stretch of sidewalk that he didn't wish to. He had his pick of cases, and most of his time was spent as an ambassador to the high society, representing the police at dinner parties and costume balls.

It was in this capacity that he had received an invitation to the old house out in the bayou. He had come with two other gentlemen—a solicitor of some great influence, who was being positioned to run for public office, and the owner of several textile factories in the north who preferred the warmer climes—and the three shared a table near the impromptu stage.

"My impressions when she first appeared were those of scale," the detective later wrote in memoirs that were never published, the pages expurgated and burned. "She seemed too small to create the sounds that would soon roll from her throat. Her yellow dress all but glowed in the light, but she seemed a shadow within it. That, of course, was before she began to sing."

When the detective arrived at the house a second time, the place was in an uproar. The drivers from the side lot had come around to the front, cars were parked in a jumble in the circle drive, where it rounded the dry fountain with its sea-foam horses and gladiatorial fish. Behind the windows of the parlor room, fire still burned, though a truck was parked and already pumping water.

As near as the detective could reconstruct the night's events, they happened roughly like this:

The Canary was singing her usual song, to a more than usually packed house. Abruptly, a woman rose from the crowd and shouted something before drawing a snub-nosed gun from her purse and firing once, twice, three times.

The detective spoke with those onlookers he could find among the chaotic crowd that surrounded the house. "You took him from me," is how one woman recalled the shooter's words, while a man who had burned his hand in the course of trying to prevent a young lady from being trampled swore blind that she had said the name of some place, "it sounded like one of those Greek islands."

One thing that everyone seemed to agree upon was that one of the three shots had struck the Canary, while others buried themselves in the piano, the wainscotting, or the ceiling. Whether a bullet struck one of the dim lamps that decorated the tables or whether the fire began in the crush of bodies that followed the shots, none could say for certain.

Later, when the fire was out and the detective combed the house with other officers, they dug spent bullets from the wood of the piano and the parquet floor. In the rush and press that followed the shooting, much was lost, yet it was not the end of the night.

The big men who would normally have interceded with the shooter found themselves stymied by the sudden panic. It wasn't just the shooting that caused the change in the crowd, however, the detective gathered.

"When the bullet struck, the song ended," one shaken woman later told the detective. "The note just broke, like a piece of stained glass. The Canary, she stumbled back and I could see her eyes. She was *terrified*, the poor creature. Not just that, though. She was … relieved, I guess?"

The detective would eventually identify the woman with the gun as Eileen Buchanan. She had been engaged to Albert Romano, a rising star at a firm of solicitors who had been one of the frequent guests at the old house, until he blew himself up in a firebomb targeting the office of the district attorney.

On her way out the door, Miss Buchanan put another bullet into the phone in the hall. "Let it all burn," she said, before the shot rang out, according to a witness who was rushing past to escape the flames.

Once outside, backlit by the inferno in the parlor, Miss Buchanan put the barrel of the pistol against her bottom jaw and pulled the trigger. Another man, who, along with the witness in the hall, had pushed out in time to see Miss Buchanan take her own life at the edge of the fountain, repeated her final words, which he told not to the detective, but to a reporter from the *Post-Gazette*, "Out, out are the lights, out all."

"An intentional reference to Mr. Edgar Allan Poe," the reporter wondered in his piece, "or simply a description of the grisly deed she was about to accomplish?"

The medical examiner later pulled gobs of melted candle wax from Miss Buchanan's ears. "Put there, I can only infer," the detective wrote in those expurgated memoirs, "to prevent her from hearing the Canary's song."

With the phone in the hall destroyed, one of the first survivors out of the house ordered his driver to hurry to the next home down the road and alert the authorities. By the time the driver arrived, however, the neighbors, who tended to watch the comings and goings at the old house with interest, had already seen the orange glow and phoned the fire brigade.

"We never knew the folks who lived there," the house's nearest neighbor told the detective. "We just called it the yellow house. This whole area used to be one big plantation, you know? There were slave cabins right there where our carriage house is now."

As the detective uncovered more and more strange things about the house in the bayou, he went to the county assessor's office and, from there, traced the records of the land holdings as they had passed down, finding that the house's original owner had been a miser and a veteran of the War of Northern Aggression, who left the property not to his children, who had moved to cities on the coast, but to an organization known as the Sign of Hali.

"I think it was one of those spiritual societies," the records clerk told the detective. "You know the kind. They were thick on the ground in those days."

The society had gradually sold off bits of the original plantation, until they owned only the old house and the grounds immediately surrounding it. The back of the place abutted the swamp almost directly, though old plats and cadastral maps showed that this was a relatively new development, and that the murky, black water had incrementally been encroaching on the region, which seemed to be sinking into the bayou year by year.

"Why the yellow house?" the detective asked the neighbors, who seemed embarrassed by the question, as the house, in the warm light of day, was clearly white, albeit faded and peeling.

"It's a bit silly," the man of the house said finally, "but our daughter Rosie was the first to point it out. At night, there was something about the place—swamp gas, or just a trick of the foliage—but that place seemed to glow in the dark a bit. Yellowish, you know? Like a fungus."

Some of the house's many servants—the cooks and wait staff, the big men who acted as bouncers—perished in the fire, as did so many others. Some were trampled, some died choking on smoke or were scorched by the flames themselves. Those who survived were either picked up by the police or never heard from again.

Those whom the authorities questioned—some hauled into wagons and dragged to the station, some interrogated there on the wet front lawn—all reported that they took orders from a woman who they called Mama C. The detective asked only a few to identify her as the body that he discovered in the back garden, the livid white marks of fingers found dug into her throat.

When he asked them about the Canary, they had even less information. "She was a Angel," one of the big men told him reluctantly, after several dry hours in an interrogation room. "A Angel a the Lord. She come down to show us why we ought to pray for Heaven."

In the attic of the house, the detective found trunks filled with yellow robes sewn with a triune pattern that would have been familiar to any of the house's frequent daytime visitors. He also found an old wheelchair of wood and wicker, with a porcelain mask lying on its seat. Unlike most masks of its kind, it was not intended to be smooth, almost featureless, but was carefully painted to look like a woman's face, the white porcelain made up with pinks and rouges to simulate the tone of living skin.

Of the house's other residents, besides Mama C and the servants, there was no sign. It was in the garden shed that one of the detective's underlings made the final discovery. "I think you need to see this, sir," he said, covering his mouth with a handkerchief as he stood at the edge of the stagnant water that now threatened the fringes of the carefully cultivated garden.

The shed was a few short strides from the door that led into the solarium where the Canary had performed. It looked, from the outside, like any other garden shed, its one small window covered from within. When he opened the door, however, he found something quite different.

"Do I now say that the room had the aspect of a crypt because of its dim closeness and the dimensions that it shares with those grim abodes of the deceased," he wrote in his unpublished memoir, "or is it only the hindsight of what I found there that lets me pretend that I imagined what was coming?"

Inside the room were shelves lined with books and candles. Against the back wall, farthest from the door, a stone sarcophagus leaned, its lid set carefully to one side, its occupant missing. No, not missing. It simply lay on the stone floor of the shed, its right hand extended above its head, so that its fingers alone were within the stone of its eternal bed.

The county medical examiner later confirmed what the detective could tell with no more than a glance. Though the body was that of a young woman, it had been dead for hundreds of years. "It's mummified," the medical examiner told the detective. "Not the kind you see in museums, though. The kind they haul out of peat bogs back in England."

What the medical examiner could not account for was the fact that the mummified body was wearing a bright, new yellow dress, or that there was fresh damage to its fingernails, one of which was embedded in the earthen floor of the shed. At the detective's insistence, the medical examiner cut the ancient body open, and pulled out a bullet from a snub-nosed pistol.

Despite the best efforts of the fire brigade, the blaze destroyed the parlor and much of the first floor of what the neighbors called the "yellow house." Those rooms that were not entirely gutted—mainly on the second floor—suffered from smoke and water damage, leaving behind vast swatches of black mold that grew in strange patterns.

The place was never repaired, never inhabited, and the hole that the fire had burned through the parlor, a wound that ran from the front of the house out through the broken glass of the old solarium, stayed open until the day the house was swallowed by the brackish water of the swamp.

Fifteen people perished in the conflagration and the rout that followed, not counting the two bodies that were discovered in the garden and the shed. From that point on, the house developed a reputation as haunted, and neighbors and young people who visited the area on a dare reported seeing floating orbs and strange yellow and violet lights within the ruins at night.

Under pressure from local politicians, the detective closed the case quickly, but was never satisfied with its resolution. Unable to drive a car himself, when he needed to get someplace in the city that he could not walk, he almost always employed the same driver.

"He asked me to take him out to that road," the driver later said, remembering the detective to a prospective biographer whose project never got off the ground. "Not up to the house itself, just to the end of the lane, where you coulda seen the house, if it had been light. We didn't go ever night, but more than a few times. He'd call up at two in the morning, three, four. He was always apologetic, always paid extra, and I was happy for the dough, and a cushy job, at that.

"I'd drive us out and park. Shut off the engine and we'd sit. He'd roll down the window and listen, though as near as I could tell there weren't nothin' to hear but crickets and peeper frogs. Sometimes he'd listen for five minutes, sometimes he'd listen for half-a-hour. Then I'd drive him back to town and that was that. We never did talk about it."

In all, the detective never spoke much about the events of that night, or about the impact that it all had on him. He lived a long life and died in his bed, and only one small section of his unpublished memoir dealt with the old house and the Canary at all, and that part he burned in his own fireplace.

One part of one page survived, while others were recorded, from memory, by his nurse and amanuensis at the time. The one scrap she saved, its edges burned, was, by her own admission, more rambling diary entry than finished manuscript.

"I find myself plagued by impalpable worries," he wrote. "I have bad dreams. So long as the Canary sings in the coal mine, the rest of us know that we are safe in the dark."

Author's Notes:

One of the more recent stories in this book, "The Cult and the Canary" was written while a pandemic gripped the land. So it only felt natural, somehow, to tap the apocalyptic mythos of the King in Yellow. The invite this time was from Simon Brake, for an anthology of KiY stories called, simply, *Y* from Stygian Fox.

I have, of course, read Robert Chambers' works, and many (though nowhere near all) of their various imitators and adulators—this isn't even the first time I have played in the sandbox, which I dipped into perhaps most notably back in "The Seventh Picture," in my first collection.

This time around, though, I think it was the writings of my friend Selena Chambers, as much as or more than that other Chambers, that influenced the ultimate form this story took—an almost *Rashomon*-like reconstruction of a single, fateful moment at a roadhouse in the bayou.

Nor is it the only time I've mixed roadhouses and jazz music with mythos elements. See "Count Brass" in my first collection and, even more so, "The Lesser Keys" in *Guignol & Other Sardonic Tales*. And then, of course, there was that irresistible urge to do a play on the classic title, *The Cat and the Canary*.

MASKS

"You were his friend, right?"

His granddaughter's voice on the other end of the phone, her words clear and free from static. I wait to answer, don't want to, because how do I say, "I don't know?" For months now, he has been coming over to my house to play xiangqi two or three nights a week while we drink hard cider and talk about bullshit. Does that make us friends, or just two lonely old guys with nobody else to talk to?

Whatever I feel in my heart, what comes out of my mouth is bound to be an affirmative, because what else can I say? And besides, she is so far away—London, of all places, with children of her own that I can hear in the background—while I am so close, his own townhouse just two doors down from mine, only empty space between us because this neighborhood is dying, just as he was dying, just as we all are dying. One uncomfortable phone call at a time.

She hasn't said the words, but the implication is clear in her voice. If I don't do it, men will come. Strangers. Impersonal men who will throw it all into boxes and, from there, who knows? The Goodwill? The landfill? No place where it matters. No place where it will be appreciated.

Am I the old man's friend? I don't think so. Do I want to do it? No. So why do I say yes into the receiver, my voice bounced across thousands of miles to his granddaughter in London?

The answer is guilt. No more noble a motive than that.

I think that I know what to expect, when I open the door. He came to my house so often, after all. I couldn't help but smell it on him. Dust, old food smells, stale cigarettes, the scent of clothes left too long in a closet. All the aromas of a college professor gone to pot.

That there are drifts of paper and takeout food containers keeping the door from opening all the way comes as no surprise, either. The old man was a hoarder. No shock there. Piles of things in every corner. A microwave, door hanging partway open. One blender, another. A DVD player still in its original box, the tape unbroken.

The layout of his house is identical to mine, so stepping inside feels both familiar and strange; a post-apocalyptic movie in which well-known landmarks lie in ruins, or are half-consumed by plant life run riot.

Just as in my place, the living room is the largest one in the house, eating up much of the ground floor. Books lie piled on the carpet, along with cup noodles, coffee filters filled with old grounds, overflowing ash trays. There is almost no furniture in this room. Just an amber floor lamp and a purple recliner that looks to be made of lichen, as if I would sink into it forever were I to sit, sending up a cloud of recliner spores in my wake.

In the fireplace, where my TV sits, he has piled empty bottles, jars, old photographs, hand-written letters. A nonsense shrine, built by a man whose religion was his own and no one else's. In one bottle, a beetle crawls, too large to ever escape its prison.

My eyes skim it all but they settle, of course, on the masks. I knew, dimly, that the old man had once worked in Poverty Row Hollywood, but I had forgotten what job he did: makeup, set painting, and masks. He said once, "Whenever a detective or a tortured academic stood in front of a wall of masks—masks from

Bali, from Africa, from wherever the studio thought conjured the exotic—those might have been mine. I was cheaper than shipping something in. Easier than doing your own homework."

The masks on the living room wall aren't those, though. No studio in the forties would have let even Patric Knowles or Ann Sheridan stand in front of these things. The faces, trapped somewhere between human and monster, between being faces at all and being something else: stars, galaxies, other organs. Melting, running, racing from one to the other and back again, only to become lost somewhere in the middle.

In the dim light struggling in through faded, half-closed blinds they seem damp, alive. Many tongues twitching, many eyes darting. Where did these masks come from? How did the old man come by them? Do they predate the old movie masks, or did they inspire them? Did they come *from* the old man or did they come *to* him? Muse or creation?

These are the questions that assail me as I stand in the quiet of the house, dust motes surrounding me as I breathe in the smell of rotting food and spores and who knows what else. When my house is quiet, I can hear the traffic on the highway, but in his living room I seem to hear something else. Scuffling. Breathing. Panting. Clawing.

I walk nearer to the masks, and the sound rises. Do they see me, as I see them? They look agonized, starving, desperate. They remind me of the old man. I reach up my hand, let it hover in the air in front of the nearest mask, and I *know* that its features recede even as they also creep closer, though I could never prove it.

I feel the purple recliner against my thigh, and when I look down it seems so *inviting*. I could sink into it, I think, chair spores floating up and into my lungs. I could wait there, keeping the masks company until someone else comes to try to take them down. An hour, a minute, a second ago the idea would have appalled me, but now?

Now it sounds so fine...

Author's Notes:

Another short—and rare—one, "Masks" has only ever previously appeared in *Forbidden Futures*, where it accompanied art by Mike Dubisch. In fact, it was actually *written* to accompany that art. The impetus here was that I was given a few pieces of artwork to pick from and told to choose one and write a story to complement it. Hopefully, I did. But, just as hopefully, the work also stands on its own, here.

It's a story, like so many of mine are, with the ghost of Old Hollywood hanging over it, if only at a distance. And it's also probably got a little of William Mortensen in there, too. Not for the first time and, again, probably not for the last…

THE HOUSE OF MARS

Stop me if you've heard this one: There are three dead bodies in a house in the Hills. One of them wakes up.

It was 3 a.m. when we got the call, because those calls never happen in the afternoon, or first thing when you come on shift. They happen after you've already been working an hour past when you were supposed to go home, after you've already spent the night pulling a carved-up hooker out of the trash behind the Red Windmill and writing up the paperwork knowing that you're never gonna haul in the sonofabitch who did it. They happen when you're already tired, when you're already wired, when you don't want anything but a belt of the good stuff and maybe a little bit of the *other* good stuff and then to sleep for a week. That's when those calls come in, always.

Apparently, someone had complained about seeing weird lights in a house up in the Hills. A house that was supposed to be abandoned. "Why the hell was it abandoned?" I asked the desk sergeant, and he said, "How am I supposed to know? That's just what they told me."

When the beat cop they sent out to check on the weird lights knocked on the door and got no answer, he should've just logged it and gone home. But he was new—damp-haired and pale, his eyes as big as saucers over that unfortunately big schnoz of his—and so he'd gone in.

I wanted to break that nose for him. Not because I knew him, or because he'd done anything really wrong, just because I knew that it was his fault I was there, his fault my night wasn't going to end up the way I'd wanted.

Inside the house was about what you'd expect from "abandoned." Big and nice, but not much in the way of furniture, except in the room with all the bodies. That place was done up like a mad scientist's lab from the movies, all boxes and dials and neon glass tubes. So that explained the weird lights.

The bodies were weird, too. Carefully arranged, laid out on cots like they'd all decided to take a nap. One of their throats was slit, the other had a hole burned straight through his chest, and the third one, a girl not hardly old enough to be outta school, was untouched, as near as I could tell, but the coroner said they were dead, all right, "as doornails."

I called him some choice names, and told Polanski to have the rookie talk to whoever had called in the complaint about the weird lights. I sent two other uniforms out to chat up the neighbors in the big houses, see if anyone else had seen anything unusual. Then I stood out in the cool air, under the big stars, and I muttered about god and the devil and everything in between while I wished I hadn't given up smoking two weeks before.

Dawn was rosy-ing up the sky by the time I got to leave the place, and I got a decent look at the house before I rolled out. It was black and gray, big as anything, but not the kind of fancy crap that the Hollywood kooks were building out in the Hills in those days. Old, Victorian, like something an oil baron would have built in the middle of the desert fifty years ago.

When I got back to the apartment, Linda was sleeping in the big chair in the front room. She was wearing her sheer shift, the one that let me see tantalizing glimpses of all her pink parts, which got me all the more pissed that I hadn't gotten home earlier the night before. Her lip was still swollen up a little from where I'd belted her a few nights ago. I couldn't remember why I'd done it, and I felt like hell about it, which didn't do a goddamn thing to un-sour my mood.

I woke her up by overfilling my glass of Scotch and pouring it all over the sideboard. The first words out of her mouth were, "For breakfast?"

"For dinner," I replied without looking.

"Then pour me one, if there's any left."

I took a pull off the glass so it wouldn't spill, then handed it over to her and sank down onto the floor next to the chair with the bottle in my hand. I let my head roll back onto her lap, and she ran her fingers through my hair in that way I like. "Hard night?"

I nodded, as best I could how I was sitting, and she didn't say anything more, which was good, because I wasn't in the mood to talk.

An hour later, the telephone rang.

By the time I got down to the station, they'd already moved the girl out of the morgue and into a holding cell. Which is good, because if the coroner had tried to explain to me how she'd been dead a couple of hours ago but now wasn't anymore, I might have broken his jaw.

As it was, I asked Polanski, the poor bastard, who was still on duty, even though I'd gone home. He looked like he always looked: haggard and drawn, dark hair stringy, eyes big and black. He looked like an addict, or like a guy in a movie from before the talkies, but he was a good cop.

I was hard on him that night because I was pissed, and there wasn't anything for me to be pissed at, so Polanski got it. He understood, just like Linda understood when she got it. The world was a rough place, and sometimes that roughness spilled over. That was the way it went. I saw it every day. Sometimes it spilled over onto junkies and whores and pimps, sometimes it spilled over onto cops and their girls, sometimes it even spilled so deep that it reached movie stars and politicians.

I stood for a long time and looked in at the girl in the holding cell. Living in Hollywood, you saw a lot of movies. Linda liked 'em; she'd wanted to be an actress when she first came out here, just like most girls. The world had knocked that outta her since, but she still liked to go sit in the dark and look up at the screen, so when I was feeling magnanimous, I'd take her.

In the movies, cops were good guys. They caught the bad guys, made people safe. I guessed I could see the appeal. Better that than the truth: that we're the can where the world throws its garbage until there isn't any more room anymore, and it gets all over everything else.

The night before, we were supposed to see something called *The New Frontier* before I got the call. Linda had showed me a poster for it: William Holden in a spacesuit—bubble helmet and all—a curly-haired redhead gripping his leg, staring out across some alien landscape. That's what all the movies were these days, it seemed like. "Space belongs to America," and all that jazz. I guessed now I'd probably never see it, and I hoped that Linda went without me. She'd like it better than I would anyhow.

If life was like the movies, the girl in the cell would have been a beauty, with hair that golden color that turns to pure light up on the screen. Instead, she was a Chicana, or some kind of half-breed, mousy and small, with dark, straight hair and thick glasses. Not anyone who would ever be an actress. Someone who'd be lucky to clean a movie star's mansion.

Polanski told me that she worked at the university, where she was an assistant to Professor Rice—the corpse with the hole burned through his chest—who was a doctor of something dealing with outer space. The other body was a guy name of Tomas Edgar, a hood of no consequence with a few burglaries on his rap sheet. Word was he sometimes helped the professor out acquiring things he needed for his work, whatever that meant.

"Looks like they had a disagreement," I'd have said under other circumstances, but what kind of disagreement leaves one guy with his throat slit and the other with a hole the size of a baseball where his heart used to be? This case was already giving me a headache, and I needed something or somebody I could take it out on.

"Rebecca Gonzalez?" I asked when I walked into the room with the girl, though I knew damn well who she was. She looked up at me, and she seemed confused, which I guess was fair enough, considering that she'd been dead not two hours before.

"Why am I here?" she asked. "Where's Professor Rice?"

"Professor Rice is dead," I told her. "And you're here because you're my only witness, which also makes you my only suspect, 'til you tell me different."

She shook her head at me, pulled one lip in under the other, like she was trying to figure out how to explain something to a dullard in the quickest way possible. And next to a college girl, or some hotshot space professor, a dullard is probably exactly what I was.

"Are you sure?" she asked. "Let me see him. He might just be… sleeping."

"Like you were?" I asked, and she nodded. "Not unless he can sleep with a hole this big straight through him." I may've exaggerated the hole a little bit.

She tucked her chin, slumped down some in the chair. Like she hadn't expected that, but wasn't all the way surprised, either.

"Maybe you'd better tell me exactly what was going on up there," I said. "From the beginning."

She nodded mutely, so I pulled up a chair, and I sat down across from her, and she told me a story. And it was a whale, let me tell you.

To understand the significance of what was going on in that house (she said), you've got to go back a long way. Back before the invasion of '38, before you were born, before Hollywood and the United States and any of this. By the time the Spaniards made their way out here in the 1500s, the natives already knew about that piece of land. Knew that it was special. They called it the Cave of Sleep in their language, and they avoided it, put up these… scarecrows to mark it. Wooden sculptures with a rod down the center and then two arms coming off each side, like this (and she drew one on a piece of paper and slid it across to me).

The first white man to discover the cave was a conquistador named Valdez. He got separated from his party and must have gone into the cave to seek shelter. What he saw in there nobody knows, but some of the men in his party wrote letters back home that talked about finding him there, sleeping "the sleep of the dead." They carried his body away to bury it, but in the process of burial he woke up ("Like you did," I said to her, and she nodded), and they took him for a vampire. A stake was driven through his heart, and his head and hands were cut off and buried separately.

("What does any of this have to do with—" I started to ask her, but she interrupted, said "Please, Detective," so I let her go on.)

The next mention of the cave on record comes after the gold rush had hit California. A prospector named Josiah Carver, who made his camp in the cave, stumbled into town three weeks later, talking about a vision he'd been given "from on high." In it, he'd seen a strange landscape populated by beautiful red-skinned humans who built massive cities, and huge, four-armed devils with whom they were at constant war. He took his vision to be a warning about the encroaching of the white man on the lands of the Indians, and he did everything he could to stop California from entering the Union.

Carver founded a sort of doomsday church that preached against gold and free enterprise, and warned that our sins would be punished from on high. This was the symbol of his church (and here she tapped the drawing she'd made of the stick with the X through it).

Carver's church gained some traction, and he had a structure built directly on top of the cave where he'd had the vision, in the same spot where the house you found me in now stands. What's more, according to newspaper reports from the time, others in his congregations sometimes experienced similar visions after entering "trance states" in the church, and they came to call the place they'd visited "Barsoom."

(Once again I tried to stop her, because "Barsoom" was a word I'd heard from the newsreels that came back from Mars, but she had warmed to her topic and pressed on before I could get a word in.)

In 1894, Carver went into the cave below his church and never came out alive. His body was buried nearby. Other members of his congregation fought over the church for a few years, and then it was shut down by a Pinkerton raid and burned to the ground in 1912. When Hollywood sprang up, and people started building houses out in the Hills, the land was purchased by a man from back east named Aberhausen Tolbert. And no, I don't know what kind of a name Aberhausen is. What we *do* know is that he commissioned the building of a house for his new wife, the same house that still stands there now, and it was completed in 1929.

On the first night that Tolbert and his wife spent in the house, something happened. Tolbert was found that morning wandering the streets, shrieking and gibbering, talking about terrible things, bulbous, tentacled things with beaks and great eyes. He said that they were watching us from the sky, that they were coming here to destroy us, that he had been given a vision, a warning.

He refused to go back to his house, and when it was broken open, they found that his young wife had been torn apart in her bed. Tolbert was put in an asylum for the criminally insane, and his house sat empty for years because no one wanted to buy the house where such a grisly crime had been committed. Tolbert remained in the asylum—raving, writing letters that the wardens never sent, scribbling warnings on the walls of his cell—until the night of October 30, 1938, when he saw the culmination of his vision. As the first of the canisters fell and delivered the tripods, he gnawed through his own wrists and bled to death in his cell.

***

There, I had to stop her, which I did by banging a fist down on the table hard enough to stop the flow of words that had been, until then, streaming out of her mouth. "Are you trying to tell me," I started, but she didn't wait for me to finish.

"The house is a portal," she said. "That's what Professor Rice figured out. Or rather, not a portal, but something else. Nobody could put it together before because nobody had ever been to Mars, and so nobody knew that's where the sleepers were going. Nobody knew what it was like there. Nobody knew the history."

I shook my head. "Even if I bought this," I said, "I went in there, about a dozen other flatfoots, the coroner and his boys, and none of us went to Mars."

"It doesn't work if you just go in. You have to go to sleep. And it isn't your body that goes. *That* stays here, though you have a body on Mars when you get there, even if we're not sure yet what it's made up of. That's why we were studying it, trying to figure out what it is, how it works. Is it some kind of spatial anomaly? The professor also believed that there was a time differential. That the date when you went to sleep on Earth didn't line up with the date when you woke up on Mars. The Mars described by men like Carver would've already been dust and ruins by the time they traveled there, so people from a hundred years ago here may have visited a Mars from thousands of years ago. We had to figure out how the time differential worked, why what happened to your Mars body happened to you on Earth, all that kind of thing, before we could publish our findings."

I waited for her to wind down. "Look, lady," I said. "I hear a lot of bullshit in my line of work. I've hauled people in an' heard 'em tell me every story in the book. The Devil made me do it, Jesus made me do it, and yeah, these days, the Martians made me do it. Hauled in a guy the other day with aluminum foil on his head, said it kept out their mind-control rays. But this? This is the biggest cock-and-bull story I ever heard, so unless you want me to throw you in the pen for the rest of your natural life, an' you can sleep there and see where you go, I suggest you tell me a better one."

"I know it sounds far-fetched, Detective, but everything I've told you is a matter of public record. There are files in the professor's office that support all of this and more. You can follow it up, check it out, verify it. And just think about what it could mean for us if I'm telling the truth. If we can work out the time differential. For America, for everyone. An instantaneous gateway to Mars at our fingertips. Not a slow boat, not even a torch boat, but a crossing that can be made in the literal blink of an eye. It would change *everything*. And if the professor and Mr. Edgar are really dead, then you and I are the only ones who know about it, Detective, so you have to believe me. At least check out what I've told you."

When I walked out of the interrogation room, Polanksi was waiting for me on the other side of the door. "Are you buying any of that?" he asked.

"On a cop's salary? I don't get paid enough to buy any of that. She's a nut. Haul her out to Sybil Brand. Let them worry about her."

That's how you close cases. Not by listening to some little girl's story about Martians and magic houses.

Back at my place, Linda was sleeping again, this time in bed, and there was nothing I wanted more than to crawl in there with her. I stood in the doorway and watched her, thought about how good she'd feel under my palms. She muttered something in her sleep and turned over. Her split lip was a dark smudge in the light from outside the window, like she'd put on too much lipstick in just that one spot. The world was a lousy place, lousier for some than others. She deserved better.

Instead of crawling in bed, I went for a walk. I walked until I found myself on Hollywood Boulevard. They say that you can see

Mars up in the sky if you know where to look, but when I squinted up past the city lights, all I saw were stars, brighter and cleaner than the ones under my feet.

I didn't go back home. Instead, I drove back out to the Hills. It didn't take much doing to find the house again. The cruisers and wagons were all gone, and the house was a dark shape against the starry sky. I walked up to the front door and pushed it open. I didn't bother with my flashlight. The night let in enough light through the windows, and I wasn't there to look for clues.

In the room full of mad-science gear, I found the three cots. One was stained with blood, a darker shadow in the darkened room, the other scorched from the burn through the professor's heart. I lay down on the one where the girl had been.

Up above me, the ceiling was dark, and I tried to imagine what the stars looked like, up there above it. Tried to imagine that I could see Mars up there in the night sky. I'd seen newsreel footage of Mars, of course. Seen the bases up there, the cities, but I'd never been. I was a cop; I didn't have the time or the money to take a slow boat. But I knew enough to know that Mars wasn't any better than this place. No more real, no less cruel. Not now, at any rate. But maybe a hundred years from now, or a hundred years ago.

I closed my eyes and hoped that when I opened them again, it would be on some new frontier.

Author's Notes:

Speaking of odd projects in the shadow of Old Hollywood, "The House of Mars" is an example of something I basically never do. Written as part of a shared-world anthology that Sean Demory put together called *Slow Boat to Fast City*, the premise was basically that every story ever written about Mars was all true, all simultaneously.

Naturally, me being me, the Mars I wrote about was more Burroughs than anything, complete with the absolutely ridiculous method of reaching the Red Planet employed in the John Carter stories. The story didn't take place on Mars, though. It took place in Hollywood, and it had more of *L.A. Confidential* and De Palma's *Black Dahlia* in its DNA than any science fiction story.

Originally, "The House of Mars" was going to go into *Guignol & Other Sardonic Tales*, but my partner pointed out that it didn't fit, and they were right. So it found its way here, instead, where I think it makes a nice Hollywood-adjacent one-two with "Masks."

THE DOUBLE-GOER

I'm at Jules' party because it's where everyone says I need to be. "You have to get back on the horse," they tell me. "Otherwise he wins." As though we're talking about terrorism or a game of chess, not my boyfriend of six years moving to California with another man. Not even a friend; someone I never met, never even *saw*, though I do know that Kenneth had sex with him several times in our bed while I was gone to work, a revelation that I didn't really need from his angry/tearful/boozy good-bye speech on our back patio, under the blue and green incandescent bulbs.

It's the first time I've really been out since Kenneth left, and I don't know how to tell Jules or Luca or anyone else that I don't *want* to get back on the horse. I know that if I try to explain I'll just sound self-pitying, or worse, like I'm in denial.

I cried for two days when Kenneth moved out, but not because I was missing him. I was pissed at the years I had wasted, thinking that I needed to stay because I had said I would, more than because I wanted to. Now I just want to be on my own for a while. I want to listen to my music at whatever volume I please; I want to watch whatever movie tickles my fancy and stop in the middle if I so goddamn desire; I want to order Chinese takeout without getting a lecture about MSGs; I want to stay up all night reading and not have to worry about anything but paying for it the next day at work. A few months without sex or the smell of his shirts or someone to curl up against while I sleep seems like a small price to pay for such luxuries.

Jules' apartment—which he shares with Damien and Marco and a girl named Karen—occupies the whole top floor of a brownstone-style walk-up downtown. It stretches along three sides of the landing, and there are many doors going in and out, all of them thrown open wide for the party, so that it spills out onto the stairs and can be heard as soon as I open the street door. Once upon a time each floor of this building was home to several apartments, but the walls have all been knocked out to make big lofts, ideal for social butterflies like Jules. You could fit our whole place—no, scratch that, just *my* place now—into the kitchen.

I've been at the party for maybe twenty minutes, and I'm trying to decide how much longer I have to wait before I can start making excuses, when Marybeth—said like that, breathless, all one word—comes in, her hair dyed burgundy this time and a guy I don't recognize on her arm, five o'clock shadow and gelled hair. She sees me and does a double take, says, "Avery, how did you get up here?" a little too loud.

"What do you mean?" I ask, and she says, "I just saw you on the landing downstairs, didn't I? How did you beat us up here?"

"I've been up here," I pretend to check my phone, keep up the pretense that I'm not counting minutes, "almost half an hour."

"Oh," she says, suddenly distracted by the next shiny thing, giving me a kiss on the cheek. "Must have been your evil twin," the boyfriend says with a wicked half-smile that might have melted my heart if I were ten years younger.

He disappears with Marybeth into the crowd, and I let myself drift, pushed by the current of bodies to the wall with the other flotsam and jetsam. I strain to my tiptoes and look out across the sea of heads for someone I recognize. Jules and Marco are in the kitchen playing bartender, but nobody else seems familiar, and no one is paying attention to me. So with my alibi now in hand, I slip out of the nearest door and onto the landing.

From below, couples and groups are still coming up the stairs from the street entrance, and a pair of girls have found an out-of-the-way corner for some heavy petting. I lean over the banister and look down.

The apartment below is like an antimatter duplicate of Jules'. Closed up where his is open, empty where his is full, dark and silent where his blazes and resounds. The occupant passed away a few weeks before, or so Jules told me when he was exhorting me to come to the party. It was the impetus, in fact. "Nothing more depressing than an empty place," he said over the phone, a sentiment that I'm afraid I couldn't share.

When I go down, there's no one on the landing. No one who looks like me, or otherwise. It's quieter, the noise from the party above receding into a dull bass thump and the roar of distant traffic or the wind through the trees; the susurrus of dozens of voices all blending into one river of sound.

At a glance the doors are all shut, but as I walk around the landing I see that I'm wrong. One stands open a crack, white wood against the darkness within. I push it open farther. Curiosity, I suppose, though I tell myself that I'm making sure no one from the party has drifted down here. Disrespectful of the dead to be drinking in his kitchen, fornicating in his bed.

The layout of the apartment is familiar, because it is the same as Jules', but here all is shadows and silence, the sound of the party fading even further as I pass through the doorway, becoming just the pulse of my own heart, the rush of blood in my veins. The only light that gets in comes through windows stripped of blinds or curtains.

I struggle to remember anything that Jules may ever have told me about the apartment's occupant. An older man, what little hair he had gone to gray. Dressed like a professor or something. Had grandkids who came to see him from time to time, but mostly lived alone, kept to himself, though he was friendly enough when you saw him on the stairs, and never complained about the noise from the apartment above.

Most of his belongings have already been removed, but the furniture remains. A well-worn wingback chair next to a bookshelf that stretches to the ceiling. I can imagine him sitting there, in the quiet echo of one of Jules' parties, sipping tea and reading Ralph Ellison or Haruki Murakami for the umpteenth time, though I admit that I'm projecting more than a little.

As I walk through the apartment from room to room I notice something. The mirrors have all been draped with white sheets, though the other furniture remains uncovered. It's a practice that I've heard about, read about, but never actually *seen*. My grandmother told me about it, remembered from when she was a girl. "They cover the mirror to keep evil spirits from coming and taking the place of the person who died," she said. "Or maybe because they think whoever sees his reflection in the mirror will be the next to go. Me, I think they're afraid, but not of that. They're afraid of seeing someone standing over their shoulder."

At the far end of the apartment, I find what must have been the old man's bedroom, and in it a full-length dressing mirror. I can just make out its shape under the sheet; oval, and positioned on a swivel so that you can tilt it up to see your full figure. My fingers find the sheet, my fingertips tingling with an almost electric thrill, and I feel in my arm an itch to pull, but I leave it alone, unsure why I'm walking around in a dead man's apartment in the first place, and unwilling to go the extra mile of disturbing his possessions while I'm at it.

On the landing, I consider just turning and going down to the street, making my apologies to Jules and the rest tomorrow, if they even notice at all. It's what I want to do, go home and have the apartment, small as it is, all to myself. Make a cup of tea, read one of those books I was just daydreaming about. But instead I go back upstairs.

When I get there someone is calling my name, and I look and see a tall guy I've never met, Latino maybe, dressed to the nines with a red pocket square and a slicked black hairdo. He's walking toward me, holding a drink in each hand, and he's asking me why I took off so suddenly. "Weren't we having a good time?" he asks, standing too close to me. "I got you that drink," and he hands me a cold glass full of something that smells fruity and heady with a strong undercurrent of tequila.

I say something noncommittal in response, because I don't know what he's talking about, and his hand is on the wall above my head, my forehead only coming up to his nose, and he's leaning in. The sideboard is biting into the back of my thigh, and I'm trying to set my glass down on it, because I know that he's going to kiss me, though I don't know why, and when he does I taste whatever it is that he's been drinking on his tongue; cold and alcoholic, with a slight aftertaste of licorice.

He's pretty, and the kiss is nice. I feel a warmth spreading through my stomach, a hardening in my cock. But I'm not ready yet, and besides, I don't know what kind of game he's playing, with the pretending to recognize me. It's what Luca would call a "red flag."

I break away, make some excuse about needing some air, or the restroom. He calls out something to my retreating back, but it's lost to the music and the noise of the crowd. Instead of air—there's no place to get it anyway, not without going down the street where the smokers are loitering—I head to the kitchen, looking for Jules.

When I find him he's a few to the wind, and he looks up at me with eyes that, for a moment, are empty of recognition, before they snap back into focus. "Avery?" he says, as though he's surprised to see me there. I say something to him, some stammering attempt at an excuse to leave, but I don't finish before he has his hand on my shoulder. "Why did you change your shirt?" he's asking. "The other one was better. If you spilled something on it, you can borrow one of Marco's. I think he's about your size."

I stumble back, crash into some girl I don't recognize and spill the drink she's carrying across her sequined shirt. Muttering apologies, I make for the door, back out onto the landing, where the bright doorways offering ingress into the party seem to spin around me. I brace myself against the banister, and wait to feel the inevitable hand on my arm, the voice asking what's wrong, but it never comes.

Once my head has cleared, I go to the stairs and down them, to the empty apartment below, where I know, somehow, my double will be waiting for me. Walking back through the apartment again, my eyes scan for subtle changes. I see a glass on a mantel that wasn't there before, mostly empty of some amber liquid. I see a single crushed petal from some pale flower.

In the bedroom, I stand in front of the dressing mirror, my fingers twined in the sheet. I pull the cover off, and for a moment my reflection is something monstrous. Skeletal thin and misshapen, skin like mangrove wood, eyes like blue fires that burn in the sockets of an unfinished skull. But then I blink and it's just me, but now my reflection is doubled. No, that isn't quite right. Someone is standing behind me, just over my shoulder.

This, I know even before I turn, is the person responsible for all the confusion. He's my spit-and-image, as my grandmother used to say. Skin the same shade of brown, eyes the same. His hair has been cut more recently than mine, his shirt *is* nicer, but it's something I would wear. Something I would have worn, had I actually wanted to "get back on the horse," the kind of thing I used to wear when Kenneth and I went out on dates, before dates became takeout in front of episodes of *NCIS* on Netflix. Like a version of me that was never domesticated.

I turn and stick out my hand, as though we're just strangers being introduced at a party. "Avery," I say, but am I telling him my name, or asking him his? He starts to grip my hand, then hesitates, our fingers a few inches apart, as though some static spark has jumped between us. He draws his hand back, watching me with a gleam in his eye, half predatory and half sensual. I see now that he's in better shape than I am, in little ways. A few pounds lighter, muscles and cheekbones a little better defined. Is this what I could have been, in another life?

In any other place, at any other time, I would react differently. I would feel threatened by this man who looks so much like me, who refuses to shake my hand, who looks at me so aggressively. Alone in a dead man's apartment, I simply accept the inevitable.

"What's it like on the other side of the mirror?" I ask, and in answer he simply reaches past me, hooks his fingers around the edge of the frame, and pulls it open like a door.

Beyond it I see darkness and trees and stars that glow in unfamiliar constellations. I turn to look at him, and he nods, the same way that I nod, and juts his chin toward the doorway.

"Enjoy the party," I say, putting my hand on his shoulder, careful to touch only fabric and not flesh, and then I step through the space behind the mirror, into whatever is waiting on the other side. If he wants to occupy the empty space that my life has become, then let him. Perhaps my place *should* be taken by someone who wants to "get back on the horse." For me, I'll just stay here behind the glass and watch. It's quiet here, and they leave me alone. That'll do for now.

Author's Notes:

Returning readers will probably already know that my collections tend to develop themes that I don't really notice until I'm putting them together. In this case, one of those themes is almost certainly "longing."

While the stories that go into this volume run the gamut as far as subgenres, topics, and styles, almost all of them feature characters who *want* something very deeply, even (and especially) when they aren't sure what that something *is*.

"The Double-Goer" is a good example. Once again, it's the result of an invitation to a themed anthology, though in this case not the theme you might expect. *Between Twilight and Dawn* was an anthology from Golden Goblin Press, edited by Brian Sammons and Oscar Rios. It concerned exclusively stories that took place over the course of a single night.

When I got the invitation, though, I was already working on "The Double-Goer," which happened to fit the bill. I don't remember *why* I was set on exploring the concept of the doppelganger and what it would mean for a person who maybe wasn't that comfortable in his own skin to begin with, but I certainly was and here we are.

THE HUMBUG

Joshua caught it in a glass jar with holes poked in the lid. He came running up to the cabin with it, shouting, "I found a bug! I found a bug!"

"There aren't any bugs in winter," Amanda said crossly, though no snow had fallen yet and the trees and ground outside were simply bare and gray.

When Joshua placed the jar on the big, heavy dining table, however, there was no mistaking that a bug rested on the bottom, lying on its back with its unpleasantly segmented legs folded up toward its abdomen.

"Then it's dead," Amanda huffed.

She was the middle child, and seemed to have reached a stage in her development where she felt the need to compensate for being neither youngest nor oldest by always knowing everything.

"Or hibernating," Alice quickly added, having only recently learned that some insects burrowed down into the ground and slept a deathlike sleep through the winter. "Cicadas do it for years and years!" she added cheerily.

But when Joshua tapped on the side of the jar, the bug inside sprang to life like a clockwork toy. Righting itself with a strangely mechanical hop, it scuttled to the edge farthest from where Joshua's fingertip still rested against the glass.

"You'll have to put some sticks or dead leaves in there for it," I told him, "or it really will die." He dutifully ran out to gather up some twigs and bits of fallen foliage, leaving the insect in its jar on the table.

I bent down to examine it as Alice climbed up on a chair to do the same and Amanda pretended disinterest by going to the sink and rattling glasses around in an exaggerated pantomime of getting a drink of water.

The insect itself was uniquely ugly, and of a type that I had never seen before, in spite of spending my own childhood among these trees and mountains. In shape, it was a bit like a poorly-wrought shield. Its color was uniformly gray, except for green bands and red spots which decorated its back and abdomen.

"It's a Christmas bug," Alice observed, thumping her small hand against the glass in an effort to point out the colors. I simply bit my lip and nodded.

I was never one to shy away from what my father had called "creeper crawlers." My own girlhood had been spent turning over rocks in search of snakes and splashing in shallow pools looking for newts and salamanders. Even had that not been the case, a willingness to handle—and, indeed, admire—just about every manner of odd creature is all but a prerequisite for being a good governess, in my experience.

No, it was something peculiar about *this* insect that made me loathe to handle the jar, that sent an impulse to my arm to slap away Alice's hand as I would from a hot stove. It evoked a shudder of the grotesque, as some insects and spiders instinctively do, even while others seem harmless or even adorable.

The bug's head was not at the point of the shield, as I might have imagined, but instead along its "top" end; the eyes red grills, the mouth a sort of hinged contraption from which poked a stunted and somehow obscene proboscis.

When the insect was in motion, its legs appeared to jut first upward from its body, then hinge suddenly down like a surgeon's needle. In every aspect of its movement it seemed somehow mechanical; as though it was a simulacrum of an insect, fashioned by someone who had received only a cursory explanation of the breed.

I say that I was loathe to handle the jar, and that's true enough, but I also found it hard to look away from the squat, ugly gargoyle within. In fact, I only realized how long I had been staring, watching the insect explore its small, round prison, when Joshua came back with a handful of twigs and dirty leaves, his hands smeared with black.

"I want to put them in," he said, dropping his handfuls on the table.

"No outside things on the table!" Amanda shouted from over by the sink. It was something she had heard her mother say, and I could even hear a childish attempt at approximating her mother's voice. Nor was she wrong. In fact, their mother would probably not have wanted the insect in the jar on the table in the first place, though rules were somewhat more lax in the cabin.

"I just need to get the lid," Joshua shouted back, the jar already in his hands, the black residue from the leaves slipping as he tried to unscrew the top. With the jar tilted, the insect was rapidly making its way up the side—which was now the bottom—toward the lid.

"Why don't *you* wash up your hands," I said, suppressing a shudder as I scooped the jar away from Joshua, "and I'll give these to your friend. Amanda, bring me a towel."

Amanda smirked as she gathered up a yellowish towel from the drying rack next to the sink and brought it over to me. I wiped off the lid of the jar and placed it back onto the table, then unscrewed it, picked up the twigs and bits of rotting vegetation, and quickly stuffed them through a small gap that I opened between the lid and the jar.

The insect sat at the bottom looking up at the opening, and didn't so much as twitch as the sticks and dirty leaves rained down on its face.

"I want to arrange them," Joshua said, coming back from pumping the water to wash his hands.

"You can arrange them later," I said, wiping my hands off on the towel. "For now, it's time for little children to eat their lunch."

"What do bugs eat?" Alice asked.

"Oh, bugs eat all sorts of things," I said. "I'm sure this fellow will enjoy eating some of those leaves we just dropped in there, but unless you want to eat leaves, you should start getting out your plates and things."

The children scurried to do as I asked, and I made sure I tightened the lid down extra tight before I placed the jar on the mantel.

In spite of my assurances, the insect did not eat any of the plants or sticks that Joshua had put in the jar. After lunch, the children went outside for a while, and I tidied up while watching them through the cabin windows.

When they came back in, their cheeks and noses red from the cold that hadn't fully set in yet, there was already a fire and hot cocoa to distract them for a time, but it only worked for so long. Joshua wanted to rearrange the sticks and twigs inside the bug's jar, and I hadn't been able, in the intervening few hours, to come up with any good reason why he shouldn't.

I watched him carefully as he placed the jar on the card table and poked at the sticks with a long spoon. I had already cautioned him against poking his hand down into the jar. "You may hurt your friend," I had said, though I was actually more concerned with the other way around.

"He isn't eating," Joshua said, a note of worry edging toward panic in his voice.

"He may not feel hungry just yet," I said in an attempt to placate him. "He's had a big day, after all."

"If he doesn't eat, he'll die," Joshua complained.

"He'll die anyway," Amanda said. "He should be dead already. He's an anomaly."

"He is *not* an anomaly," Joshua said, clutching the jar to his chest. "He's mine!"

"He may well be an anomaly," I said, interposing myself between the two children and—surreptitiously, I hoped—screwing the lid of the jar back on. "An anomaly just means something that's unusual or unique, and I've certainly never seen anything like him around here before."

"What does he like to eat?" Alice asked again.

"I'll tell you what," I said, directing my sentence at Joshua, who looked like he was about to cry, "let's try to find out what he is tomorrow, and then we'll know what he eats."

Mollified somewhat by this, I was able to convince Joshua to relinquish the jar, partly by telling him that the insect would be warmer on the mantel than anyplace else in the cabin, and get all the children into bed.

Joshua named the bug Henry, and it accompanied us on the train ride from the cabin back home to Gillford, where the children's parents were supposed to be waiting for us. Waiting instead was a telegram saying that their trip to the continent had been prolonged unavoidably but that they should be back in London within a fortnight and, if so, the children could come down and spend Christmas Eve in the city.

The rest of the telegram—the part which I didn't read aloud to the children—thanked me for my forbearance and promised a substantial bonus for my troubles upon their return, though it wasn't any inconvenience on my part that irked me, it was the crestfallen faces of the children themselves when they heard the news.

Little Alice began to cry, asking when Mummy and Daddy would be home, while Amanda stormed up to her room and slammed the door. Joshua simply asked if he could go outside and play, to which I told him that he could, so long as he returned promptly within a half-hour. He took the jar containing Henry with him, and I confess to a secret hope that he would release the insect into the wild and we would be rid of it for good.

"Mummy and Daddy do very important work," I told Alice as I held her in my arms, "and sometimes our work takes longer than we mean it to."

"I want them to come home," she sobbed, her face red and wet with tears.

"They'll be home very soon," I said, "and you'll see them for Christmas Eve." But even as I reassured her, I feared that I was lying.

The appointed time came and went, and with it another telegram explaining their continued absence in words that might have appeased another adult but held little balm for children. "If we cannot make London by Christmas Eve, we promise a grand celebration upon our return," the telegram ended.

On the day that the second telegram arrived, I took all the children into town to browse for things to put in their letters to Santa, or so I told them, though really it was to take their minds off the absence of their parents.

Joshua had continued to keep Henry in his jar, and had begun to drop other small bugs in with it, which promptly disappeared, neatly solving the problem of what Henry ate. As to what sort of insect it was, we had exhausted all the information that was to be found in the encyclopedias at home, and were no closer to identifying the unusual bug. So, while we were in town, we stopped into the tobacconist's shop, which doubled as a bookseller's, and asked Mr. Keene if he had any books about insects.

He brought out one that was filled with sketches of all kinds of insects from all over the world—insects that looked like sticks and leaves and everything else you could imagine, but though Joshua and I sat on the bench inside the shop and turned every page in the book, the warm smell of tobacco settling around me and reminding me of my own pa, who always smoked a pipe in front of the fire before turning in for the night, we could find nothing that matched the creature he had found.

"Mine isn't in here," he indignantly said to Mr. Keene. A smile crinkled the old man's weathered features, his red nose shining in the afternoon sunlight as he leaned over so that his face was closer to Joshua's level.

"Well, son, there's all kinds of insects in the world, you know? Thousands and thousands. Millions, even. For every beast and bird and fish in the whole world, there's probably at least ten different insects. So, it only stands to reason that we haven't found 'em all and named 'em all and wrote 'em all down yet. Who knows but that you may be the first to find a whole new species, eh?"

"How would we know if I'd found a new species?" Joshua asked as we left the shop. He struggled with the last word, pronouncing it "spee-see."

"Well," I replied, "I guess we'd have to write to a scientist or someone who works in a museum. How about we do that as soon as your parents get home?"

When we got home, I had the children write their letters to Santa. Amanda insisted that it was silly. "Mom and Dad get us presents," she informed her two siblings hotly.

"And me," I reminded her.

"And you. But not Santa."

"And how do you know that Santa doesn't pass them along to us? Do you know where we get them from?"

"The shops in town."

"But certainly not everything that you get is something that you've seen in the shops in town. Don't your mother and father give you things that you've never seen anywhere else?"

She conceded this point, but remained convinced that it was, at best, impractical for Santa to work through such a middleman.

When all the children had gone to bed, I opened the envelopes into which they had carefully placed their letters but which they had not sealed, and read their lists by the light of the fire. I sucked in my lip when Alice asked for Mommy and Daddy to be home.

In contrast to his extensive lists from previous years, there was only one item on the list that Joshua left for Santa: a terrarium home for his new six-legged friend. Feeling guilty for the absence of his parents, I caved in and bought it for him early, from a little shop down in the village while one of the maids watched over the children. I had the shopkeeper deliver it.

"Why does Joshua get one of his presents early?" Amanda asked, when I told him that he could open it a week before the holiday.

"You may all open one present this evening," I said, not willing to tell her that the reason I had rushed it was because Henry was already very near to outgrowing the jar in which Joshua kept him.

The snow began on the night that the children opened their one present. "Does this mean Mommy and Daddy won't be able to make it home?" Alice asked as the three of them pressed their noses against the cold glass the following morning and watched the blanket of white grow deeper.

"There are lots of ways to get through snow," I replied. "Sleighs and skates and those sleds pulled by lots and lots of dogs…"

"Can we make snow angels?" Amanda asked, her perpetual ill-temper momentarily forgotten.

"As long as you watch Alice, and come right back in when you start to get cold," I said.

It would have been one thing if the snow had fallen and then stopped. We might even have still enjoyed a white Christmas, if the temperature didn't climb too high during the day. But that isn't what happened. The snow didn't let up. Not that day, when the children came in rosy-cheeked and damp with sweat and melted snow, and not that night, as we all sat gathered around the fire drinking cocoa.

The next morning, it was still snowing, and that day it never seemed to get bright. It was as if the dawn struggled and failed to climb over the edge of the world, and the low clouds gave us perpetual twilight as the snow piled soundlessly higher and higher.

For the first few days, we still saw carriages and horses passing along the road from time to time. The mail came and went. By three days before Christmas, however, we saw not a soul, and the snow had piled to the bottom edges of the windows.

"What happens if snow buries the house?" Joshua asked.

"Well, the chimney is at the top," I replied, "so Santa can still get in."

Yet, I was growing concerned. The maids and cooks had not arrived, stuck in town due to the growing mounds of snow that continued to bury the world outside. I had been quick-thinking enough to bring in extra wood from the pile outside and stack it in the pantry, but even so it would only last for so long. I encouraged the children to leave their bedrooms and come sleep down near the fireplace, next to the Christmas tree. I told them it would be cozy.

That's where we were on the chilly, dim afternoon of December the 23rd, when we heard the sound of breaking glass from upstairs.

"Could it be Santa?" Alice asked.

"Santa doesn't break windows," Amanda said.

"It's too early for Santa," I cut her off. A kinder explanation, anyway. "It was probably just the wind. The three of you wait here, and I'll go see what it is."

I genuinely believed my own explanation, but I felt a shiver of fear as I left the warmth of the hearth and headed up the stairs. I told myself that it was worry over the plunging temperature inside the house, which would only get worse if a window had, in fact, been broken, say by the branch of a nearby tree. But I knew that it was something else.

On the second floor, I walked from outside window to outside window, trying to find the source of the noise, expecting to see snow piling on the windowsill and drifting to the floor. All the windows appeared to be intact, however, and I was about to give up and head up to the third floor where the lumber room and now-unused servants' quarters were, when I noticed the bits of glass next to Joshua's bed.

He had placed Henry's terrarium on his desk, and now the side of it was shattered, as though it had been hit with a mallet. The glass wasn't *inside* the terrarium, though, it was all over the floor, where dirty, round spots the size of a pencil eraser led away in two uneven lines until they vanished not far from the door.

"What was it?" Joshua asked as I came back downstairs, hoping that the firelight would hide how pale and drawn my face had become.

"Your terrarium fell over," I said. "I think Henry got out."

Joshua made to rise and go look for him, but I grabbed him around the waist. "I don't think you should," I said. "There's broken glass and you could cut yourself. We'll clean it up when it's more light outside."

"But what about Henry?" Joshua objected. "He'll freeze."

Somehow, I doubted it, but what I said was, "Insects know how to survive. You found him in the winter, so obviously he can withstand some cold, and it's not so cold in here. Besides, he'll know to go someplace warm."

Looking at the fireplace, I hoped it wasn't true.

That evening, we heard a sound from the upstairs. A clicking sound, like two sticks rapping together. "Branches," I told the children, as we all looked up at the ceiling above our heads, "tapping on the windowpanes." In silence, we listened to the sound moving from one side of the house to the other; searching.

"How big was Henry when you last saw him?" I thought to ask Joshua at one point, when the noises had subsided. I realized that I had been avoiding the terrarium since it was installed, hadn't even peered inside. Joshua held up his hands a little way apart, indicating a space the size of a large man's boot.

"Bugs don't get that big," Amanda told him.

"Henry did," Joshua replied. I didn't argue, though I wanted to.

***

"I have to go to the bathroom," Alice said, tugging on the sleeve of my dressing gown. I looked at the big clock that stood upon the mantel and saw that it was a little after three in the morning, making it officially Christmas Eve.

"It's just down the hall," I said.

"I'm scared," she replied.

So am I, I wanted to say, but I knew better. Looking at the other two children where they lay on the rug in front of the orange glow of the hearth, I nodded and took her small hand and led her out of the parlor and toward the water closet.

The door to the washroom was just beyond the base of the stairs, and when we got there I asked if she wanted to go in by herself. "As long as you promise to wait right here," she said, and I held out my pinkie, which she wrapped in hers and gave it a firm shake.

She went into the room and shut the door, and I leaned against the wall and felt how cold the house was already growing everywhere except in the parlor, where I was keeping the fire tended. The snow outside had drifted higher than the bottoms of the windows, now, and in places it blacked out the glass. I could feel the cold oozing in.

On the stairs, I heard a sound. A familiar clatter. It was one I had heard many times before. The children's mother kept a brass statue of a cat on a small table on the landing, and every time one of the children went barreling down the stairs—or up them—and took that corner too quickly, they knocked into the table and sent that brass cat clattering to the floor.

The sound was so familiar that I even assumed I knew the entire story of its origin in a moment. Joshua had awakened and, noticing my absence, had decided to slip upstairs to look for his lost pet. I pushed myself off the wall and stepped around the corner, expecting to see his feet disappearing up the stairs and readying my voice to call up and scold him.

Something was on the stairs, but it wasn't Joshua. It was the size of a small pony, and even in the dim light I could see the color of its boxy body, gray with green bands and red spots. Its squat proboscis was the length and girth of my forearm, and its legs hinged up and down with that horridly mechanical jerkiness as it came hurtling down the steps toward me.

I might have been frozen there until it arrived had Alice not chosen that moment to step out of the washroom and, when she saw the massive monster coming, let out a high-pitched scream. This seemed to stop the creature in its tracks for a moment, and when Joshua and Amanda appeared in the doorway, I saw that Joshua was holding a fireplace poker.

Unsure of what I was doing, save that I had to keep the children safe, I grabbed the poker from him and advanced on the demon on the stairs. At first it seemed uncertain how to proceed, and then it lunged forward. I brought the poker down and struck it, the pointed end glancing off one of its red eyes.

Though seemingly uninjured, the creature drew back, and I pressed my advantage, forcing my way up the stairs, batting at it with the poker. On the same landing where it had, indeed, knocked the cat statue from its perch, there was a round, stained glass window the size of a dinner table, and with a single, mechanical hop, the thing propelled itself away from me and through the glass, out into the snowy night.

Now it is midnight on Christmas Eve. Immediately after the creature's departure, we retreated to the parlor, and I stoked the fire as bright as it would go. We heard it moving outside the windows, against the walls. I built the fire up until it was blazing, thinking of that hideously segmented body coming down the chimney like some profane Santa Claus.

Now, however, the fire has died to embers, and I have nothing left at hand to throw on the flames. I made an effort at breaking down the furniture earlier in the day, but most of it is too sturdily constructed for the tools at hand.

The children are sleeping fitfully, huddled as close to the fire as I will allow. They should be harassing me to open their presents early, not wanting to wait for Santa to come, and I should be giving in, as their mother always does, and allowing them to each unwrap one present tonight—just one!—and save the rest for the morning.

Instead, most of the presents are burnt, still in their boxes and shiny paper. I've taken a heavy knife from the kitchen and sheared most of the branches from the tree and burned those as well. I have made two trips to the pantry for more wood, but the pile there is dwindling to nothing, and I am loathe to leave the children alone for long.

The back door is snowed shut, even if I were willing to open it, which I am not. I've seen the shadow moving outside the windows, and the last time it passed, it must have been as big as a horse. It has been hours since I saw it last, but I know that it's still out there, waiting for us. I can hear it now, up on the rooftop, click click click...

Author's Notes:

I've always loved the ghost stories of M. R. James and E. F. Benson and the like, and those classic, turn-of-the-century spectral yarns are often set around Christmas. The tradition of ghost stories at Christmas seems to be one that we've lost, over the years, though it also seems ripe for a comeback—but as much as I loved them, I'd never really written one.

I resolved to correct that oversight, and this very Benson-ish tale was the result. It wasn't written for any specific invitation or anthology, just for me to exorcise the bug (pun intended) of a Christmas ghost story. It was broadcast on Pseudopod on Christmas Eve 2021—my eighth appearance on that venerable podcast, if I'm doing my math right—but this is its first time in print.

DOCTOR PITT'S MENAGERIE

Archie Pitt had worked in the movies until computers drove him out—building razor-toothed cannibal plants for *Seeds of Change* (aka *Terror Harvest*), creating the crystalline thing that crawled out of the well at the end of *Out of Space*, and masterminding the vampire-to-giant-bat transformation effects for *Blood Night*.

Rolling into the aughts, though, demand for his work started to dry up and blow away. He still got a gig every now and again; cheapie homages to the campy monster movies of the '80s, stuff like *Beyond the Void*, but he dropped out of sight before the advent of crowdfunding and VOD, when his talents might *really* have come back into use.

"Retired" was the word we used, but "disappeared" was probably more apt. We heard that he left California, moved back to his old hometown. There was no shortage of money in his family coffers; at least, that was the rumor. What he had done he did for the love of it, and now that the love was gone, well, so was he.

Which was why the invitations came as such a shock. Not all of us were in L.A. by then; not all of us ever had been. The changing tides of cinematic fortunes hadn't been kind of most of us. We weren't the sorts of people who weathered such seismic shifts well.

Gabe was a screenwriter who had worked on *Out of Space* and written early treatments for some post-slasher schlock as recently as 2014's *Doctor Slaughter*, but paychecks these days were few and far between, and he did construction jobs on the side to help pay the mortgage on his shitty house up near Laurel Canyon.

The death of the VHS tape had closed down Something Strange video, which Sabrina had owned outright ever since her second husband Mick died, and she didn't have the liquidity to get back in on the boom in VHS nostalgia that was just now raising certain boats. She worked at a lingerie store, last any of us knew. Someplace with a crescent moon in the logo.

Walter had never lived in L.A. Never lived anyplace but the big, rambling house in Ohio that he inherited from his folks when they passed away. But he flew out once a year, like clockwork, to go shopping. He was a regular Forry Ackerman in the making, collecting the monster movie memorabilia that stuffed his house to bursting.

Lanie had played bass in the band Sex Creep—which showed up in the club in *Blood Night*—and put out one studio album before the whole thing fell apart. She lived up in Petaluma now, and worked in a bookstore that also sold vinyl records. It always had, she said, but now that hipsters had rediscovered vinyl, their selection was a whole lot bigger.

What we all had in common—the *only* thing we all had in common, besides an affection for cheesy monster movies—was that we had all known Archie in a more-than-professional capacity. We had been his friends; had been to his house, back when he still lived in town. We had seen his private collection. And we were the ones who got the invitations.

They looked like something between an invite to a kid's birthday party, a school flyer, and the ad for one of those midnight horror shows that movie theatres and drive-ins used to put on. Big letters in grainy, photocopied black on yellow, magenta, and sickly blue paper inviting us to the grand opening of "Doctor Pitt's Menagerie."

Cartoony drawings of cobwebs and coffins and a crawling hand decorated the margins, and we all recognized the art as being from Archie's pen, even though none of us had seen him draw anything in more than a decade. The words, in their hand-lettered fonts, promised "Chills! Thrills! Fun for all ages!" And each invitation, folded carefully in two places and tucked inside a regular-sized envelope with no return address, held a plane ticket that dropped out when we opened it up.

Was it arrogance for Archie to assume that we would drop everything—our lives, such as they were, in all their various states of disarray—and get on board the flights he had arranged for us? That he could beckon, with the paper equivalent of one of Christopher Lee's raised eyebrows, and we would come somnolently to him like a hypnotized victim in some black-and-white horror flick? If so, his arrogance was not misplaced.

Some of us had stayed in touch, over the years, and we called each other, or exchanged the Facebook equivalent of hushed messages back-and-forth, speculating on what the invitations could mean. Had Archie been working on something all this time? And, perhaps more pressingly, was there something in this for us?

Others of us had dropped out of contact, but we all recognized each other when we arrived at the Kansas City International Airport around the same time. Those of us whose flights arrived first were greeted outside the gates by a tall figure in a chauffeur's outfit. His face was angular and waxy, the stubble on his chin strangely staged, like the perpetual five o'clock shadow of an action movie hero. His eyes were hidden behind mirrored aviators even though it was the dead of night, and he held a white sign. It didn't say our names, though. It said, "Pitt's Menagerie."

We guessed, for the time being, that meant us. "The others will be here shortly," the chauffeur said, when the first of us approached him. "Then it will be my pleasure to take you where you're all going." His words seemed to contain an odd mixture of formality and teasing casualness. They lacked any discernable accent, any hint of a midwestern twang.

Lanie was one of the first ones there, her hair now unfashionably big and out-of-the-bottle blond, probably to hide the fact that she was going gray. She and Gabe were actually on the same flight, though they didn't realize it until they were disembarking, Lanie's flight having jogged down from SFO to LAX where she boarded the same plane that brought Gabe to Kansas City. We hugged, Lanie running her hand over Gabe's still stubble-bald head, jokingly disparaging the gray hairs in his beard. He asked about the others and Lanie said that she had talked to Sabrina on the phone, that she was going to be here. None of us knew for sure about Walter, until he walked up behind.

While we had all gotten older, Walter had changed in some other, less definable way. His skin didn't actually look any more lined, and his hair was still as black and slick as it had ever been, falling over his forehead in a clumsy wave, but there was something about him that made it look as if he had exchanged skeletons over the intervening years, his skin now hanging off him like an ill-fitting suit. "I've had some health troubles," he said, by way of answer to a question that we were all too polite—or too uncomfortable—to ask.

Sabrina was the last to arrive, and she came with a younger girl on her arm. The girl wore fishnets under a denim skirt, and a leather jacket over a Dokken T-shirt that was manufactured to look faded. Her hair was dyed with one green stripe, and she smiled nervously at all of us while Sabrina introduced her as Megan. A glance at Lanie told us that she didn't know any more about this than we did, and Sabrina didn't offer much in the way of explanation, as Megan flashed a smile that showed small, round teeth and shook each of our hands in turn.

"I was able to get Megan a ticket last minute," Sabrina said, casting a defiant glance at the statuesque chauffeur. "I hope Archie won't mind?"

"The more the merrier," the chauffeur said with a smile. His teeth were almost blindingly white, and much sharper-looking than Megan's were.

The black SUV seated all seven of us, counting the chauffeur, with Megan squeezed between Lanie and Sabrina in the third row. Sabrina's hand settled on Megan's thigh, Walter slumped against the window, and Gabe leaned forward in his seat, looking out as we passed the lights of Kansas City. "Where are we going?" Lanie asked from the back, crinkling the paper of the invitation as she pulled it out of her bag, which led to all of us doing the same, comparing colors, passing them around to see that they were, in fact, all identical, except for the shade of paper upon which they were printed.

"It's a surprise," the chauffeur said from the driver's seat, his hands on the steering wheel, encased in black gloves like the killer in a *giallo* movie. Even with its flyover sprawl, Kansas City seemed small and dim to those of us who were used to the City of Angels, but as we turned from one highway to another—the numbers on the signs we passed meaning nothing to us, lost to our memories as soon as they were out of sight—those lights gradually grew farther apart, the sodium orange night glow of downtown appearing and then fading as we drove into the sparser lights of the suburbs.

It got darker the farther we went, and we passed empty storefronts and a long, concrete wall slowly being overtaken by some sort of creeping vine. "Kudzu?" Lanie asked, but, "We're not far enough south for that," Walter said, his voice sounding like it was dredged up from someplace far away.

When we stopped, it was in the parking lot of an abandoned mall. The pavement spiderwebbed with cracks, the building a darkened monolith against the city lights in the distance. We weren't exactly out in the boonies or anything—there were lit storefronts close enough that we could see them; a Shell station on one corner—but they felt far away, somehow, and the parking lot seemed like the surface of a dead world.

"So, this doesn't feel like we're going to be murdered or *anything*," Lanie said, bending her neck to peer out the windshield toward the darkened mall.

The chauffeur didn't reply, just opened his door—which beeped to let him know that the keys were still in the ignition, even as the dome light came on, permitting a reflected glimpse of that too-white smile in the rearview mirror—and stepped out onto the cracked pavement.

One by one, the rest of us did the same because, honestly, what else were we going to do? We had already come this far.

The moon looked red—stained by the light pollution from the nearby city—but also big, close, pressed tight against the bulk of the mall. The lights on the tops of the tall poles in the parking lot were dark, with only the streetlights from the intersection at our backs to light our way, glowing off the glass doors ahead of us. Taped to those doors was a ghost; a white shape blotched with black that, upon closer inspection, resolved into a larger version of the invitations that we had, by then, all crammed back into our bags or pockets. "Doctor Pitt's Menagerie," it said. "Come one, come all…but NOT FOR THE FAINT OF HEART!"

The headlights of the SUV were still on, but they were pointed off at an angle, illuminating a brown expanse of wall, nothing more. The chauffeur walked unerringly to the glass doors and held one of them open for us—a practiced motion—while his other hand swept down in a gesture for us to enter. Those aviators still wrapped his eyes, mirrors shining back darkness and tiny spots of distant light. That smile still decorated his face. It seemed like a rictus then, calling to mind *Mr. Sardonicus* and *The Man Who Laughs*.

We walked through the door, into the dark, Sabrina and Megan holding hands, the rest of us wishing we had someone's hand to hold.

The glass door closed behind us with none of the gothic finality that we had all, by then, come to expect. Just a gentle whoosh of displaced air, not even the faint click of a lock. The chauffeur and the night left outside.

We found ourselves in an empty store, a Sears or a Dillard's, it was almost impossible to tell now. Mannequins jutted out in half-completed disarray, like figureheads on a ship's prow, and up ahead the empty glass coffins of disused jewelry cases formed a vanguard around escalators frozen into stairs.

We expected it to be dark, but it wasn't, not entirely. There was a dim light from up ahead, an otherworldly glow with a color that was, as we drew closer, actually more than one color. Pinks and blues, greens and purples all rubbing up against one another but never quite mixing.

Beyond the entrance to the empty department store, the rest of the mall opened out. It was built into a hillside and now, as if by some act of prestidigitation, we found ourselves on the second floor. Here the light was clearer, and it illuminated the polished floors, the glassy storefronts. The source of the light was somewhere up ahead, and we all walked toward it, huddling close together through some unspoken herd instinct, our eyes scouring around at the shadows that closed in on us.

The lights came from the sign. They illuminated it almost sourcelessly, glowing up from some hidden recess to paint the letters in silhouette and chiaroscuro: DOCTOR PITT'S MENAGERIE.

Whatever the storefront beneath the sign had once been, it was now transformed. The windows covered over by brick, painted a blue so dark it turned to black in the shadows of the deserted mall. In place of the usual rolling metal gate, the entry was closed off by a pair of ornate wooden double-doors, closed save for a single crack which leaked out a violet glow across the polished white floor.

"I guess this is the place," Gabe said, but none of us made the first move to swing those doors wide and see what lay beyond.

We didn't need to. As if activated by his voice, the partially-open door swung the rest of the way outward, spilling out that strange pink-purple light and silhouetting a massive shape that stood on the other side.

For a moment there was just the outline—human-shaped but also wrong, somehow, its edges at once too jagged and too smooth—and then another shadow moved in front of it, and a familiar figure stepped forward. Archie had changed over the years, as had we all, but he had also remained the same. His once bushy beard was tamed now, and he wore a white suit in place of the jeans and button-up, short-sleeved shirts that he had always sported when he was at work, but otherwise he looked more like the intervening years hadn't touched him than any of us did. It wasn't until he moved again, stepping forward with a visible limp that hadn't been there before, that he felt less like a photo from some old issue of *Gorezone* come to life.

"You all made it," he said, the smile on his lips also in his voice. When he shook our hands and pulled us into hugs, we saw that he was wearing a glove on his right hand but not his left. A new affectation, perhaps? Like the suit?

"Megan, this is Archie," Sabrina said, by way of introduction.

"The Doctor Pitt from the sign?" Megan asked as he shook her hand.

"He's not really a doctor," Walter chimed in.

"Actually, I am," Archie replied. "I finished my doctoral thesis after I moved back here. I was already about halfway along when I dropped out and ran off to California to make movie monsters."

Deftly, artfully, so that we didn't even notice it was happening, Archie maneuvered us through the greetings, the been-a-whiles, until we were on the threshold of the open door, our feet scuffling the last edges of the shining mall floors and the beginnings of the night-dark carpets, specked with flakes like polygonal stars, that lay on the other side.

Up close, the other figure hove into greater resolution. It wore an old-fashioned tuxedo, like the butler in an old dark house picture, but beneath that its skin was the gray of putty, and seemingly of a similar consistency. It didn't have features as much as it did the general impression of them, crude thumbprints dug into its pulpy face.

"Don't mind Bulwark," Archie said, and the shape stepped back, pivoting on one foot and turning in the open doorway, to let us pass. We all sucked in breaths then, took involuntary half-steps back, because we had all assumed that it was just a statue, and weren't prepared to see it move.

"Is it a suit?" Walter asked, reaching out a tentative hand to touch it, first his fingertips and then his palm resting against the hard surface of the thing.

"Bulwark was an early attempt," Archie said, reaching up to lay a paternal hand on the big figure's hulking shoulder. "Not as successful as my others, but still, I wouldn't trade him for anything."

A person in a suit, we all decided. A big man, bulky as a wrestler, boiling and sweating under pounds and pounds of heavy latex. We had all seen suits like it before. If this one seemed different, well, it was dark in here, and we were all keyed up.

"What is all this?" Gabe asked as we stepped inside. Because, after all, whatever lay beyond those doors was obviously what we had come for, what Archie had summoned us from halfway across the continent to see.

"It's what we talked about," Archie said. "I finally did it."

Did any of us really remember that night, fourteen years ago, when we were standing in Archie's house, the one we didn't then know how he could afford out in Venice Beach? Not the way that Archie remembered it.

"I never felt comfortable in my skin," Archie told us that night, standing behind his converted tiki bar, looking out the sliding glass doors at the pool which glowed like some deep-sea animal. "Never felt at home with people. I got along with everyone okay,

I suppose. I went to work, I made my monsters. I did what the bosses told me to do, and nobody ever complained very much. I went out for drinks after work, sometimes, and everybody laughed when I told a joke, and I laughed at theirs. We got on, but I didn't *feel* anything."

While he talked, our weirdly-colored drinks sweated in our hands, our eyes traveled across the framed posters that decorated the walls of the room, the wax figures that stood in the corners. Archie had made the figures himself, he told us earlier in the night. The same figures that decorated the posters, folded and creased, from first runs and special engagements. Posters for *The Reptile* and *Plague of the Zombies* and *The Devil Rides Out*. Those were the monsters that stood in the room, too. Not the kinds of things Archie was hired to make for the studios nowadays. Gothic terrors from the silver screens of yesteryear, bug-eyed and green in their housedress, furred and pointy-toothed.

"The only place I ever felt anything was in the theater," Archie went on. "I belonged in ruined castles and rotten crypts, in dark mountain forests and villages beset by terrors. I lived in a world of monsters. A world not only gone by, but that had never really existed. So I tried to make it, but I never went about it the right way."

None of us knew what to say to him that night. We knew that he was saying goodbye, that he was leaving Hollywood, leaving the business, but we didn't yet know for how long. Not that he seemed to expect us to say anything as he continued his soliloquy, his eyes fixed on the moon which was now visible above the fence and the trees, bright and almost white. An eye that the darkness had developed to look back at Archie Pitt.

"I'm sure that I'm making you all uncomfortable," he said, with a sad smile. "I truly don't mean to be. This isn't supposed to be a sad night. I'm leaving, but I'll see you all again. This town, this world," and here he had gestured with his glass to take in, we assumed at the time, Hollywood, with all its many promises and limitations, "has no place left for me. Or, I think, for any of you. We're all going our separate ways, but we'll meet again. Of all the people I have known since I came west, the five of you are the only ones who ever seemed to really understand."

He had turned from the door, then. Turned away from the pool and the moon and back into the dimly-lit room, with its monsters and us. "You *do* understand, don't you?"

And we had all murmured our assent, because what else could we have done? We were his friends, and you don't tell your friend that you don't know what the hell he's talking about. Not on his last night in town. But still, there was something in his brown eyes, shadowed and dark and gone in a moment, replaced by the glitter of a smile only slightly forced, that told us, even then, that we had failed him somehow.

After that night, none of us ever saw him again, until he stepped out of that purple light and into the darkened mall. He disappeared off the face of the earth. No forwarding address, no phone number. By the next week, when Gabe drove by in his shitty van, Archie's house was empty. By the week after that, it was sold.

Could we have tracked him down? Almost certainly. We all knew that he had come to California from Kansas City. We knew that his family had money. We knew his name, his predilections. But none of us ever tried. Yet now, here we all were.

How to describe the place? The massive expanse beyond those double-doors, the room that was Doctor Pitt's Menagerie. There was a smell to it, first of all. Not obvious but subtle, loamy and coppery, buried deep under the scent of sawdust and polish, a smell that conjured to mind workshops and basement laboratories and…something else.

"It was one of those blacklight miniature golf courses before I bought it," Archie said as he led the way deeper into his creation. You could see where those elements still remained. The geometric flecks in the carpeting, the occasional stripe of neon along one wall, but the décor had otherwise changed considerably.

Candelabras taller than our shoulders stood here and there, filled with multicolored candles that remained unlit. Old furniture, a globe the size of a dining room table, bookshelves filled with musty tomes. Cobwebs connected the bits of décor, and the fact that they were the kind that you buy in a store around Halloween did little to detract from their ambiance, especially in the sourceless purple glow that enveloped the entire place.

Where the greens and holes of the miniature golf course had once been there were now great cavities carved into the floor. Gaping maws that opened down into the lower story of the mall, their sides lined with glass railings like animal enclosures at the zoo, allowing you to look down at hippos or lions or tigers or bears, oh my. Except Doctor Pitt's Menagerie contained nothing so mundane.

Each of the nine openings was walled off at its base, so that it formed an irregularly-shaped room, larger at the bottom than at the top through some optical illusion, and each room contained a tableau. Something between a wax museum and a scene from a Halloween haunted house. In the nearest one was a cemetery. Bright green moss dotted the headstones, and a low-lying fog clung thick as soup to the floor, which was made to look like earth and grass, complete with slight rises and hillocks.

Farther on there was the pillared edifice of a southern plantation house, the trees that lined the front drive reaching up as high as where we stood, their branches draped with Spanish moss. On another side was what looked to be a tomb, but not Egyptian. The angular carvings on the walls depicted some other style, likely fanciful, inspired by the cultural artwork of Central America.

Each of the settings seemed to be slightly in miniature, but the same optical illusion which made them appear larger at the bottom than at the top made them feel life-size. They were impressive enough on their own—certainly, they were the first things that caught the eye—but they weren't intended to be the main focus. Within each scene were figures. From the graves of the cemetery came, not rotten zombies or fleshless bones but lantern-eyed ghouls up from subterranean staircases, their skin the leathery green of reptiles. On the front steps of the southern manor stood a woman in a fine dress, her face that of a serpent, her hand, where it rested on a pillar, a glittering claw. In the tomb, a desiccated mummy was caught in mid-transformation, its arm halfway to a bat's wing, its face morphing from human to upturned nose and radar ears.

That would all have been one thing—more than enough—but the menagerie was more than just a wax museum. Each of the figures moved. Not with the stuttering, jarring motion of animatronics, but fluidly, smoothly, naturally. The only thing to break the illusion, to give away that we were looking at anything besides real creatures, acting out their real lives—or whatever such things had in place of life—was that they repeated their motions again and again. Like watching an animated .gif as it cycled through its handful of frames then started over.

The ghouls rose from their graves, padded across the loamy earth to the crest of the hill, raising their heads high, turning their lantern eyes toward us before making their way back, again and again. A loop of film, playing over and over.

"What the hell is this?" one of us asked. It could have been any of us. Was it a haunted house? A wax museum? A haunted wax museum? Were these things animatronics? People in suits? Even advanced holograms of some kind, their movements so precise, over and over again.

"It's our home," Archie said, and it was like he had just shattered a plate in a silent room. Since we first entered, we had been preparing ourselves for something like this, or we had thought we had been. We had expected something, but we had also known, from the moment that smell touched our nostrils, from the moment that light spilled out of the door, from the moment Walter touched that big figure and felt—there is no doubt about it—some kind of living thrum underneath, that we had walked into something terribly *wrong*.

It should probably have been Megan who ran. She was the one of us who didn't belong, who had been brought by accident, rather than design. And she *did* pull her hand free of Sabrina's, leaving the older woman listing slightly as Megan stepped forward, instead of back, her hands on the railing around the chamber full of ghouls.

Instead, Walter was the one who bolted.

"Bulwark, not yet," Archie said loudly, over his shoulder, and the dark shape stepped back in front of the door, and began to change.

One moment it was shaped like a big man, the next it began to flow into something else. Its feet rooted into the carpet like trees, and one of its arms became a tendril of clay that lashed out, caught Walter around his chest, and smashed him against the wall. Like a flood of water from a fire hydrant the gray stuff pushed him flat, pinioned his arms, lapped against the bottom of his jaw, and then hardened again, trapping him there.

"I was afraid of this," Archie said sadly, as we all shuffled our feet and looked this way and that, first toward the pits, then toward the door, guarded by whatever the hell the figure had become. Only Megan stayed still, her eyes on the ghouls making their rounds, grave to hilltop and back again.

"I'm not doing this to hurt any of you," Archie continued. He wasn't looking at us, or at the figure he called Bulwark that now stood stock still again, Walter no longer struggling in its grasp. Instead, he looked out across his menagerie. "I did this to save you. To save us all. To give us a place where we could finally belong.

"The others were volunteers, if you can believe that. And, if you search your hearts, I think you'll find that you can. I had to make sure that I got it right, before I brought you all here. But it was never the same with them. I never felt comfortable with anyone but you."

He turned back to us. The menagerie was filled with the opportunity for shadows, but his eyes caught some fragment of light. His suit seemed almost to glow in the dark.

"I'll do it," Megan said, her voice small at first, little more than a squeak, but then she found her confidence, repeated herself, louder now. "I've never seen anything I wanted so much in my life."

With a sound like someone pulling a suction cup off a window, Bulwark wrenched its arm free from the wall and, with Walter still ensconced in its muddy grip, uprooted itself from the carpet and walked on elephant feet over to where we stood, looming behind us. Archie turned to look at Megan. All of us turned to look at Megan. Sabrina went pale, her fingers twitched.

Archie walked up to the girl, put his ungloved hand out, onto her shoulder. "You were never a part of this," he said. "You can go, if you wish to go."

Megan bit her bottom lip, shook her head. "I want to stay, if I can. I want to be one of them," and she gestured down into the pit.

"You're sure?"

She nodded, and Archie raised his right arm, used the first finger and thumb of his left hand to pull off the black glove that sheathed his right. What he revealed was not a human hand. It was a twisted claw of amethyst crystal, inside which neon embers burned. He laid it on Megan's forehead, the dyed-green streak in her hair brushing the claw with a faint and distant music. For a moment she was surrounded in shadowy crackle, black against the purple light, and she fell to her knees and began to change.

Have you ever seen a werewolf in a movie? Imagine one of those, but hairless save for a single shock of green hanging over its forehead, albino pale like marble or bone, with the mouth of a crocodile and arms longer than its legs. That is what clambered over the side into the pit, which was decorated to look like a hunting lodge, complete with fire burning in the hearth and the heads of animals up on the walls, their glossy black eyes reflecting the flickering light.

Those of us who remained watched the thing that had been Megan, the thing that *was* Megan now, clamber eagerly over the side and down into the pit. We watched her begin her strange pantomime, her series of seemingly pre-recorded movements. Down the stairs, prowling, glowing eyes searching for prey that had not yet been brought in to populate the once-opulent room, its furniture soon to be overturned, soon to be splintered by her own great claws. Trapped in that amber moment of potentiality. Caught forever in the heartbeat before action.

Was there any sweeter trap?

"I'm not going to force any of you into this," Archie said, and though we felt the living wall of protean flesh standing behind us, we all believed him. "Not yet," he had said to the nightmare creature, and he had meant it, this man we had known years ago, but never as well as he now proved that he knew us.

"I sent you the invitations for a reason. I'm not your father, your ex-husband, your boss. I'm your friend, and I'm inviting you to do this with me. To become a part of something. And when you think about it, reach all the way down inside, I don't think you will find my offer so much less appealing than the tracks you already run, from your work to your home, from your kitchen to your bed. If you do, if you find my menagerie repulsive, then say so now, and you can walk out that door and never return."

Walter slipped from Bulwark's tendrils, his feet unsteady on the carpeted floor. The door to the mall still stood ajar, and we all knew that Archie was telling the truth. He would let us leave this instant, if we could just tell him that we had something better to return to.

I looked him in the eyes, and I couldn't think of a thing.

Author's Notes:

This is one that I don't think a lot of my readers have seen before. It was first published in an anthology called *Bargains*, edited by Darren Hennessy and put out by Pine Float Press. The theme, well, I think the title kinda covers it.

This is another one that sits adjacent to the movies, especially the cheap monster movies released by Full Moon Video. And the stop-motion tableaus of the eponymous menagerie were inspired, in part, by moments from Mike Mignola and Christopher Golden's *Baltimore* comics, not to mention Hammer's gothic horror films.

ANUM'S FIRE (1987)—ANNOTATED

Anum was his name, but they called him the Machine Man from the Haunted Ruins *(also the title under which the movie was released in Spain and Mexico).*

At night, he stood in the courtyard and looked up at the stars, trying to remember a time before the ruins. If he ever did, he never spoke of it, for Anum spoke seldom. He wept no tears for the past he had lost, for his burning eyes could shed none. So Arrestes the Bold wept for him, standing in the shadows of the columns and looking out at the huge golem of gold that loomed there in the semi-darkness.

(Was there some gay subtext between Arrestes and Anum, as Sophia Serano argues in her biography, The Black Beyond? *It's hard to say, especially since it would have been difficult to consummate any such romance given the … unorthodox nature of Anum's physiology.)*

Anum had vanquished the ghosts of the haunted ruins *(in the montage that opens the film)*, for what fear could grave-cold spirits hold for a being of such metal and heat? He had blazed a trail from those ruins to the palace he now occupied—*(itself a combination of soundstages, interiors shot in the Museo di Storia Naturale, and the ruins of the Castle of San Sebastiano on the island of Sardenia)*—yet he felt uncontented.

"Sleep now," said the Princess Ilia, whom Anum had saved from the clutches of the Web People *(also in the montage)*. She laid her small, pale hand upon the metal of his chest and felt the heat that was his heart. Heat enough, she knew, that it could burn her, should her hand linger too long.

"I need no sleep," Anum told her.

(Was she attempting, at this point, to woo the metal giant? Her later betrayal and the words of the snake/queen would certainly indicate so, though what she was hoping to accomplish is unclear—see above re: his unusual physiology.)

So rejected by her savior, the Princess retreated to her chambers and threw herself upon her bed of silks and satins. Standing outside, her two bodyguards—topless, muscular women wearing long skirts and visored headdresses like metal fans—could hear her weeping.

Someone else heard, too. A serpent, black as pitch, its back a string of red diamonds—*(there is no such snake in the wild; apocryphally, the crew painted a boa)*—crawled from the mouth of a statue of the god Orr and spoke *(in the same echoing voice as Queen Zorena, regardless of which version of the film you're watching)*.

"Your hero turns his back on you," it said. "He seeks other flesh now. Other lands to conquer. He uses your throne to advance his own ambitions, and soon he will cast you aside and your kingdom will come tumbling into the sea. I have seen it come to pass. Yet, you may still prevent this calamity."

(The Biblical allegory needs no interpreter, though it's said that in the original shooting script it was a spider, rather than a snake, that spoke to Ilia. Perhaps this was rejected for being too close to the Web People.)

"Speak, spirit," Princess Ilia said, "and I will harken carefully to your words."

Outside, in the courtyard, Anum stared up at the stars, unaware that those who owed him everything were, even then, plotting against him.

We never get an origin for Anum. In his book, Orgy of the Dead, *William Teague argues that Anum was a robot from a civilization so advanced that their technology appears as magic to the people of the film. That, in fact, the "haunted ruins" in which he first appears are the remains of this lost civilization.*

Another theory is that Anum was an alien. "When I saw the movie as a kid," filmmaker Wayne Bartalos says in the commentary track on the Severin release, "I just assumed he was from another planet. It explains why he was always looking up at the night sky, right? He was looking for home."

Even as the snake was spilling its honeyed poison into the ears of Princess Ilia, Queen Zorena waited in her throne room. *(Like most of the women we see in the film, Queen Zorena is mostly naked, save for a suggestively furred thong and a golden mask, its eyes slits, the nose almost batlike. The visual synchrony between Zorena's mask and Anum's coloration serves to connect the two in some tenuous way that the film never really explores.)*

One of the armored Ogre Legion who served her—in their faceless iron masks—brought her a human skull, the top neatly removed, from which the Queen extracted with her fingers a handful of pink mush, shoving it up beneath her mask.

"Show me what you knew," she said, as she consumed the dripping gore with a terrible slurping. *(This is the first time we hear Queen Zorena speak directly, though we have already heard her voice from the snake. In at least the American dub, her voice is provided by Althea Chambers, but run through a filter to make it sound distorted and almost mechanical.)* "Show me the land of the Ghouls."

In a flash of white *(that blanks out the screen and blinds the viewer)*, Queen Zorena saw what she sought. A land of rank grasses and sere hillocks, separated by pools of rancid water. Smoke billowed from holes in the ground and rolled across the land, half-obscuring standing stones carved to resemble human figures. *(There's no record of where this was shot, but the smoking holes in the ground were likely created simply by burying some of the smoke machines.)*

Among these stones, shadows moved. Hidden by the blowing smoke, shapes capered and darted, then abruptly stilled, so motionless that they could be the stones themselves. *(Then, what we thought was a stone suddenly moves, revealing that it was a Ghoul all along, an effect achieved through careful edits, camera trickery, and the obscuring mist pumped in from offscreen.)*

These were the Ghouls. Human once, they had renounced their previous nature due to their lust for pain and flesh—that of others, certainly, but also their own. Flaying the skin from their faces and heads to leave dripping red skulls that nonetheless lived, they drove iron spikes through the meat of their limbs and hacked off their own hands to replace them with wicked blades.

It is here that the director's trademark rancid mutton gore first really reveals itself in the film. Rumor has it that actual amputees were recruited to play some of the Ghouls, though they are only ever seen in group sequences and none are credited, so that claim may be nothing more than the exploitation glee of the gorehound.

The connection between this sequence and the next is so jarring—even for this picture—as to lead many to speculate that there must be some footage missing, though so far none has ever been found in any of the no less than five cuts of the film that have been exhibited or released on home video over the years.

As it stands, it must simply be inferred that Queen Zorena commands the Ghouls, as she later does others, and that they find their way into the chambers of the Princess through some agreement that Ilia and the Queen have reached offscreen—though whether the viewer is meant to assume *that or whether, in spite of the scene with the snake, Ilia's betrayal is meant to come as a surprise is a question we cannot answer.*

Into the chambers of the Princess poured the Ghouls, coming

from some hidden passage in the wall, their bony maws dripping blood onto the marble tiles. She shrieked as they tore at her silken clothes, their hands—where hands they still possessed—smearing her pale flesh with crimson.

And then, all were gone.

(It is one of the film's most haunting moments. The bedchamber is a riot of Ghouls and the Princess; close-ups of grue and monstrous bodies juxtaposed with the finery of the palace. Then, in one still shot, the empty chamber, the Princess and her captors gone, the silks and satins in disarray, the floor streaked with red.)

Anum strode across a field of stiff grasses blowing in the wind, Arrestes loping at his side, bow and quiver slung across his back. In the distance, hazy mountain peaks reached cold fingers toward the purple sky.

(Here as well the connective tissue of the film is missing, the scene of Anum and Arrestes discovering the bloody chamber and the missing princess merely implied.)

"Come winds," the voice of Queen Zorena echoed over the grasslands. "Come beasts of the field. Come darkness upon the face of the land." *(Zorena's voice here is apparently diegetic, for Anum and Arrestes stop and look around when she begins to speak.)*

The wind picked up, blowing smoke across the landscape as clouds scudded *(in time-lapse speed)* across the sky and the sun went dark, as though a hand had stretched forth to cover it. "People of the Mud Tribes," the voice of the Queen boomed across the land, "the time has come to pay your debt to me."

From out of *(previously unseen)* pools of standing water rose those peoples of the Mud Tribes *(simply stunt performers plastered with dried mud and cheesecloth, ping pong balls cut in half and placed over their eyes)* while Flesh Tearers sprang from the tall grasses, their muscular legs devouring the ground in loping strides. Black *(ragged, stop-motion)* birds began to pour from the darkened sky.

Arrestes drew his bow as the nightmare tide surged toward them and nocked a black-fletched arrow, letting it fly. It shattered the eye of one of the Mud Tribe in a spray of yellow gore, and the creature collapsed to the ground.

Anum reached out a hand, staying Arrestes from his next shot. Then a glow began to build beneath the square plates that made up his golden body. First at his feet and then up across his broad torso to his shoulders and finally pouring from his eyes in two radiant beams, bright as the sun. These he swept across the grasslands before him, and wherever they touched, the rank vegetation blossomed into flame.

(This is the first time we ever see the super weapon for which the film is titled in its most commonly-seen American release. There are no records of how the lights within Anum's suit were accomplished, though the twin beams—which can also be seen on the film's poster art—are pretty clearly optical effects. They destroy the grasslands and, mostly by implication, the majority of the Mud Tribe.)

Racing ahead of the devastation, one of the Flesh Tearers leapt upon Anum, the hot metal of his torso burning its paws, even as the darkened sky seemed to descend in a vast cloud of tearing beaks.

(In the earlier shot, there are three visible "Flesh Tearers," each one a female lion, apparently rented from a local zoo and fitted with a hasty horned helm of papier-mâché for that one sequence. The Flesh Tearer that reaches Anum is, in actuality, a different *lion, this one trained by the studio animal handler and fitted with a similar, though sturdier, headdress to make it look more monstrous. Even then, it is used only for the shot of it leaping, combined with intercuts of its slavering jaws. The rest of the time, the stuntman under Anum's suit simply wrestles with an inanimate bag of fur thrown over an armature, while the attack of the vicious birds is simulated with black "noise" added to the individual frames of the film.)*

The monster bit at the metal man, its teeth denting his armored hide, but it could find no jugular to rip, no hot blood to gush forth. Anum wrestled it to the ground and snapped its neck, leaving its body to lie as he turned to his friend.

The black birds had come too close for arrows, and so Arrestes had drawn his brace of curved blades and with them he lay about himself, an ashy snowfall of feathers and avian bodies dropping around him. *(The withdrawal of the birds, too, is implied. One frame they are filling the air around Arrestes, the next he is putting his blades away, small cuts from beaks and talons peppering his face and arms.)*

"The tower of the Queen lies there," Arrestes said, pointing toward a peak that rose above the others. "Yet, to approach, we will have to cross the Valley of the Dead. I know an herb that, when crushed and mixed with this burned mud, will render me invisible to them. But what of you?"

"I have no fear of the dead," Anum replied. "They are the past."

(This is the first time the movie makes reference to a major theme. While Anum's Fire *was released to international markets nearly a full decade before the director's death, alone in his cramped apartment in Rome, there are elements of the screenplay that seem to foreshadow an artist turning his back on his past and striking out into the great unknown.)*

The Valley of the Dead was a place of twisted, gnarled trees *(actually pieces of driftwood)* in which the dead lay tangled, half-sunk in a rotting bog. It was a place where death was arrested but never halted. A place of eternal decay. A place of stasis.

Into this place walked Anum, a thing which could not decay. The gold of his armored body seemed to shine brighter in the gloom of the valley—*(a trick the director purportedly pulled off by shining pin lights at the figure from off-screen)*—and the mist parted to let him pass.

By his side strode Arrestes, his skin smeared with the greenish paste made from the magical herb. At their approach, the dead stirred from where they lay, gripped in the branches of the blighted trees, but they did not intercede.

As they reached the far side of the Valley, however, Arrestes wiped the back of his hand across his forehead *(this preceded by an uncomfortable close-up of sweat trickling down his face, carving channels through the greenish muck)*, wiping away the magical herb. His hand falling again to his side, he saw the green smear across its back and realized his danger, even as all of the dead, who had closed ranks behind them, rushed forward as one.

"Run," Anum said, extending one of his mighty arms between Arrestes and the dead, and then he once more unleashed that terrible light from his eyes. *(This time we get to see a stuntman doing a full-body burn as pyrotechnics light up the Valley.)*

In the smoky, blazing aftermath, several of the dead stumbled forward, but made it only a few steps beyond the fire before Anum's hands crushed them to dust. *(Nice close-ups of those big, golden gloves crushing dusty skulls here, and one of a sizzling gold fist going through a much juicier ribcage.)*

For a moment, Anum stood, meat cooking on the surface of his metal skin. He tilted his head back and looked up toward the sky, but no stars were visible in the depths of the Valley, through air choked with smoke. "Perhaps I have seen the last of them," he said.

(One imagines that anyone to whom the film might have been accountable at the studio assumed Anum to be talking about the living corpses he had just vanquished, rather than the stars. For anyone who has paid any attention to the strange air of tragedy that surrounds the unstoppable metal man, however, rather than simply figures of dollars and cents, it's impossible to think he means anything else.)

A cry *(from off-screen)* that struggled into a wet choking and then a thud echoed through the Valley, and Anum turned from his silent contemplation of the night to lope into the darkness, up a hillside strewn with boulders.

"Arrestes?" he asked, his voice reverberating through the orange dark, before spotting first the puddle of blood and then the body of his friend, its neck a red welter of *(extreme close-up, complete with severed bones and the wet ruin of a throat)* gore, its head missing.

The body of Arrestes lay at the edge of that pool of blood, a tributary for a red river that became a crimson lake. The gaze of the metal man traveled from all that remained of his friend up the hillside to a red-spattered boulder *(this is all night-for-night shots, with an orange haze that could be the fire in the Valley below casting everything in smoky dimness, except for this one boulder, which is lit in red, probably from a gel light suspended above)* where the head of Arrestes was balanced on its frayed neck, mouth agape, eyes bloody.

Next to the severed head stood a warrior in black armor. Blood ran in syrupy, congealing rivulets down the head of its massive axe *(a weapon shaped more like an enormous meat cleaver than the image the word 'axe' might normally conjure)*. The black helm encasing its head was spiked, as was the breastplate that strained to cover the bulging muscles of its chest. Its arms were uncovered, the skin ashen, while the legs terminated in heavy, cloven hooves *(fur leggings and hoof-shaped boots)*.

"I drank your friend's hot blood," the warrior said. "I tasted his fear and knew his despair, when my axe slew him. They tell me you have no blood, but I will make you die nonetheless, and I will forge a great weapon from the ichor of your heart."

(The clash that follows is one of the strangest parts of an already bizarre—even for the director's admittedly eccentric filmography—picture. What seems like it will be a major encounter ends in a matter of seconds. Anum stands stock still as the warrior swings its bloody axe, reaching up one hand, in an insert shot, just in time to catch the blade in its palm. Cracks of light run across the surface of the blade—optical effects, again—and it shatters in slow motion. Then we see a close-up of Anum's other hand as it closes over the spiked, black helm of the warrior and squeezes, *blood running in rivers from between those golden fingers. The last shot of the fight is a pulled back image of the warrior's body, already having crumpled to the ground, as Anum steps over it.)*

The warrior slain, Anum raised the body of his fallen friend and roared his anger and his grief into the heavens. But he did not weep, for his eyes could still make no tears, and now there was no one left to weep for him.

Inside the tower, Queen Zorena waited. In the room were no soldiers, no guards. Princess Ilia sat on the steps at the Queen's feet, a delicate gold chain fastened by a jewel-studded choker around her neck, leading to a ring on the arm of the throne. Queen Zorena rested a hand atop the golden locks of the Princess.

(While we have previously seen the inside of the Queen's throne room in earlier sequences, this is the first time the camera has been pulled back enough to get a sense of the chamber. It is surprisingly organic, like the interior of a massive stone heart, with mist-filled passages leading off in almost every direction. In the center, the Queen's throne rears high above her, carved in the shape of a horned bat, its wings spread.)

From beyond the chamber, the sounds of battle could be heard. Then, a tide of blood poured from the door in front of the throne. *(The effect is like someone dashing a bucket of fake blood on the floor—but it never stops. The frothy wave comes from nowhere and begins to fill the room, Princess Ilia retreating up the steps to escape it.)*

Only when the Queen and the Princess sat alone on an island in the midst of a sea of red did Anum appear in the doorway. *(The figure of Anum is backlit by a cheat light; the only details of him we can see are the glowing edges of the square plates of his body, and the twin beacons of his eyes.)* In his right hand, he held a helm of one of the Ogre Legion, and as he crushed it like pot metal, blood poured forth.

"Have you come to rescue this morsel?" the Queen asked. "Can you show her the love her young body desires?"

"Once, I came to save her," Anum said. "I sought to preserve something of beauty in a savage world. Now, my heart is gone, and I have come only to destroy. I care not what or who."

(At his declaration, Princess Ilia, her pride presumably wounded

by the fact that he's no longer there to save her, stands and reveals her treachery. Anum seems no more surprised by it than we are.)

"You then," he said, his eyes still burning. "All this blood is on your hands, because of wounded vanity."

The metal man stepped forward, the blood boiling as his boot sank into its red depths. Queen Zorena smiled beneath her mask *(how can we tell? I don't know, but we can)* and raised her arms above her head. "Come figures," she called out. "Come shadows."

(A wind machine kicks on from offstage, behind the throne. It billows the Princess's hair and her silk garments. Mist fills the room. When the camera pulls back, we see the transformation it has wrought.)

The horned bat that had been the throne became a living, breathing *(animatronic)* creature, the heavy flesh of its wings folded down now, a tent around the two women. Its shaggy head, with four horns—two jutting upward, two curving toward its slavering jaws—hung low, eyes red as it dragged itself forward, toward Anum.

Where the front of the monster was all bat, its back half was reptilian. Scales covered its haunches, its tail lashed against the walls of the cavern. *(In the shots of the bat monster, the blood on the floor is all gone. We can only assume that it proved too challenging to set up for each relatively expensive shot.)*

Anum met it where it came, his hands locking onto those curving horns as the jaws bit for him. It raised one huge, clawed wing, and raked it down his side, opening rents in the metal that bled white-hot fire *(literally created using a cutting torch, as near as anyone can tell).*

For several moments the two titans struggled, and then, with a terrible crack, Anum shattered one of the horns, snapping it from the creature's head *(close up of a gruesome stump)* and jamming it up under the bat's jaw, through its mouth, and out one of its red eye sockets. With one final thrash, the monster slumped and lay still.

"No," Princess Ilia cried, trying to back away, finding herself at the end of the chain that bound her to the throne. "She captured me. She hypnotized me. I was not myself."

"I care not," Anum said, his hand closing heavy around the Princess's pale throat. *(In the American version, what happens next is—perhaps blissfully—cut short, though we can see the headless body of the Princess in the background of a later scene. There's rumor of an unexpurgated "gore cut" that shows him squeezing her head from her body, but it has never yet surfaced.)*

"You are indeed mighty," Queen Zorena said. She threw her arms around the shoulders of the metal man, a feat only possible because of the height of the throne compared to where he stood. *(The Queen's flesh does not sizzle when it contacts Anum, though whether this is an intentional artistic choice—another way to subtly connect the two—or a simple continuity error is impossible to say.)* "Think what we could accomplish together."

"I have accomplished too much," he replied.

(This is the scene where, in some cuts, Zorena asks "Who made you? Where did you come from?" and Anum replies "No one. Nowhere. Nothing." Then he turns those eye beams on again, directing them straight into the eye slits of Zorena's mask, which heats up like a filament bulb and when the camera once more shows a wide shot, there is nothing but a cooked skeleton hanging from the golden mask, the bones all collapsing onto the throne.)

Anum stood on the top of a cliff as the sun rose. Before him was the sea, the waves crashing against the rock, drowning out all other sound. The fire inside him had all but died out. He looked like nothing more than a suit of armor, propped up there to catch the first rays of the sun as they glinted off his golden body. The crashing of the waves grew louder and louder.

The final shot of the film, before the brief roll of the credits, is a black screen with a quote from Lord Byron, the sound of the waves still audible beneath it: "I am ashes where once I was fire."

Author's Notes:

Every now and then, I write a story that I can't believe somebody lets me get away with, let alone pays me to publish. "Baron von Werewolf Presents: Frankenstein Against the Phantom Planet" was one such, originally published in *Eternal Frankenstein*, edited by Ross Lockhart, later collected in *Guignol & Other Sardonic Tales*—so yes, Ross was reckless enough to pay me for that one *twice*.

This is another. Written for a Lucio Fulci tribute anthology, when editors Perry Ruhland and Astrid Rose pitched the project to me, they mentioned that they were hoping to get some stories that dug into the *rest* of Fulci's filmography, not just his zombie and gore pictures. So I decided to write a sword and sorcery tale, inspired by (mostly the poster for) Fulci's *Conquest*. Except, this being me, I decided to do it in a roundabout way. I would do it as annotations to a Fulci film that didn't exist—the film that *Conquest* might have been, in another universe, while also trading in the tragedy of Fulci's final years.

It's one of the weirdest things I've ever written, but so far readers seem to be pretty happy with it, and I'm grateful for that.

THE PEPYS LAKE MONSTER

The Wikipedia page for "Pepys Lake Monster," accessed 2015

> Pepys (/ˈpiːps/PEEPS) Lake refers to both a lake and neighboring town located in northeastern Connecticut, near the borders of Massachusetts and Rhode Island. Pepys Lake is best known for a series of monster sightings that occurred there in the early 1900s, and *The Pepys Lake Monster*, a 1963 black-and-white science fiction monster film directed by Graham Ward inspired by the sightings. *The Secret of Pepys Lake*, a documentary film about the monster and the making of the movie, was released in 2012 and won the Raab Prize at the High Strange Film Festival in Golden, Colorado.

Pepys Lake, 1959

Michael Deschutes was out too late on a rainy Sunday in his father's scow when he saw the monster. It wasn't quite dark, but the thick, low clouds made it nearly so, and the rain fell in a steady tap, like fingers on typewriter keys, making the early evening a miserable one. Mike sat near the rear of the boat, his shoulders hunched, the hood of his slicker pulled up over his head.

He was in that place, at that moment, because earlier in the day he had neglected his chores in favor of watching Cynthia Carter practice high kicks in her father's barn. She was performing a dance number for the talent show that was to be held at nearby Padgett's Mill High, where all the kids in Pepys Lake went to school, and that day she had invited Mike over to watch her practice, and he had simply lost track of time.

The explanation had done nothing to palliate his father, however, and as punishment for his negligence he had been sent out in the little scow and the thickening weather, which is why he was the one who saw the monster.

He had heard stories about it since he was a kid, of course, but he had never seen it himself, nor known of anyone whose tales of its sightings seemed more credible than those of drunkards seeing snakes. Yet here it was, rising up from the lake not twenty yards from the bow of the boat, rising and rising on a neck that was taller than the mast.

Mike would later attempt to describe the creature, first to his father, then the police, and then to the *Pepys Lake Observer* and even the *Padgett's Mill Herald*. The head was long and angular, almost equine, but the neck was like that of a prehistoric beast. Mike had never seen a giraffe, even in a picture, but if he had then that's what he would have compared it to, save for the huge, froggy eyes that blazed like lamps. It made a sound, "like a train chugging along a track," and when it opened its mouth it spit forth a geyser of flame.

Somewhere in Germany, the 1940s

Reinhardt had been a puppeteer before the war. Every year, during the summer months, he had set out his little stage in the town square and re-enacted the story of *Der Rattenfänger*. The animatronic figure of the piper was the star of the show in his multi-hued clothes made of candy glass, belling out around his mechanical legs so that the light filtered through them. Inside the figure's back was a music box, a spiked cylinder that turned on a spindle as carefully-tuned metal fingers plinked over the raised knobs to create the tinkling music that summoned the rats.

Each rat was not distinct, but a single organism, a mass of rabbit fur laid over wheels and gears and red eyes that lit from within, all rolling along behind the piper as he led them out of the city and into the mountain, which opened wide on its clockwork hinges to receive them. And then the curtain closed, and when it opened again the piper was being denied his due payment by the townspeople, simple automata in black robes who bobbed their heads and held bags painted with *pfennig* signs so that the children would recognize them as money. When the piper reached for the bags, the townspeople pulled them away with a jerk, their arms bending backward on a hinge.

The curtains closed and opened once again, and there was the piper, once more leading a huddled mass through the town square to the hungry mountain. This time, the mass was made up of children. They spun on their bases, to indicate that they were dancing, though once again they were truly just one figure, like a wagon that the piper pulled behind himself, their wheels hidden in tracks sunk into the base of the puppet stage. They disappeared into the mountain and it snapped closed behind them, the piper's tune dwindling off gradually into silence. In the town square, the real children clapped and clapped, even though he had just shown them a vision of their own untimely deaths.

Reinhardt's father had been a shoemaker by trade, but a stage magician by choice. He had gone off to the bigger cities a few times a year, to perform tricks on disreputable stages for crowds of drunkards and harlots. In their rooms above his father's shop, the old man had created the tricks that he would perform. Mechanical birds and spring-loaded mechanisms that he tucked up his sleeves. Boxes with hidden compartments, and plants that seemed to grow in a matter of moments.

These had always been what fascinated Reinhardt. Not the tricks themselves, but their secrets. The mechanisms that made them work. He knew that for the children, the illusion was the thing; that's why he worked so hard to hide the machinery that drove his puppets. But for him, it was the building, not the performing, that gave him joy. He loved the secret gears and wheels that made his creations live.

As for the story, he never understood its appeal, not until the soldiers came and began rounding people up. Some were conscripted into the army, to serve the cause, while others were taken off to someplace worse. Once again a piper came and took the children of Reinhardt's town, though this time the mountains that opened wide to claim them had other names: Dachau and Buchenwald and Auschwitz.

When the first of the soldiers marched through the cobblestoned streets, Reinhardt hid in the rooms above his father's old shop, where he now made puppets and automata, instead of shoes. His father had been a cobbler and a magician, but he had also been a Jew. Fortunately, he was four years in the ground by the time the soldiers arrived, and Reinhardt hadn't kept the faith, had never been interested in miracles, only in the solid and the mechanical, what he could touch and build. Still, when he heard the gloved fist on his door, he was afraid that he had been found out, but instead of the camps he was told that the Fuhrer required his special skills for a project that would help the war effort.

It didn't make much difference, as it turned out. He was taken away by car, instead of by train, but at the end of the ride he found himself no less a prisoner. He was given a workshop much grander than the one he had made in his father's old store, and he was given the tools and assistants that he would need to complete his labors—other Jews like himself, though ones who had been identified already, turned in by their own neighbors, marked by their names and their features and the yellow stars that they wore on their sleeves—who were there to help him build mechanical monsters for the man who planned to exterminate them all, for the piper who would lead them into the mountain.

Soldiers stood outside the workshop with rifles in their hands at all hours, but Reinhardt was considered loyal, and so he was given much more leniency than he might otherwise have enjoyed. While he labored building infernal devices, he had an apartment nearby that was vastly richer than anything he had enjoyed in his home town, and he had the run of at least some parts of the city, though he seldom traveled far without seeing soldiers in their crisp uniforms.

He could almost have enjoyed the relative luxury, the work. Could almost have forgotten the purpose to which his labor was being turned, had it not been for the poor wretches who toiled alongside him, their ultimate fates written in every flinch when a soldier spoke, every line etched into their gaunt faces. Had it not been for the knowledge that he was like them, in the eyes of the men who kept him so luxuriously, and that one day they would realize it, too. So Reinhardt used his father's show business contacts—such as they were—to eventually meet with an actress who was sympathetic to the resistance, and who was, herself, in contact with filmmakers in Britain and beyond, who saw the benefit that his work could bring to their ventures instead.

So it was that one night Reinhardt, who had been a puppeteer before the war, was smuggled out of Germany under the cover of darkness to become a puppeteer of a very different sort, on a very different stage.

Pepys Lake, 2010

The diving machine was named *Nemo*—not, its inventor was quick to point out in an interview to be included in the documentary, after the fish from the movie, but rather the captain from Jules Verne. It looked like an aquatic beetle, with a turbine on its back and a light in the nose and small arms that allowed it to manipulate, however crudely, any obstacles that it might encounter, all controlled by a bank of switches and joysticks floating in a rented boat on the surface of the lake.

Sealed inside *Nemo*'s watertight outer casing was a camera, the thing for which it had been built. The camera recorded everything that *Nemo*'s searchlight shone upon, broadcasting it back up to the waiting boat above.

The resulting footage appears almost colorless in the documentary, the only light that reaches the black bottom of the lake that which *Nemo* makes itself. The film seems grainy with all the particles and motes that hang in the still water. This effect, almost like looking through night-vision goggles, heightens rather than reduces the ultimate revelation, as *Nemo* drifts over a hillock of silt on the lake bottom and we get our first glimpse of the monster.

Pepys Lake, 1954

Reinhardt's workshop in the small Connecticut town was much different than the one in his father's old shoe shop, or even the big empty warehouse where he had toiled for the Nazis. Now it was a repurposed boathouse, long as an airplane hangar and low-ceilinged, hung with chains and tackles and winches that allowed him to move the various parts that he used in his work.

Down the center of the boathouse was a strip of open water, which he could hear at all times lapping at the pilings that held up the floor beneath him. Here and there this strip of water was crossed by small walkways of metal and wood that could be slid aside when they weren't needed, so that the thing he was building could be lowered fully into the lake.

His assistants were different here, too. A young man and woman, barely out of their teens, rather than the sallow-faced slaves who had labored for him in Germany, though, from what he gathered, the studio wasn't paying them a whole lot more. They worked with him because they wanted to work in the moving pictures, the strange and golden empire that had rescued him from beneath the boots of the Nazis.

Though he tried to forget, he still had dreams in which he woke up on the hard wooden floor of a train car, not a small town in America, not rescued after all, surrounded by the gray faces and shining eyes of ghosts that stared down at him. The train, he knew, passed into the mountain, which closed like a mouth behind it.

Since coming to America, Reinhardt had built many ingenious devices for the motion picture studios. "Special effects," they called them. Everything from tables that were built to collapse on command to hanging harnesses, mock guillotines, and reproductions of torture devices from ages past. He had built creatures, like the puppets of his youth, which moved and acted at his accord, powered by wheels and pistons.

Even the engines of war that he had been asked to create for the Nazis were not as ambitious as the project he labored over in Pepys Lake, however, and it wasn't even going to be put on film. "Then why build it?" Reinhardt had asked, and the producer, a man named Marsh, had put his hand on Reinhardt's shoulder and pointed up into the sky, as though at something Reinhardt should have been able to see, but couldn't.

"We're going to stir up a little publicity first," he had said. "Give them a *real* monster, something they can believe in. And once there have been a few sightings of *that*, we'll make sure that the word gets spread. National newspapers, the works. And once everyone knows the name...bam! *Then* we make our movie."

To that end, Reinhardt and his assistants labored in secrecy, under strict orders not to touch a drop of alcohol, or to fraternize with the locals any more than was necessary. When asked what they were working on, they had been given falsified credentials claiming that they were civilian contractors for the Army Corps of Engineers, and that they were engaged in testing various materials for buoyancy. "Why not just say that it's classified?" Reinhardt had asked the producer.

"If it's classified, then people are curious. They'll snoop," Marsh had replied. "If it's boring, then they're much less likely to stick their noses in."

The Dark of the Matinee blog, accessed 2009

The Pepys Lake Monster (1963) originally screened as the back half of a double-bill with the spiritualism shocker *The Final Session*, but is mostly familiar to viewers today from its occasional showing on Saturday afternoon monster movie broadcasts throughout the '70s and into the '80s. Ultimately directed by Graham Ward, it was originally intended to be produced by schlock movie legend Kirby Marsh, but by the time it finally went in front of cameras he was already in England directing a pair of British horror pictures, so his credit is that of executive producer, instead.

Three things distinguish *The Pepys Lake Monster* from its peers: its unlikely "inspired by true events" logline, a surprisingly restrained screenplay by Gavin Summers, and, perhaps more than anything else, its monster, created by the underappreciated German special effects genius Carl Reinhardt.

The titular monster itself is pretty much all head and neck, though we do get a brief glimpse of a gigantic clawed paddle foot, and a tail fin in one shot. The neck is little more than a column of scaly darkness rising up from the water, surmounted by a long, tapered head with lantern eyes and knobby antennae like a giraffe. The eyes are, at first glance, the most striking feature. Round and bulbous, they give off a somehow pumpkin-like effulgence, even on the black-and-white film, and if you squint closely you can see that they are compound, like the eyes of an insect. Then you are distracted as the monster delivers its coup de grace: opening wide those horse-skull jaws and blowing out a spray of sparks.

Though obviously mechanical to our modern eye, the effect remains impressive, and precisely how Reinhardt pulled it off remains a mystery, one that he took to his grave only two years after the film was released. According to studio records, the monster mechanism employed in the film was sold for parts as soon as principal photography was completed, but documentary filmmaker Gale Chambers thinks that there might be another way to get an idea of how the effect was achieved.

According to the premise of her planned film, which is currently seeking funding under the working title *The Secret of Pepys Lake*, the spike in sightings of the Pepys Lake Monster in the late 1950s was not, as originally believed, the impetus for the film of the same name, but rather the other way around. She claims to have uncovered documents alleging that Kirby Marsh and Carl Reinhardt built a previous mechanical Pepys Lake Monster, one that they deployed in the lake itself for years to startle the locals and help build the legend, before filming of the actual picture got underway.

Her pitch email asserts that she intends to prove this hypothesis by using a newly-invented diving robot to explore the bottom of the lake and find the remains of the original "monster," which her records say was sunk there in order to prevent it ever being found once the picture was released.

Loch Ness, 1948

Reinhardt stood next to the American producer whose name had escaped him and looked out across the water of the lake, or "loch" as their guide had pronounced it. Everywhere around them and across the flat gray water mist hung in thick clouds and tatters.

"They say there's a monster under the water," the producer was telling him. "A serpent, or a dragon, or even a dinosaur, surviving on to this very day. They've been talking about it since the seventh century, when a visiting saint is said to have driven it back with the sign of the cross."

"I've seen enough monsters in my day," Reinhardt replied, "and known enough men that I don't believe in saints."

"Still," the producer said, smiling out over the water, "you've got to admit that it would make for one hell of a movie."

Bartlett University, 2016

The documentary film *The Secret of Pepys Lake* ends with shots of the documentary crew recovering the head of the original Pepys Lake Monster, built by Reinhardt in a boathouse on the lake and used to create hoax sightings throughout the latter half of the 1950s. The head has been badly damaged by its time at the bottom of the lake—one of the eyes is cracked, a blackened chasm in the candy glass exterior through which the incandescent bulb that once illuminated it is now visible—but it remains mostly intact.

A text crawl at the end of the film assures us that the mechanisms inside the head have been examined by engineers and special effects technicians, but they are too damaged for anyone to get a very good idea of how the creature must have originally worked. The text crawl is interrupted by a snippet of interview with special effects guru Scott Cole. He wears a red-and-black flannel shirt and is shaking his head, rubbing at his beard as he talks.

"There's nothing in here to indicate how it did any of the things that we know it did," he's saying. "Where did the sparks come from? And how did he provide power to it under water? The outer shell isn't watertight, and even if it was, there's no visible method of producing those effects. There must have been some additional mechanisms that were damaged or removed before the monster was sunk into the lake, so that other people who found it one day couldn't copy his methods. Reinhardt learned his craft from magicians, after all."

What the documentary doesn't say is what happened to the remains of the monster after they were recovered. Gale Chambers donated them to the Bartlett University Museum of History in Maryland, where they now lie in a wooden crate in the back of a storeroom largely given over to items of historical significance that are too damaged to make them suitable for public display. Two smaller crates—containing pottery—are stacked atop it, and several paintings packed in cardboard have been leaned against its front.

Because the storeroom is rarely entered except to add new pieces to its ever-growing stockpile, no one has ever seen the jack-o-lantern glow that sometimes emanates from the slats of the crate, or smelled the whiff of smoke as the sparks sizzle against the wood inside. But perhaps someday, they will.

Author's Notes:

I had already written this story when the invitation to contribute something to the second volume of Planet X's (sadly short-lived) *Test Patterns* anthology series came along. With the subtitle being "Creature Features," this seemed like a perfect fit.

I don't remember what I originally wrote it *for*, or where the hell I came up with the idea of combining an animatronic Loch Ness Monster with the Pied Piper myth, but I can recall that I had just written an article about the history of the Pied Piper for a freelance client, and so a lot of that stuff was still fresh in my mind.

This one samples influences from all over the place. The title is a nod to the classic Bernie Wrightson comic, "The Pepper Lake Monster," which also influenced the tale itself, but I changed the name of the lake just slightly, borrowing from Samuel Pepys because he, in turn, had been borrowed for one of my favorite horror video games, *Nightmare Creatures*. The weirdo Werner Herzog/Zak Penn mockumentary *Incident at Loch Ness* is in here, too, along with maybe a little of Caitlin R. Kiernan's "The Lovesong of Lady Ratteanrufer." And I used the faux-documentary format to drop in some names of a few of my favorite contemporary horror writers, while I was at it.

THE POWER OF THE DEAD

For this story, pretend that you've never heard of me. Pretend you never read any of my pieces in *Harper's* or *Rolling Stone*, never saw those photos of me on his arm, wearing dresses I couldn't have afforded to even dream about five years ago.

Pretend that you don't already know the story, that you don't already know how it ends, that you didn't watch it over and over again on all the major news channels just like everybody did. Pretend that you don't know who he was. That he wasn't your golden boy, the way he was everyone's golden boy. Pretend he was only mine, as this story is only mine, and just listen…

There are parts that you probably *don't* know. In interviews, he seldom talked about the early years, the ways in which it all began. How the first time it happened he was walking alone down the side of a country road…

He was sixteen. He'd driven his little Volkswagen to a party and run out of gas, and rather than be stranded there he decided to walk home. He didn't have a good reason, or at least not one that he remembered. No one stood him up or insulted him, he wasn't dating anyone and so no one told him she thought they should maybe just be friends. It wasn't anger or grief that triggered what happened, just a kind of sullen absentmindedness.

The walk back to his house was maybe four miles. He didn't

know, when he told me about this later, how long he'd been walking, or how long since the last car had passed. His head was down, his hands shoved in his pockets, and he was kicking rocks.

There was a car passing, coming up from behind, and it startled him as it laid on its horn. He turned, and he remembered later that some circumstance of the lighting let him see the face of the car's passenger—a girl, maybe twelve or thirteen—as she turned in her seat to try to get a look back the way they had come.

He followed the inferred trajectory of her gaze, and saw that he was being trailed by a ghoulish menagerie that straggled behind him for perhaps a quarter of a mile. Here was a deer, one eye glassy and white, the other swarming with maggots. There was a possum dragging its hideously broken hind legs stiff as drumsticks behind it. A friendly-looking mongrel gazed at him with blank eyes while garlands of intestine dangled from its burst stomach.

He said that he remembered running, after that. Running all the way home, though his breath was like septic fire in his mouth and his chest hammered with spikes. And every piece of roadkill between the party and his house got up and followed.

Even in the months we spent together, he never gave me any coherent narrative of his life between that first night and the day when he became famous. One can extrapolate, though. The terror, the guilt, the slow, fumbling, macabre steps toward understanding.

The loneliness.

As we would all learn later, as would appear in every news story and every interview, he couldn't actually return the dead to life. He was more of a puppeteer, galvanizing the dead into movement, lending stolen fire to the decaying cells and making them dance.

In my efforts to give a name to his ability I once called him a remote-control Dr. Frankenstein. His smile was unreadable to me then, as always.

There was a time, as he was learning to control his power, that he put it to the sorts of uses that you'd expect from a young man. Making all the frogs in the biology class jump, going to funerals and causing the cadavers to suddenly sit up or thump around in their caskets.

In our third interview, after we had already begun sleeping together, I asked him what it had been like, to be a friend of the dead. I still remember what he said then, and I'll always remember it because I kept the original transcript of the interview, though these words never made it into the November issue of *Rolling Stone*:

"It's not like that," he said, growing suddenly serious. "What I do isn't like having friends. The bodies I control aren't like people, or even pets. They're like rocks. And when I animate them it's like throwing a rock. They aren't friends or companions, they're remote control limbs. Remote control limbs that rot."

The day that he became famous was the day Governor Rosen visited the natural history museum. He was in the crowd when a would-be assassin pulled a ceramic knife. A hundred and thirty people saw the Tyrannosaurus Rex skeleton tear itself free of its moorings and snap its dagger teeth around the assassin like a bear trap, scissoring him in half.

By the time he and I met he was already working for the government. They didn't kill him or dissect him or imprison him, not like in the movies. I can't say if they would have, in a different situation, but they couldn't. He was too high profile. He had become a celebrity overnight. He had to stay in the public eye or else people would find out what had happened to him.

They *did* study him, though, subjecting him to MRIs and CAT scans. And when they realized that they couldn't learn how he did it, or replicate it, they put him to work doing it for them.

Sometimes what he did was obvious, like walking the victims of a plane crash up out of a swamp or using the dead to help rebuild cemeteries washed out by a hurricane. He did other things, too, but they were always classified. He told me stories sometimes, when we were together, always off the record. Stories about marching unkillable soldiers into hot zones, or remote-piloting already-dead bombers on suicide missions.

Eventually, though, the government asked him to do something that he wouldn't. I never learned what it was. I still don't know and probably never will. By then he and I were already living together, in a big loft apartment on the government's dime. There were two agents assigned to guard us at all times. When he was on a mission, there were still two agents who followed me around.

When he left that morning, it wasn't any different than any of a hundred other times. We said goodbye at the door to the apartment, and I watched at the window as he got into the car that was waiting for him. He knew I was watching, and he looked up and waved once to let me know, like he always did.

When he refused to do whatever it was they'd ordered him to do, they took me.

No one ever referred to it as a kidnapping. They never told me I was a hostage. I was asked to come down to the local office, they sent a car to pick me up. When I asked the driver why I'd been sent for he just shrugged, and when I got to the office they said we were just waiting for him to come back.

For awhile that's what I did. I had some coffee, did a crossword puzzle, watched what was going on around me. By the time I tried to leave I'd already figured out that they weren't going to let me.

Everyone was very polite about it all. I was never hit or bound or threatened. They brought me just about anything I asked for. They just wouldn't let me leave. The doors were all locked, my phone wouldn't work, and there wasn't any other phone to be found.

My attempts to leave were, at first, just as polite as their imprisonment. I asked to go, they asked me to be patient "just a little while longer." I asked for a phone, they said they'd "see what they could do." But while *their* politeness remained consistent, mine crumbled. Shouting followed demands and was followed, in turn, by tears and then resignation.

They brought in a television, when I requested one, and a stack of movies, but the TV wouldn't get any channels and so I didn't hear about what was happening until later. I saw it on their faces, though, and I could guess.

I picture him coming home from god-knows-where, a coffee cup in each hand. When he knocks on the door and I don't answer he transfers both cups to one hand to unlock the door, expecting to find me asleep or in the shower. In my imagination, the cups fall from nerveless fingers when he finds that I'm gone and he can locate no note, but knowing him as I do I know that he probably set them down on the hall table before he even started looking, if he ever had them at all.

When he couldn't find me his first call would've been to Sanderson, the day agent in charge of our comfort and safety from Monday through Thursday. I don't know how many people he had to talk to before he figured out what happened, but I doubt it was many. Maybe they just told him right away.

If they ever reconstructed how the first three agents were killed, it never made it into the news and I never heard about it. All I know is what everyone knows: that he slipped his handlers and disappeared, though not for long.

The random string of letters that employed him had several offices all over the city. I wasn't being held in the main one. If I had been, I would've been able to see what happened next by looking out the window.

The main office overlooked the veterans' cemetery, with its identical rows of white markers. Two hundred and seventy-seven actual bodies were interred there, and that afternoon every last one of them got up.

No one knew he could do it. Previously, the largest number of human remains I'd ever heard of him animating at once was around twenty, though maybe he'd done more on some of the secret missions they sent him on.

The powers-that-be must've been impressed enough to negotiate a ceasefire with him. I learned later that the negotiations were handled with him speaking remotely through the lips of a recently dead agent, another trick that I don't think anyone knew he was capable of. The pretense, I guess, was that the whole thing had been some sort of epic misunderstanding.

A black sedan picked me up and took me to a crypt guarded by the walking dead.

I remember stepping into the crypt, and I remember very clearly those first few blind, blinking seconds as my eyes adjusted to the dark and saw the thing that was waiting for me there.

It was dressed like him, and for a second it even *looked* like him in the bad light, but it wasn't. It was just a corpse that he'd given his coat to.

It said my name with a voice that was close to his, if his had come from down a long metal tube, but also weirdly overlapped by another voice. "Whatever happens," he said, "don't be scared."

The corpse reached out and took my hand, and I tried not to flinch away. The flesh felt strange; not clammy, exactly, but not the right temperature or moisture for a living hand, either. It squeezed my hand just the way he always had, though, so I followed it as it walked outside.

Hand-in-hand, like lovers, we stepped out of the crypt and back into the sunlight. The first sniper's bullet caught the corpse in the shoulder, jerking it to the side. The second entered the bridge of the nose and the skull collapsed like a rotten melon. The corpse staggered twice and I felt the terrible sensation of its fingers slipping out of mine as it fell.

The rest is the ending, the part you already know. You saw it on the news, read it in the papers, watched the clips on YouTube. You know what happened next, that for three hours all the dead in the city went to war against the living.

No one knows where he got the power; if he'd had it all along and kept it hidden, or if his rage gave it to him. The corpses in dozens of cemeteries all over town clawed their way to the surface all at once. The antique bits of crushed bone that made up the petroleum in gasoline formed rippling golems that tore their way free from cars and the underground storage tanks at convenience stores. For three long hours, the dead ripped the city apart.

The real ending was a mocking reflection of the false one that I had witnessed. The only footage ever captured just shows a distant black blot that jerks and then crumples to the ground as the sniper's bullet finds its target.

I wasn't there with him when he really died. That black blot was the last time I got to see him alive, even on film. In my imagination, being there would have been like it was when I saw the bullet take the zombie that was wearing his coat, but I know that in reality it would've been a hundred times worse.

No one was with him when he died, no one but the sniper and that lone and distant cameraman, but we all knew exactly when it happened. It was the moment when everything else in the city went back to being dead, too.

I don't know what would have happened to me in a movie. Movies never go past the ending, never tell what happens next. In real life, the government let me go, cut me loose. Whenever I tried to contact someone from the old offices, I was handed through a never-ending chain of polite secretaries and underlings who never knew anything. They continued to pay for my housing and a stipend just as they always had, though. I don't know if it was their way of saying they were sorry, or their way of keeping me placated so I wouldn't talk.

A lot of people *expected* me to talk. To write a memoir or return to journalism, but I didn't have anything left to say. Nothing until this, and even this isn't enough.

Though I loved him—and I *did* love him—I don't think I ever really understood him when we were together. Not like I do now that he's gone.

Sometimes I imagine that he'll come back. Claw his way up through the ground like the corpses he gave life to. But I know that he won't. And even if he did, it wouldn't really be him. I know that for certain, because he taught it to me. Whatever powers the living can assert over the dead, their power over us lies in their absence, and in our inability to bring them back.

Author's Notes:

This is, without a doubt, the oldest *published* story in this volume, tracing its first appearance all the way back to 2009, when it was in the tenth issue of a now-defunct magazine of superhero stories called *A Thousand Faces*. It's never been reprinted before and, given the print run of that magazine, I doubt many of my fans have ever read it.

As long ago as I wrote this story, the idea of it—the remote-control necromancer—is one that I'd been toying with even longer. Since college, at least. At once point, I wanted to turn the thing into a whole novel, but this is the only finished version that ever came to pass. For the most part, stories from so long ago are consigned to the dustbin of history, but this one felt like a good fit with the themes that were coming together in this collection—especially given its coda.

The title—and from the title, that coda I mentioned—comes from a line in the movie *The Dungeonmaster*. A line that I first discovered *not* via the movie itself, but because it was sampled in the Skinny Puppy song "Hexonxonx."

THE SPLITFOOT REEL

I

The first time I ever heard the Splitfoot Reel was in the alley behind Marcus Treacher's loft. He had an LP called *Bremen Town* by Albert Gidney, the cover like a Fuseli painting of blanched animal faces with bright, blank eyes peering in through a darkened window. He showed it to me earlier in the night, spinning the sleeve between his two hands and snatching it back when I reached for it.

"Look wit' y'eyes, girl," he said, "not wit' y'hands. This thing wasn't easy to come by."

I had never heard of Albert Gidney or the Splitfoot Reel before that night, but Marcus acted like the album was a big deal, and even then I knew enough to know that Marcus wasn't wrong about those sorts of things. I kept loitering around, waiting for him to put it on, but the loft echoed with the beats of Sonic Sum and Stereolab instead, and finally I retreated down the big fire escape out back to smoke a cigarette in the alley.

They told me later that's what saved my life. Not something the Surgeon General's ever going to put on a pack. I was huddled up against the wall because the night was cold, my hood up, my hands cupped around the cig when I heard the beats from up above stop. Marcus had dropped the needle on something different.

The song started with a sound like the band tuning up—scratches and screeches. Even that early, I knew what I was hearing. The Splitfoot Reel had been the first track listed on the back of that album cover, and as the notes started to swell out from Marcus's hi-fi, I dropped my cigarette, cherry embers spilling across the damp concrete. My sneakers pounded back up the fire escape stairs in time to the music, one-two one-two.

Marcus's loft was a KC fixture in those days. It occupied the entire top floor of the building, one end wrapped floor-to-ceiling in windows that overlooked McGee Street on one side, and east toward the Tension Envelopes building on the other. That half of the loft was mostly clear of any furnishings, the hardwood floor decked out with nothing but a few couches that could easily be pushed up against the windows to clear some space. Everyone just called it the dance floor.

I was young then, but I already had smoker's lungs, and it took me a few bars to make it up the five flights of metal stairs. Above me, I could hear the reel playing, picking up steam as it went along. From the fire escape landing, I could see through those big windows and onto the dance floor. That's where the light was coming from, and the music.

The dance floor was full of people. Everyone from the party must have been there, except me. People dancing and stomping and twirling amid the smoke, their feet already leaving bloody prints when they came down hard on the wood floor.

I couldn't pick out anyone I knew. Couldn't see Marcus through the haze, or Donna, who I had come with, or anything but bodies moving to the rhythm of that song, which, even through the windows, I could feel in every drop of my blood. My heart was beating in time with it.

Heat poured off those windows. Heat that I could feel on the fire escape, pushing back the cool night air, forcing the breath from my lungs.

The fire escape access was through a window in the kitchen, and we always propped it open so we could come and go, but now it was closed. I tried to force it, but the glass was hot against my hands, like a pan straight out of the oven.

The smoke on the dance floor was getting thicker. I banged my palm against the window, but all I got for my trouble was blisters. It couldn't compete with the sound of the song, the sound that was making me dance, my feet doing a little jig—though no, of course, they were doing a little reel—under my body even as I tried to think of what to do.

Squinting through that smoke, I saw the figure. Golden eyes, split like a goat's, bulging out of a head like a burned-up mask. Black clothes made of burned paper. A fiddle the size of a cello held up to its chin, while a big, black claw drew the bow across the strings. Then the windows burst and the fire came out.

The fire department found me in the alley behind Marcus's loft. I had burns on my face, arms, and hands, and I had inhaled a lot of smoke, but I fared better than anyone else at the party. Nobody else made it out alive.

When they loaded me into the ambulance and pulled off my sneakers they found the soles melted, my shoes full of blood. The bottoms of my feet were bruised and split. The doctors decided it was from running pell-mell down the fire escape to get away from the flames, but I knew that it was from dancing.

II

My graduate thesis was a performance called "A Night on Bald Mountain." The theme was witchcraft in music, or maybe music in witchcraft. The cover of the program was a black-and-white image of a famous Goya painting—*Witches' Flight*—with figures in tall, brightly-colored hats bearing a naked man writhing in ecstasy or delirium into the air above another man who rushed underneath with a sheet over his head. In the background was a donkey, my little nod to that cover of *Bremen Town*.

Inside was a quote from the *Newes from Scotland. Declaring the damnable life of Doctor Fian a notable sorcerer*, in which the accused was reported to have "daunced this reill," presumably with the devil. Below the quote was a notation: "The earliest written reference to the reel as a dance dates back to a witch trial in 16th century Scotland."

I had a few other musicians with me on the darkened stage, playing hornpipes and mandolins and the bodhran, but mostly it was me, standing in one small pool of light, the fiddle pressed against my chin, my other hand curled into a claw to draw the bow across the strings again and again.

For the last song of my performance, I played the Splitfoot Reel. I hadn't ever practiced it, and I was alone upon the stage. I knew the notes by heart—they were branded into my brain, so that when I closed my eyes, I could see them burning there in the warm dark.

I didn't have the band supporting me that had been on Albert Gidney's album, so I replicated that strange opening by rubbing the bow across the strings to create a dissonant susurrus that filled the auditorium, and then I began to play.

The assumption, later, was that there had been some kind of panic when the lights went out. Several people were hospitalized with injuries to their feet and hands that they couldn't explain. My faculty advisor told me that I collapsed after the end of the song, but I can't remember playing it at all. They said that I just kept sawing away in the dark, while the people stampeded around, or whatever it is they did until the lights came back on.

When they found me I was huddled in a twitching mass on the stage, cradling my violin. There were ugly blisters along the palms of my hands and the insides of my fingers, and I was dehydrated and malnourished. I stayed in the hospital for three days while they pumped fluids back into my body. The doctors insisted that I must have been working too hard leading up to my performance, that I hadn't been eating or drinking. Nobody but me knows that I had a big meal that day at lunch; that I had a bottle of water in the car before the show.

***

After the fire at Marcus's loft, it would have made sense if I had never crossed paths with the Splitfoot Reel again, but I was never that kind of person. My momma used to tell me that I was born unlucky. "If you want anything in this life, you're going to have to work twice as hard for it." In the bio of my thesis program, it said "Marley Sommer is the seventh child of a seventh child." I didn't have to make it up.

I had been playing the violin since the fourth grade, and by the time of the fire I was already doing postgrad work. After that night, however, I poured myself into the music overtime. I played reels until the people in the apartment downstairs beat on the ceiling with broom handles, and I did everything I could to track down the Splitfoot Reel once again.

I couldn't get it out of my head. I would tap it out while I was trying to study, and then, when I realized what I was doing and tried to stop and write it down, the notes fled from my mind, evaporated.

No one really knows who originally wrote the Splitfoot Reel. When it can be found at all, the music is usually credited to a man by the name of Giles Montague, but he claimed to have found it in a fiddle case in the ruins of an old plantation house that had burned down.

Giles and the song comprised a sort of folk story dyad. The song was supposed to be cursed. If you had an enemy, someone you wanted to lay a hex on—say your fella was fixing to marry some other girl—then you could hire Giles to play the Splitfoot Reel at their wedding, and things would go poorly for them in short order.

Giles never wrote the song down, though. He said that the "devil hisself" whispered the notes in his ear as he played. "He puts his big, black claws on my elbow, on my arm, and he guides that there bow." I found that in a book on *Spiritual Music & Mysticism from Africa to the American South*, where it was attributed to Giles Montague, anyway.

The first person to *record* the Splitfoot Reel was Albert Gidney. During my graduate studies, I was able to track down the man who had produced that *Bremen Town* LP. His name was Marion O'Conner, and he lived in Birmingham, which is where he met me in an apartment above a laundromat. By that time he didn't look like much—an old white man with a big belly, pearl buttons on a stained shirt and a white cowboy hat.

"Gidney never believed in none of that hoodoo stuff," he said. "He just wanted a challenge. That boy was a born musician. The good Lord never made an instrument that Gidney couldn't play. He was best on the fiddle, though. Played it like nobody I ever seen. But the Reel," the old man shook his head, spat tobacco into a Coke can by curling his lip up and around the side. "That was a whole other thing.

"Gidney'd never tell me where he got the music from. Just showed up with it one day and was itchin' to play it. Said that it was impossible, unplayable, an' that meant he *had* to play it.

"Like I said, Gidney didn't believe in curses or whatnot, and neither do I, but you don't work in music for long without you learn to believe in yer gut. Instinct, y'know? There are places, people, instruments, days, an' you better believe it, pieces of music, and there's somethin' *wrong* with 'em. Call it a curse if you want, but they're just not right. We've all met folks like that. Folks who just ain't right. We know 'em the minute we sees 'em. We *know* the wrong just comin' off 'em, even if we can't explain it. They make our hackles rise up, make us start lookin' fer the door. That song was like that, but it was hard as hell to play, an' that's all Gidney cared about.

"We recorded that album in a studio off Canal. Little place, it burned down the next week. Rats got into the wiring, is what they said. They only pressed a few hundred copies, and most of those was lost in a warehouse fire. Rats again, most like. We recorded in November and by the first of the next year, Gidney was dead. Hung himself in the rooms he was renting. They had me identify the body an' he'd purpled all up, his eyes poppin' out.

"They said that music was scattered all over the place, an' it looked like he'd had a roaring big fire a'goin'. If they found the Reel they never said, an' I never asked too hard."

I offered to take Mr. O'Conner out somewhere, but he shook that old, white cowboy hat side-to-side. "Don't care much fer goin' out these days," he said. As he showed me to the door, I asked him the question that had been scratching around inside my brain the whole time he was telling me the story.

"Do you know where I can find a copy of the music?"

"You got the bug, ain't ya?" he asked, smiling a brown-toothed smile. "That's a shame," and he shut the door in my face.

There were practice rooms at the UMKC Conservatory of Music and Dance where I was doing my graduate work, but I tended to rent space in a little labyrinth of whitewashed rooms under a strip mall out in Prairie Village. It was closer to my apartment, and I liked the distance from the other students.

The practice rooms there were blank and identical—dark and windowless when not occupied, flooded with harsh fluorescent light inside. The hallways felt like a Gordian knot of low corners, flanked by featureless doors numbered off 11-12-13-14. I was practicing in room 14 when I heard the knock, just a week after I had gone to see Mr. O'Conner, with three weeks left until my thesis performance.

There was a rhythm to it, familiar. Not shave-and-a-haircut, but something I had heard before. It sounded like it came from low down on the door, as if a child was knocking, which wasn't out of the question; little kids sometimes rented the practice spaces, just like I did.

When I opened the door to number 14, I just saw a shadow disappearing around one of the corners. The ragged streamers of a coat, the black feathers of a raven's wing. A manila envelope fell inward from where it had been leaned against the door. It was dirty, with black smudges on the paper. I opened the envelope and pulled out the sheet music; hand-written on yellowed paper—even the staves hand-drawn in thick black ink that seemed almost tacky. The words at the top said: The Splitfoot Reel.

I shouted before I ran, gripping the neck of my violin in one hand, the envelope full of music in the other. Turning the corner I had seen the shadow turn down, I saw it turn another, up ahead. I shouted again. "Wait," or even, "stop," but there was no response.

Down one white hallway, then another, the room numbers flashing past on either side, climbing, climbing, higher than the number of rooms I had known were down here. 237, 238, 239.

Finally, I stopped at the head of a set of stairs leading down. The first few steps were covered with gray rubber, but the rubber soon tapered off, ragged at the edges, melted and warped in spots, grown over with black mold in others. Below that the steps were concrete.

The lights here flickered, and down the stairs they were off entirely, but they illuminated far enough for me to know that these steps went down much farther than they should have. From below I could hear music reverberating up, the bass beat of a cellar club, but this was a different kind of music. On the wall was a handprint, black ash, but it wasn't shaped like a human hand.

The janitor at the place found me there, his hand on my shoulder rousing me from whatever stupor I had fallen into. I was sitting cross-legged on the floor, my right hand gripping my violin so hard that the strings had cut into my fingers and blood was dripping onto the rough, off-blue carpet. I was facing a concrete wall, where the hallway dead-ended.

When I asked him if there was anything under the music rooms he just laughed and shook his head. "Under here? No ma'am. Just dirt and pipes and China, I guess, if you dig far enough."

The music for the Splitfoot Reel was still in my other hand.

III

I called my first album *Bremen Town.* On the cover was a photo of me, my hair falling curly across my shoulders, my fiddle held in my left hand, behind my back. I was standing in a blinding white art gallery, looking up at a painting on the wall that must have been at least eight feet tall. It was of animals, bright, blank eyes and faces that looked washed out, like they were caught in a flashbulb, peering in through a darkened farmhouse window.

The painting was called *Bremen Town Musicians*, and it was by an artist named Christoph St. Vincent who grew up on a sugar plantation in Barbados. I found it in a museum in Key West, which is where the photograph was taken.

For the songs on the album, I played with a band. We were Marley Sommer and the Night Hags. The other women all wore masks—blank white, with black-rimmed, staring eyes and open mouths, meant to call to mind the masks of a Greek chorus—and switched instruments from song to song, but I only ever played the fiddle.

The songs on the album were all songs that I had written. *Fire on the Mountain*, *Walpurgisnacht*, *Black Paintings*, *Notes from Underground.* I played them at my concerts, in front of crowds of people, who stomped and clapped and cheered. I felt the music reverberating through my body, and I knew that I was waiting, that I would know when the time was right.

My first tour ended where it had all began, in Kansas City. We played the Midland, with a line stretching out and around the block. From the stage, the audience was a black shadow tinged with red, but I knew that they were there. I could hear them moving out in the dark before the curtains pulled aside.

Every other concert had ended with *Fire on the Mountain*, but this time, after the last note had faded and the curtains had closed, I stepped back out on the other side, framed in the halo of a single spotlight. The other Night Hags were backstage already, putting away their instruments, as I raised my fiddle to my shoulder one last time.

I could feel the audience out there in the dark. Every shuffled foot, every inheld breath, every person sliding their thumb across the screen of their phone. I could feel the heat that came off them, a heat that was nothing at all compared to the furnace at my back. If I closed my eyes, I could see the shadow gathering around me. Bulging golden eyes, the ruined remnants of stunted wings. The black tatters that draped it could be curtains or feathers or neither or both, and the burnt black claw that gripped my arm, that guided my hand, could have belonged to a bird.

It burned where it touched me, but the burn was so familiar. Blisters on the palms of my hands as I beat them against the glass of Marcus Treacher's loft. The burning in my lungs as I woke from the darkness of the graduate thesis, but this time I knew I would be awake for the whole thing.

When I drew my bow across the strings it unzipped the very air above that stage and the Splitfoot Reel came pouring out. It hasn't stopped yet.

I wonder if it ever will.

Author's Notes:

Another one that I don't think most readers have encountered, which is a shame, because it's probably one of my favorites. I keep a little notebook where I write down ideas for titles that I want to use someday, and this one has been in there forever. I finally got the chance when I wrote this for the souvenir book that accompanied NecronomiCon in 2019—the last one before the plague times.

This is another piece that deals in music, not to mention the story of the Bremen Town Musicians and the artwork of Goya. While plenty of modern artists have had bigger influences on my work, few classic ones have found their way in here as often as Goya.

PREHISTORIC ANIMALS

It's night when they pull Dottie's body out of the water. The cherries on top of the police cars and the ambulances paint the statues in strobing, cotton candy colors; reflect in daggers off the black pond.

They tell me not to look, that it will be better if I don't, but I have to look, because it's Dottie. I get just a glimpse of her face and I can see that it's been eaten away, those bee-sting lips now ragged and pale.

"Fish," Detective Ford tells me. "Just little fish in the pond."

At the funeral, Mrs. Weber won't look at me while the minister talks about ashes and dust and how man is filled with misery, cutteth down like a flower. The wind makes the trees rustle, and I listen to those instead, because Dottie would have liked them better. When we die young, we don't get much say in how we're disposed of. One more injustice. Add it to the pile.

The hole in the ground that they lower her into is nice and rectangular, but the shadows of the leaves look like teeth at the edges, like the ground is eating her up, and I want to tell them not to lower the casket, but I know that I'm already on thin ice, as my dad would say, so I bite my lip and keep my own counsel.

"There's nothing in there anymore," I can hear Dottie saying in my ear. "Just rotting meat. All we are is a spark, and then the spark gets put out." I'm not sure I agree with her anymore. I'm not sure I ever did.

When the casket is gone, I try to go up to Mrs. Weber, but she just walks away, and Dottie's older brother Jared gets his ex-football player shoulder in between us and says, "She just needs some time, Kat, y'know?"

I nod, but I know that there'll never be enough time. She didn't spit at me, so at least that's something.

My dad tries to keep the details from me, just like Detective Ford did. "For your own good," he says, sitting on the other side of the kitchen island, me listlessly pushing waffles around in congealing syrup on my plate. There was a pat of margarine on top for a while, but it has slowly disassembled itself into greasy bubbles.

I know that he's right, and I also know that he's wrong. She died face-down in that black water, sucking in muck and bugs. She drowned on that junk, but she was already dying. They found a wound in her chest, below her ribcage. A knife had gone in, long and straight. It hadn't pierced her heart, but it had done enough.

For a while, the police look for a perpetrator, until Mrs. Weber finds Dottie's diary behind her dresser drawer and reads about our break-up, and then the police decide it was suicide. "Where was the knife?" I try to ask, but they have their answer ready: It fell in the water, sank down to the bottom.

"Then what happened to her *teeth*?"

They don't have an answer for that one.

Two weeks, and I have to go back to school, where my grades drop a full letter, two in chemistry and Latin. The doctor gives me blue-and-white pills that make me feel thin and echoing. Sitting in class, the sun outside the window transforms the panes into fluorescent bulbs that send spikes of pain into my head until I close my eyes, tune out the teacher, go to sleep and dream about black water surrounded by monsters.

I wake up gasping for air in the twin bed of my dorm room, with no memory of how I got back. I instinctively reach for my phone to text Dottie, as I always did when I woke up from a bad dream, but she's not there and I let the phone fall onto my clothes where they're balled on the floor as I curl up tight and wish that I had tears left to cry. My chest aches, and my nails carve crescent moons into the palms of my hands.

Somehow, I make it through the semester. The counselor calls me into her office and I sit in a soft fabric chair and try hard to listen to her but it feels like I can only make out every third word, and so I just nod, working to keep my eyes focused, making sounds of agreement whenever she stops long enough for me to realize that she's waiting for an answer. Eventually, she lets me go.

My GPA suffers, but not enough for me to lose any of my student aid, and then it's time for summer and I opt not to take any electives and instead go home, move back into my old bedroom. Dad's apartment is still where it has always been—above the garage of an old house on Bleeker Street, behind the bank—and my bedroom still has its own way in and out, down a set of wooden stairs that deposit me in the alley, filled with the rubbery fragrance of trumpet vines.

My first night home, I fall asleep with my fingertips against the carving on my bedpost, the one that says D+K, done up in a handmade effort to replicate the Dead Kennedys font, inside a heart flanked by crossbones.

I'm home for most of three weeks before I drive out there. The tires of my old Subaru crunch on the gravel that has been scattered in front of the gate, which is no more imposing than it ever was. Just a chain strung between two pieces of metal pipe anchored in concrete, a "NO TRESPASSING" sign creaking in what little breeze manages to penetrate the tall pines.

I let my fingers slide along the links of the chain, like vertebrae, my fingertips coming away with a grimy coating of orange rust that I wipe on my jeans. I can see the spots where the chain has been mended, over the years. Sometimes with little c-rings that screw shut, others welded silver links. When we were younger, as often as not, we would find the chain simply lying on the ground. In high school, we would drive right on through and park out there in the darkness, among the beasts.

I leave the Subaru by the side of the road and walk around the metal pipe, along the place where dozens of other feet have worn a path. There used to be a wooden sign here that said Tar Lake Park, but it was already gone by the time Dottie and I started coming out here. My dad told me that the city tore it down. "Wood borer beetles," he said. "Got in and ate it from the inside out, 'til it was plumb hollow."

To get to the monsters, you have to go past the chain about the length of a football field. The road turns slightly there, enough to hide them from sight, and as you round the curve the first one looms up out of the dark in the glow of your headlights, because night is the best time to come out and see them.

It's just a shape, at first, big and dark and heavy. It could be a bunch of trash bags dumped in a pile, or an old car, were it not for three things: The needle teeth that fill its mouth, the eyes that still bear a few chips of reflective paint, and the sail that heaves up from its back.

In the daylight, even dim as it is, diffused by clouds and trees that gather close now, I can see that part of its mouth has been broken, its bottom jaw torn away stage left, the concrete form that it's poured from exposed, little bits of rebar jutting where teeth should be. The sail is also tattered, chewed at its edges as though a toddler has gotten hold of it, and here and there holes let the sunlight through onto the carpet of pine needles on the other side.

I guess it's supposed to be a dimetrodon, as imagined by someone who's never seen a dimetrodon skeleton—or even a half-accurate drawing—in his life. Still, it's closer than most of the others. The sail is about right, as is the tail and the broadest outlines of the head, though the eyes are much too big, and the mouth looks like the jaws of a 'gator that ran into a parked car and had its snout accordioned in, like a cartoon character. The teeth are all uniformly sized; the teeth of a toy dinosaur, not a life-size statue. I run my fingers along their points until they stop at the edge of the broken jaw, my fingertips brushing empty air.

The next statue along the road is some kind of ceratopsid with dull horns and a spiny fringe around its bull head. Dottie used to always point out that its mouth—round instead of beaked—was also full of pointy little teeth. In fact, there didn't seem to be any herbivores among the dinosaurs in the park, as if they had been designed and built by the kind of kid who finds plant-eating dinosaurs boring.

Next in line is a biped—an allosaurus, maybe, but tipped up too straight, its head positioned directly above its hips, like a person in a dinosaur costume. Its body is pear-shaped and painted umber, its eyes reflective red. Its mouth is like a gharial or an alligator gar, long and narrow and filled with teeth. Its tiny arms end in three claws, one broken off from its right hand.

The parade of weird animals continues as I walk along the road, and the farther I go from the gate, the more degraded the road becomes, until after a while it is like walking on cobblestones rather than asphalt, grass growing up through the cracks, in places as high as my thighs.

The road goes around the pond like a lasso. Most of the statues are in and around the pond; a thing with toad-like haunches and an almost canine face, a monstrous fish with eyes like peeled oranges, something wormlike with stubby legs and saber-sharp buck teeth.

They say that the pond was a tar pit once upon a time, long before people existed, let alone built the town. Where the black water is now was once naturally-occurring asphalt. Antediluvian animals became trapped, were pulled down, sucked beneath its bubbling surface, their skeletons preserved, what was the joke, "in showroom condition."

Are the skeletons down there still? Local legends were never terribly clear about how anyone knew about the tar pit under the lake, though there were certainly bones in the tiny natural history museum in city hall that were supposed to have been pulled from it.

Dean Watterslee built the park back in the 1950s. He made the molds and poured the concrete. Planned it as a big tourist attraction—it was going to put the town on the map, don't you know—but it never really did. He killed himself in the pond, they say. Just walked right into it one day. At its best, I'm told, families drove their station wagons through here in the '60s, but by the time I was a kid it was already closed, and the only people who ever came out were teenagers looking for someplace to cause trouble, or a good makeout spot.

Dottie and me, parking by the big thing that looks like an iguana with, of course, sharp little teeth; fogging up the windows until we couldn't see the round green scales in the headlights. Her fingers against my sides, up under my bra; my hand sliding along the curve of her thighs, pulling her panties to the side.

This was where I told her goodbye. I was going off to college that year, she wasn't. "It's not like you're going to war," she objected, her lip stuck out in that way she did when she was pissed off. I always thought it looked so cute, but that day I couldn't think of anything, could barely look at her. It was spitting rain, just enough to make everything wet and miserable, little ripples on the surface of the inky water. "We have cell phones. We can sext."

But I didn't want to hold her back, isn't that what I told myself? I didn't want to be the person, miles away, living my life, while she pined at home. "You should be able to do what you want," I tried to say as twilight faded the monsters outside.

"As long as it doesn't involve you, right?"

I had tried so hard to be angry with her, to tell myself that she was being childish, but really, truly, now, just between me and the dinosaurs, I had just wanted to keep my options open, right? I didn't want to go off to college with a millstone around my neck. If I met someone really fucking cute at freshman orientation, I wanted to be able to jam my tongue down her throat without feeling guilty. I didn't want to be thinking about Dottie.

After the funeral, when I tried to go to Dottie's house, Mrs. Weber refused to answer the door. When I kept ringing the bell, she came to it, her eyes still hot with tears, and slapped a piece of paper against the inside of the glass. It was a page from Dottie's journal—I knew the paper, the purple border—and the ink had run with drops of moisture that I knew were tears. Dottie was asking why, what had she done, why didn't I care anymore.

I walked away, and couldn't blame Mrs. Weber for hating me. I hated me, too.

At the far end of the pond, where the road circles around, stand the park's only two mammals. A thing with a hippopotamus head mounted on long moose legs—maybe it's supposed to be an entelodont—squares off against a giant ground sloth. The sloth may be the most accurate creature in the entire menagerie, its shaggy fur all sculpted, its claws curved. Only the eyes betray the sculptor's gift for inaccuracy—they are huge sightless discs of reflective white paint, no pupils.

"This one's my favorite," Dottie always used to say, hugging her arms around one of the sloth's big, shaggy legs. "Look at his dumb face."

The Tar Lake Gift Shop is a concrete building on the shore of the pond that looks like a cross between a filling station and a crypt. Where its front windows once were not even the hint of glass remains and years ago the city sank iron bars into the façade, blocking the windows and what was once the door.

If there were any kids who had ever been inside it when Dottie and I were coming out here, none of them ever returned with very credible stories. I remember standing with Dottie, our hands jammed through the bars across the front door, squinting inside. "Think there's a vampire's coffin in there or something?" I asked, my forehead against the bars.

"A *dinosaur* vampire," Dottie returned. Then, after a few beats, "Probably just rat nests and trash, actually."

"Probably," I agreed, but we both thought a dinosaur vampire would have been better.

When I get back to my car, the right front tire is flat. There isn't a knife sticking out of it or something, like there would be in a movie, but when I kneel on the damp ground, I can tell that it's been slashed. My dad's a mechanic out at the dealership on the highway; I've been around cars since I was a little girl.

Straightening back up, I scan the road and the woods to either side, looking for any sign that anyone is there. I try to imagine Mrs. Weber driving up in her Sonata and getting out with a shiny new kitchen knife to saw through my radials. More likely, she would have sent one of Dottie's brothers to do her dirty work.

Fortunately, there's a full-size spare in the back, and though I mutter and grumble as I hoist it down onto the damp pine needles, I'm perversely glad for the distraction from my own thoughts. I wrestle the spare into place against the car, drag out the jack and tire iron.

The sun is starting to sink, and while it won't be full dark for a while yet, here among the trees the sun goes suddenly. I've got the tire off in the gloaming and I'm off-balance trying to hold the spare in place when I sense something behind me. I start to turn as something heavy and soft lands against the back of my skull and darkness drops like a curtain. It's heavy and soft, too.

I hear voices in the dark.

"This is a mistake. We should sink her. We should have sunk the other one."

"No, this is a blessing. They believed the last suicide, this one will be even easier. Wracked by guilt, she comes to the scene of her crime to end it all. It couldn't be more perfect if we had planned it."

"We didn't plan it, but maybe the Maw did."

"Brought her to us, you mean?"

"Why not? The serpent bites its tail."

"I still think we should sink her. It worked before. We don't need people snooping around here."

Several voices talking. Bickering above me somewhere. I can't tell them all apart, but it's more than two people. There are men and women.

I'm lying someplace hard. My fingers can feel channels cut into stone. Designed, I know without looking, to carry blood. It smells damp and close, like a basement or the reptile house at the zoo. There's a bag over my head that smells like a T-shirt straight out of the dryer, cutting the smell of wherever I am.

My hands are tied at my sides—coarse rope that bites my wrists, anchored down below whatever I'm lying on. My neck and ankles too, though I can't feel it as well through my jeans, and I have a moment's relief that at least I'm still dressed, except for my shoes and socks which seem to have gone missing, as what the voices are saying tries to force its way through the cotton that still clogs my brain.

"What would we have done if she hadn't come back?"

"We have always found a way. Have a little faith, brother."

"This way we swallow two birds in one bite."

"I still think we should sink her."

The bag comes off my head and I blink against harsh light. I'm in a strange, incongruous room, and it takes my brain several precious seconds to process it, throwing the data to me in a series of staccato bursts: Roughhewn stone. Long fluorescent lights that hang from the stone ceiling. Figures in black robes, trimmed in purple. Alligator skulls on the walls, below a ledge lined with mason jars filled with…could that be human teeth?

The black robes are gathered around me, and I'm roughly the height of their navels. They aren't wearing hoods or conical hats or any of that. I recognize some of the faces looking down at me. Mr. Lowery, the bank teller. Mrs. Fowler, who taught social studies when I was in eighth grade. A woman who works at the same dealership where my dad does. Detective Ford.

"What's going on?" I ask, though when you wake up tied to a sacrificial altar, it seems a rather stupid question.

"You're not here to talk," Mrs. Kovacks, the assistant principal at the high school, says in her sharp, schoolmarm voice. I can't see her from where I'm angled, but I don't need to. Dottie and I heard that voice often enough. "You will be silent in Its presence."

"What's presence?" I ask, and feel a sharp blow against my cheek, the side of my head. Not hard enough to do much damage, but with my head still throbbing from whatever knocked me out, it sets off klaxons and fireworks in my brain.

"What did you do to her?" I ask through gritted teeth.

"Dottie received a great reward," Detective Ford says. "Now it's your turn."

"You don't get to call her that," I reply, my vision refocusing, the noise in my head quieting for a moment as rage overrides pain. I even ignore the threat implicit in his words. Right then, I don't care. "She's Dorothy to you. Nobody gets to call her Dottie but me."

This time a hand clamps down on my arm like a vise, nails digging in hard, drawing blood. It's the lady who works at the dealership. Vivian something. I try to lock my eyes with hers, and she raises her hand from my arm, licks my blood from under her nails.

"She has become a part of the Feast," Detective Ford says from off to my left, but I'm still trying to stare down Vivian. "Why are you speaking to the food?" Mrs. Kovacks asks. "Why are any of you. There is no need for her to understand. How can the fly ever understand the beauty of the spider's web?"

I part my teeth to say something else, spit some kind of epithet at them, most likely, and they take the opportunity to jam something hard down into my mouth. It smells like blood and tastes like pennies and my teeth click against metal. I remember when I was a kid, trying to bite a quarter because I had seen prospectors bite gold coins in movies, and my dad explaining to me that they bit gold because it was soft. Whatever's in my mouth isn't soft, but I bite it anyway, bite until streamers of pain run up my temples, until my vision swims with stars.

On every side of me, the black robes start a kind of low ululation. A sound that begins in the backs of their throats and hums up from their chests. At once ominous and piteous somehow. Heads begin to disappear from my view as they sink to their knees, and then I feel teeth fastening on my skin. First on my arms. My wrists just above the restraints. The soft flesh below my shoulder. They push up my pant legs and bite my ankles. One of them fastens his teeth onto the bottom of my right foot. Hard enough to bruise, but not enough to draw blood. And still that sound continues.

Then all the lights go out.

There is a beat when I think that it's all part of some sick game they're playing. Someone hit the light switch and now we're all going to play spin-the-bottle or seven minutes in heaven. Only in this case it's seven minutes in the dark with a bunch of cannibals, or whatever the hell.

Then they start letting go. First the one on my foot, then the ones farther up. Their teeth disengage, their lips come loose with a wet slurp like suction cups. There are sounds of confusion, like someone is stepping on their toes in the dark. One shouts, one screams, one pleads with something I can't see.

"Oh, Great Maw," someone is saying. "Lord of the Feast. Forgive us and show us the way."

"What happened to the light?" someone else is asking. I think it's the same person who wanted so badly to "sink" me earlier. "What did you do with the light?"

And then I realize that my right hand is free. I don't know how. I didn't feel the rope coming loose, yet I can suddenly move my hand, my arm.

I reach up to the rope around my neck. It's anchored through the stone, looped through holes and knotted on the other side. I work my fingers underneath one of the knots, trying to pry it loose with my nails, and then it's just *loose*. The knot has come untied without my help, and I'm pulling the rope up through the stone, sitting up. I can reach around to my other hand, get hold of the knot on the other side, pull it loose, pull the rope through.

On the other side of the stone slab where I lay the ropes are secured to boards, and when I pull this knot loose the rope snakes through the hole and the board clatters to the floor. I can't see it, but I hear it, and so do some of the black robes.

"She's getting loose, you idiots," someone says, and I feel hands grasping at my back. I've already moved, though, scooted up, and I'm untying my feet.

"I've got her," someone says, and there's a scuffle, then another voice, "That's me, dumbass."

It would be a Laurel and Hardy routine if they hadn't just been biting my arms and talking about how they were going to kill me.

I finally get my feet under me, and I would head for the door, if I knew where it was, and just like that, the lights flicker, and I see a bedlam of robed figures all hunching and scuttling around, and stone steps leading up and then the lights are out again but it's enough, I've got my bearings, and I'm pushing through the crowd toward those stairs I just saw.

Whenever someone tries to get a hold of me I stiff arm them as hard as I can. I feel a nose break under my palm at one point, feel lips split. They're shouting now, swinging their arms around in the dark. They can't see any better than I can, though, and they don't know where I am, while I know where the stairs are, now, so pretty soon I stub my toe against a step and I'm limping up and out.

One of them grabs me, hand sliding down my leg to wrap fingers around my ankle, and I brace against the wall and kick backward with my other foot. The grip slackens and someone hits the ground.

"She is getting away!" Mrs. Kovacks' angry voice enunciates very clearly behind me.

She's right, I am.

At the top of the stairs I hit a metal door. Heavy as shit, but it isn't locked, and I manage to wrestle it up. It feels like moving a manhole cover. Then I'm in another room. This one seems familiar, yet also wrong somehow. Like I just walked into a room that's upside down, all the furniture on the ceiling. It's not upside down, though, it's backward. I've seen this room before, but I was on the other side. This is the Tar Lake Gift Shop. Those are the bars, and beyond them the black pond. The iron door leading out is swinging on its hinges and I'm sprinting for it before my brain catches up enough to warn me about the weird light.

I run out into the old road and stop because out here all hell has broken loose.

The pond is on fire. That would be weird enough, but the fire is also purple. It doesn't cover the whole surface of the pond, just blooms up here and there, reflecting on the still water beside it, shimmering, creating an optical illusion that threatens to throw me off balance.

Behind me, I can hear the black robes coming up the stairs and out into the purple twilight. I know I should keep running, but for the moment I'm struck dumb, stunned, and I guess it's okay, because they don't come try to grab me, even though I've stopped moving. When I finally look back over my shoulder, I can see that they're piling to their knees, their faces to the dirt. Praying, sure, but also something else. Dogs heeling, showing deference to a bigger dog.

I turn back to the pond, and that's when I see it.

The Great Maw, one of them called it, and I guess that makes sense. It's made of the black muck at the bottom of the pond. Asphalt and anaerobic mud, ground up bone and the skeletons of trees. Protruding from its dripping side I can make out skulls that are lit from within by that same violet fire; some of them human, others older. Its face is simply a configuration where a head should be; crocodilian, yet formed from the same brackish stuff as the rest of its body. The ultimate predator doesn't need teeth, after all. The ultimate predator eats us all when we die.

It moves a little like a 'gator, like how the big iguana dinosaur probably would have moved if it had ever been real. Stuck like a deer in the headlights, I think about all those sculptures with their pointy little teeth, about the man who made them. They said that his arms were just stumps when they found him in the water. I think about the tar pits that were maybe here a million years ago, and all the dead things lying down at the bottom of them, getting sucked up by whatever was down there and feeding it, making it grow.

Its legs are round trunks, its feet splay-toed where they land and ooze out into a palm frond footprint before lifting up with a sucking sound and coming down again. It doesn't have four legs. It has six now, now eight, now twelve. It moves however it needs to in order to get at its prize which is, of course, me, because I've figured at least that much out by now.

I can smell it, as it looms over me, the smell of mud that's dragged up from the bottom of a stagnant pond, the breath of a snapping turtle. Water is dripping down on my face as that mouth opens above me, the alligator jaw flattening into a lamprey O as it starts to descend, and still I can't move. Even with the enormity coming toward me, my mind is pierced by a single image that holds me transfixed. Those people behind me in the dirt, sticking a long knife into Dottie's chest and leaving her to die in the water, her death more food for this thing.

"I'm sorry, Dottie," I say, as I close my eyes and wait for the bite that never comes.

It takes me a moment to realize I'm not dead. When I open my eyes, the thing is still above me, dripping its stagnant water down on me, and next to it is something else. The sloth statue, limned in green foxfire, its eyes now glowing that same brilliant green. One of its arms is wrapped around the throat of the Great Maw, which is thrashing and running under its grip. Those two long, hooked claws are dug deep into that black muck, and underneath it they're opening up streamers of purple fire.

I'm no action hero. I fall backward onto my ass as the sloth hauls the head of the black, dripping muck monster aside. Those limbs made of dirty silt hammer at the sloth's concrete body, leaving black smears wherever they touch. The sloth is unfazed. It pulls the monster's head away from me and into a bear hug, toppling it backward onto the road.

They both move in big, shuddering jerks—neither of them made of materials that are meant to be alive—the sloth statue rolling on its back like a turtle, hauling the bulk of the Great Maw up and over. The Maw is fluid, but thick and slow. Syrup rather than water. As its body twists and writhes, skulls peer out here and there, then sink back again.

"You should be running," Dottie's voice in my ear, but when I whip my head around, I don't see her. Behind me, the black robes are still prone, their heads up now, watching the strange battle taking place at the edge of the pond. Not watching me, so I take the advice of the voice, whether it was real or just in my head, and I sprint toward the gate as well as my bruised feet will allow.

At the place where the road would curve and hide the lake from sight, though, I stop. I stumble forward about three more steps, then look back. The fight is still going on. The thing in the lake has grown larger, sucking up more of the muck and death, forming itself into a pillar—pear-shaped, like the allosaurus statue—its head flattening and enlarging like a smooshed toad as its many arms now lift the sloth up from the ground.

I tell my feet to run, but they won't. Not again. I won't leave Dottie here again. I know that she's here. Not just a voice in my head, not just my guilt. That's her animating the sloth. *"Look at his dumb face."*

So instead of running away, I run back. Around the pond on the other side, keeping the black water between myself and the cultists who are now, slowly, clambering back up to their feet and... what? Biting themselves? I don't know what they're doing, and don't spend much time trying to puzzle it out.

On the far side of the lake is another dinosaur statue. Normally submerged in brackish water up to its hindquarters, the tide has gone out as the Maw rises up, so now the whole statue stands exposed. I don't know what exactly it's supposed to be. A brontosaurus, maybe, from when there was such a thing, its neck and tail too short, its head too big and, like all the dinosaurs in the park, its mouth full of pointy teeth.

More than any of the others, it always made me laugh. I named it Bill the Carnivorous Brontosaurus, and it was always my favorite, the way the sloth was Dottie's favorite. So now I put both my palms against Bill's concrete sides.

"I don't know what's left when we die," I say out loud, though nobody is listening because the monster and Dottie and the cultists all have their own problems right now. "I don't know if we're a spark that goes out, if we're just meat, or what, but there's something left here that still belongs to Dottie, and whatever it is, there must be something like it in me. So, if it can help her now, then it had better, that's all I'm saying."

Nothing happens. I look across the pond where the sloth is slowly being battered down by the Maw. It rips one concrete arm off with its toothless jaws, then spits it on the ground in disgust, as if realizing for the first time that its foe is no flesh-and-blood life that it can absorb. Sorry, guy, no Feast tonight.

But that gives me an idea. Down near Bill's back legs, where he would have been covered by the water in normal times, the concrete isn't as smooth. There are jagged places where the rebar almost pokes through, and I drag my palm across one of them, opening up a gash that looks black in the light from the purple fires.

I slap my palm against Bill's side, tears in my eyes from the pain and from Dottie and from everything. "Wake up, damn you," I'm shouting as I leave bloody handprints across his concrete scales. "Wake up and fight."

There's no transition at all. It's like a frame has been removed from the film of the world. One moment I'm beating my hands against Bill's sides, and the next I'm looking down at my body where it lies in the mud.

I'm moving, but my body isn't. My point of view is swiveling on its long-yet-stumpy neck, my feet are tearing loose from their bases with a sound like a giant bottle opener. My pointy-toothed jaws are yawning wide to roar, but no sound is coming out because inside I'm just filled with rebar and bricks.

I cross the pond at something as close to a run as I can manage. My concrete feet sink down into the muck, but fortunately the Maw has pulled most of the lake into itself by now, so there isn't much left for me to sink into.

It feels me coming, I think. I can see its head shift, sliding backward through its neck so that the face now peers out toward me. It isn't fast enough, though. My own head crashes into its body, flinging mud and bones and punching out the other side, next to the dismembered sloth, which seems to manage a slow smile before hooking its remaining arm around one of the Maw's limbs and pulling.

The sloth falls back, its legs splintering, as I push my whole body through the torso of the muck monster. It's big by now, but I'm bulkier and heavier, and I disperse it with the simple facts of my weight and my velocity.

From above, it topples onto me and pushes me over onto my side, and I know immediately that I may never be able to rise, my feet far too stubby to rock me back onto them. That's okay, though. I can just lie here, so long as the Maw does, too.

The Maw has been scattered around, and now its body is much smaller, but that mouth hasn't shrunk at all. If anything, it seems bigger than ever. It leers like a toad, its jaws full of tarry stalactites, its many eyes flickering. "Smile, motherfucker," I say, but no sound comes out because I'm a concrete brontosaurus. My pointy little teeth fasten on one edge of that gigantic mouth while a hooked claw grabs the other. Then Dottie and I pull, like we're splitting a wishbone at Thanksgiving.

It's almost soothing, in its way. I can feel the asphalt sucking at my feet. I came for water, because I was thirsty, and now the boiling mud is pulling me down and down. I know that I'm dying, but it feels pleasantly warm and close, like the nest from which I hatched, and I don't really mind going to sleep here, knowing that I'll never be alone.

I'm looking at the lake from high above. The brontosaurus and sloth statues lie broken in chunks, bricks pouring out. Black muck is everywhere, the majority of it slowly draining back into the pond. The purple fires have gone out.

Something else is happening, too. The black robes are following the murky water, climbing voluntarily into the shallow pond and crawling down into the mud. Drowning themselves, one by one, until the last one is gone and there's nothing left on the sides of the pond except broken sculptures.

My point of view is getting higher and higher up, and I can see that the sun is rising, though the battle took only minutes and began when it was still twilight. Perhaps I've been watching for a very long time. It doesn't seem to matter anymore.

"Not yet," Dottie's voice says from somewhere behind me. "It isn't time to sleep just yet."

Everything is pain. My palm, my back, my neck. The places where the cultists bit me. For a few beats of my heart, pain is all that I can process, and then I realize that I'm back in my body, if I ever really left it.

That's a copout thought, though. Something my brain is throwing out there to help distance myself from the situation. "Ah, maybe it was all in her head," we say in the movie theater, because it makes us feel better than the other explanation, the one that explains less than it asks.

It doesn't hold much water this time, because there's an empty concrete slab next to where I'm sitting painfully up in the dirt, and a broken, paleontologically-inaccurate brontosaurus statue on the far side of the pond, its pieces mixed with those from a sloth with a big, dumb face.

When I stagger back to my Subaru, I see that it's still up on the jack, but the spare tire is missing altogether. That's just as well. I'm in no shape to drive this morning. It's a long walk back to town, especially with no shoes on, but I'll make it. And besides, I need some time to think.

Author's Notes:

Very nearly the longest story in this collection, I wrote "Prehistoric Animals" for an issue of the *Weird Fiction Review*, from Centipede Press. The theme of the issue was those old, pre-Code horror comics, though what I wrote sampled perhaps as much of some of the later stuff, like the Stan Lee/Jack Kirby monster comics.

More than that, though, this was my love letter to dinosaur parks. I always drug my parents to them whenever we passed near to one when I was a kid, and I loved the statues of their—often inaccurate, even then—dinos. I loved them much more than if they had been picture-perfect, in a way that I couldn't really articulate then and can't really now, either.

The title, for no particularly good reason, comes from a line in a Shriekback song.

OLD HAUNTS

Kim Parks considered himself something of a connoisseur of the haunted attractions that sprang up every year around Halloween. While he was getting his masters, he had been to haunted attractions all over the country—New Orleans, St. Louis, New York.

He worked as a systems analyst for a major telephone company, a job that required him to travel all over but that kept him occupied only during the daylight hours. At night, he was left to his own devices, and during the month of October those devices took him unfailingly to the doorsteps of the haunted houses.

Every city had one or two, most had more. Some were professionally run, put on by people who attended the HauntWorld trade show in St. Louis every year, but Kim was particularly fond of the more amateur affairs—the haunted equivalent of putting on a show in the barn.

He was not, in any of his other habits, a morbid individual. At work he wore suits in colors with names like "charcoal" and "fawn." There was nothing to mark Kim out as a habitue of haunts, yet some exploratory urge drove him to them, time and again.

After a while, they became so uniform—dark rooms and strobe lights and men in masks wielding chainsaws with the chains removed—that every deviation was like a precious stone unearthed unexpectedly in his driveway. These deviations became what he lived for.

He had passed through a door cut in a movie screen playing *Night of the Living Dead*, seen a dragon made of sheet metal breathe real fire, walked across a pulsating floor that bucked and squirmed like a living waterbed beneath his feet, and pushed his way through "cobwebbed" rooms festooned with silly string. He had been to haunts on islands, on farms, in plantation houses, old hospitals, and even an abandoned doll factory.

The haunt he pulled up in front of that October night was just a regular house, built on a cul-de-sac off the highway, on a level above the sidewalk, separated by a low concrete retaining wall so that Kim had to climb up a short batch of stone steps to reach the front porch. Bungalow style, the house was two stories with big, square pillars supporting a deep front porch. Did it strike Kim as slightly altar-like, as he approached, or was that just an embellishment?

There was no name above the porch, nor had there been one on the listing he had seen online that brought him here. "Haunted House," was all it said, followed by an address and a ticket price.

On the porch, a man stood next to a wooden box and took Kim's money, handing over a nondescript paper ticket, orange, of the kind that could be purchased in big rolls at any party store. The man wore a costume, though Kim couldn't have said what he was supposed to be dressed *as*. Perhaps an old-fashioned carnival barker in his top hat and mantled cloak, but that didn't explain the red scarf wrapping his mouth and throat.

The ticket vendor looked tired and maybe strung out. Kim wouldn't have been surprised. Haunts could be scary for reasons besides the safe and intentional ones. They were necessarily fly-by-night operations and many, even the biggest ones, were located in the most burnt-out parts of town, where large, empty buildings could be rented for cheap.

Kim fully expected to wind up with a knife in his guts someday, or at least with tetanus from a rusty nail, or a broken ankle from falling in the dark. Oddly, the thought never dissuaded him.

There were a few other people standing around on the porch, smoking cigarettes or talking quietly, waiting for their turn to go in. It wasn't a big crowd, especially for this late in the season, but there were also much bigger and more well-publicized haunts in the city—it's why Kim had chosen this one.

A wooden porch swing still hung on rusty, squeaking chains and a young couple sat in it, the boy whispering something in his date's ear as she stifled a laugh. The only light on the porch came from two dim bulbs, one above the ticket vendor and one above the storm door. They seemed to cast their light only straight down, leaving the rest of the porch in deep shadow, made even deeper by the distant streetlights.

Kim counted six other people besides himself and the ticket man; all in pairs.

Involuntarily, Kim found his gaze drawn back to the man selling the tickets. His eyes were bloodshot and bulging; his face, where it showed above the scarf, pale and feverishly clammy, with a sickly, almost greenish tinge. In the weak light, Kim couldn't decide if it was makeup or not.

The man seemed to be waiting for something impatiently, even irritably. Kim imagined that, had he been a cartoon character, he would have checked a comically oversized pocket watch.

There was no one else behind Kim in line, and no one else coming up the walk. With a deep-body sigh, the man stepped out from behind his wooden pulpit and drew himself up as best he could. When he spoke, his voice was the croaking rasp of a heavy smoker, or someone who hasn't slept in several days.

"Ladies and gentlemen," he wheezed with a flourish. "Before we proceed, I must give you one final warning. Despite its humble appearance, this house is unlike any other haunted attraction you have ever visited. If you enter these doors, I can guarantee neither your life nor your sanity. I caution you, if you fear for either, take this opportunity to collect a full refund and depart this place without shame."

It was a good speech, and though the man was obviously exhausted and the speech clearly one that he knew by rote, he fell into it effortlessly. Still, no one took him up on his offer, of course. As he turned and opened the storm door, he seemed to almost deflate, as if he really *had* hoped that they would all just leave.

Instead, he opened the storm door and then, beyond it, the front door of the house, which was painted a kind of faded brick red. The room on the other side still looked like what it had always been—a living room. There was no TV or couch anymore, and the fireplace against the far wall had been covered up by something black and shiny that looked like garbage bags. But even though all the lights had been replaced with red bulbs that lit the room like a heat lamp, it still looked like just a room, in just a house.

In one corner, old newspapers had been taped to the walls and floor. They were covered in streaks of fake blood that looked black in the red light, like a very dull Jackson Pollock. Something was crumpled in the corner. It looked like a pile of dirty laundry, but the arm jutting out said that it was supposed to be a body.

Kim had maneuvered to place himself at the back of the group, so that he was the last one into the room, aside from the ticket seller. All of the interesting stuff tended to happen to those at the front or the back, and the people at the front were usually pushed forward by the press of those behind—their fear, sure, but also the rush of the haunt operators to get one crowd through before the next arrived. Kim liked to be in the back, so he had more time to soak up the artifice.

No one else seemed to notice anything amiss. There were the usual exclamations of giggled disgust from the girls, the usual rueful chuckle from the guys. Kim's senses had been honed by innumerable haunts by now, though, and he noticed it immediately. The door to the coat closet that should have contained the knife-wielding killer stood ajar, and inside there was nothing but a couple of coats all shoved to one side.

The ticket seller seemed to notice it, too. He walked across the red room and paused by the door on the far side, letting his bleary gaze drift around the room, as though he was equally surprised by the killer's absence. If he truly was, though, he covered it well. "Once," he croaked, "terrible atrocities were committed in this house. What you see before you is merely reenactment. The true horror lies beyond."

While this, too, sounded like a prepared speech, Kim was pretty sure it wasn't. By now, he knew the rhythms of a haunt as surely as he knew those of his own body, and he knew that there should have been someone in that closet.

As the ticket seller opened the door and ushered the others into the next room, Kim paused beside the "dead body" on the floor. Closer now, he could see the mannequin face drizzled in syrup blood, but he was actually squinting to read the headlines on the newspapers. They were about some explorer bringing back artifacts from abroad and donating them to the local museum.

"You can still depart, if you wish," the ticket seller said from the doorway, gesturing with one too-long arm toward the front door, shut once again to keep out any latecomers. Kim pulled his gaze away from the newspapers, shook his head, and followed the others into a room that had once been a kitchen.

There were things in the sink. Puddles and stains all the way up the cabinet doors. In here was the obligatory strobe light, making the room feel like it was in constant motion.

The others were most of the way through already, their limbs seeming to jerk in the flickering light like a series of still images not quite linked together—a flipbook with a few pages missing.

In one corner of the room a staircase led up to the second floor, and Kim was sure, as sure as he had been about the empty coat closet, that the tour would normally have gone that way. In the pulsing glow, he could just make out the dummy dangling from a noose above the first landing.

Instead, however, the ticket seller had somehow already crossed the kitchen ahead of him, his hand resting on the brass knob of a smaller door, set into the wall beneath the stairs. In the throbbing light, he seemed to be moving strangely, his clothes shuddering with hidden life.

"Beneath us is the true house," he said, his voice somehow thicker still, filled with mucus. "It's not too late to turn back."

Yet he didn't wait to see if anyone did, just opened the door and, one by one, the group ducked through. As he passed, Kim tried to get a closer look at the man's face, or his twitching clothes, but the light wouldn't let him. It played tricks with his vision. Was the ticket seller wearing a mask underneath the scarf after all? Out on the porch, Kim would have sworn not, but now he saw something—an expanse of damp flesh—that he was sure couldn't be a man's face, even with makeup.

As he followed the couple in front of him down creaking cellar stairs, he was blinded by the transition from the strobing light to darkness, black spots and flashbulbs dancing in front of his eyes. In time, though, his vision began to adjust, and he saw that the stairs were lit by another light that seemed to creep up from the cellar ahead.

The steps themselves were wooden slats, with spaces in between where hands could reach out to grasp unwitting ankles—another thing that *should* have happened, in a regular haunted house. The sides had been blocked with pieces of pegboard, hung with the usual detritus of fake rats and bones and shrunken heads. The violet light from the cellars below crept through the holes in the pegboard, making strange patterns on the backs of the couple in front of him.

The light was sharp yet murky and it seemed to ooze up the basement steps, following the low-hanging fog that was as much a part of haunts as strobes and defanged chainsaws. The air below smelled damp and coppery, like a reptile enclosure.

Before the bottom, the stairs turned sharply to the left. In the eerie light, Kim could see the rest of the crowd disappearing around the corner below him. He could make out a kind of quiet thrumming noise; a bunch of voices humming atonally.

As he reached the landing and that sharp left turn, his sense that something was very wrong with the haunted house came back, filled him up. It made him want to turn and flee and also eager to press on. Novelty was the high he chased through these dim labyrinths, after all, and this promised to be novel indeed.

When his sneaker touched the damp-slick basement floor, Kim's first impression was a sweeping sense of chagrin. It was just a haunted house after all; another spook show in a long line of spook shows, and he was both impressed and disappointed that it had managed to take him in.

The rest of the crowd was strung out in a loose group at the base of the stairs, as though uncertain of their place in the tableau of the room.

The basement itself was unfinished and small, with concrete walls and wood supports. Unlike the rest of the house, it hadn't been decorated except with its one central prop. In one corner, a mundane washer and dryer still sat.

The only other furnishing was a card table upon which had been placed what Kim could only think to describe as an idol, roughly three feet tall. It was carved from some kind of purple-black stone that made Kim think of the volcanic glass that his mother had brought back from a trip to Maui. He was hard-pressed to say what the thing was carved to look like. It was hunched forward, like a gargoyle, and its back was swollen and bulbous, its head a mass of holes or protrusions and how was it he couldn't tell which?

Standing around it were the rest of the haunt's staff—the ones who had been missing from the rooms above. Here was the man in stained coveralls, a bloodstained plastic knife now hanging limply from his fingers. There, a girl in a torn white dress and overdone silent movie makeup who should probably have been descending those kitchen stairs.

The atonal humming sound was coming from their throats as

they all stood around the statue, arms at their sides, heads cast back, eyes rolled up in their sockets. And though they were all wearing costumes, it was also like they were wearing *another* costume beneath it. The girl in the white dress had one arm that was *much* longer than the other; the man in coveralls had split his costume down the back to reveal a humplike, cancerous growth that swam with yellowy eyes. And though the light cast smoky, undulating shadows on the walls, *they weren't the shadows of the figures that surrounded the idol.*

No, this was not just another haunted house. Kim knew it absolutely now. Knew it in his guts and his bones, not just with the creeping sense of wrongness he had felt before. He didn't know exactly what it *was*, instead, and in the months and years that followed he would lie awake at night often, struggling with the fact that a part of him wanted to stay and find out.

He was never sure what allowed him to break away. To turn and run, only too late remembering the ticket seller behind him, blocking the foot of the stairs. Half in a fall, Kim scrabbled at the man, and the scarf wound 'round his throat came off, revealing a shuddering, clenching mass of wet, red flesh where a mouth should have been.

Behind him, there were sounds of movement now. Perhaps a choked-off scream and a breathing like a wet bellows. There was a gust of hot, fetid air at his back, but he didn't look over his shoulder. He shoved past the ticket seller, recoiling at how much his flesh felt like a great tongue.

Up he went, through the strobe-light kitchen, the murder-scene living room, leaving the storm door slapping against the siding as he crossed the altar-like porch. He didn't even stop for his car, where it was parked up the cul-de-sac. He just ran and ran.

The police called Kim at his hotel room the following day, and when he went to pick up his abandoned car, he was questioned by a Detective Stanton, though Kim learned more from the exchange than the detective did.

After several reports of abandoned vehicles along the road, police had gone door to door, eventually finding the door to the haunt ajar, just as Kim had left it. They also found $350 in the petty cash box on the front porch, but otherwise the property was vacant. Even the props that Kim remembered from the haunted house were all gone, though there were still bits of tape stuck to the walls in the living room, dried fake blood in cracks and crevices here and there.

The house had been rented by a Benjamin Jasper, who had no license to operate a haunted attraction there. Back at his hotel, Kim did some digging into Benjamin Jasper. At one time, he had inherited a small fortune from his parents, who had been big-time local investors. He had gradually squandered it all on world travel, bringing back all sorts of objets d'art, many of which he had donated to local institutions, including the museum at his alma mater.

Several were currently on display there, but Kim opted not to go pay them a visit.

Author's Notes:

While it's one of only two entirely original stories in this collection, "Old Haunts" may also be the oldest story here. I don't remember how long ago I wrote the first draft of this, but it has changed a lot over the years, with only one central idea staying intact: "What if a Halloween haunted house got hold of an object that was *actually* cursed?"

Originally, the story was going to relate more directly to Lovecraft and, indeed, in the earliest drafts of this story, the haunted house was called the "House of Cthulhu," a nod to Cthulhu's house in R'lyeh, where he waits dreaming. I try not to use actual material from Lovecraft's mythos in my stories where I can help it, though, and eventually this got adjusted until it became the story it is now.

Between then and now, it went through a lot of revisions, and spent a lot of time in the proverbial trunk. Every few years, usually around Halloween, I would pull it out and tinker with it, and I always kind of liked it, still. So, when I decided to use "How to See Ghosts" to open this collection, I realized that this story would make a good companion piece to it, and here we are.

STYGIAN CHAMBERS

—When did you first begin having the dreams?

The voice is like a recording. It scratches scratches scratches

scratches

—When did you first begin having the dreams?

It was then, which is now. After the house. After what happened in that house. They said that the girl had gone missing and we were supposed to look in that old, abandoned house.

I never even knew that it *was* a house. I always thought it was a warehouse of some sort. *How odd*, I used to think, *there being a warehouse in this neighborhood.*

That's where it is, a neighborhood. Quiet brick streets that let grass grow up, let the rain seep down, into the dirt underneath, and the things underneath the dirt. The bugs and the worms and they crawl and crawl and—

—The house.

Yes, it was in my neighborhood, the one where I grew up, but there was a wall around it. Tall and sharp, like the wall around a warehouse, which is why I thought that's what it was. The building itself was tall and square, too, the roof flat, like a warehouse. And the windows, tall and thin. Like coffins.

It had been abandoned for as long as I can remember, and when we were little, we used to dare each other to go over the wall. There was a wooden gate, big enough to drive a truck through, and a smaller pedestrian entrance, blocked by iron bars. Both were always locked when we were kids; a rusty chain flaked off little orange bits when we squeezed between the bars, which of course we did.

The ground on the other side wasn't grown up, like you might think. I guess the wall kept the sunlight from shining down, so that the only things that grew there were brittle grasses and little hollow shrubs that rattled in the wind.

One time—the *only* time—I squeezed through those bars myself. It was a sunny day, but it was never sunny on the other side of that wall. It wasn't enough to go *through* the gate, of course. You had to go a little way. Throw a rock through one of the windows, maybe, or at least peek in through the dusty glass.

Would that I had thrown a rock through a window that day. Instead, I went around the corner of the building, so that the gate was lost from sight. It seemed much braver to me than looking in a window. Gone around the corner anything could happen to me, and the kids who waited on the other side, bright-eyed and eager, would never even know.

Standing just around the corner of the building was a man. He was wearing a green raincoat, and his back was to me. He was digging a hole in the ground. Not a very big hole, but big enough. Big enough to put a person in. When I rounded the corner he stopped, his shovel sunk into the gravelly dirt, and started to turn around. The hood of his raincoat was up, but it wasn't raining.

I ran before I saw his face. Ran as hard and as fast as I could, even though it was only about thirty or forty feet to the metal gate. I crashed against the bars and tried to squeeze through but, can you believe it, suddenly I couldn't fit. I was so terrified. My face was red and I thought I was going to pass out. When the other kids saw how scared I was, they ran, too, and so I was alone, puffing and squeezing against the metal bars, willing my bones to bend, my flesh to turn to jelly so that I could ooze through. Every second, I could feel that man in the raincoat behind me, his shadow up against me, and then—

Then I was through the bars and back out on the street and I ran all the way home and didn't look back.

It would make a lot of sense if I said that I never went near that house ever again, but I was a kid, and my curiosity was stronger than my fear. I went by there every day, walking four extra blocks on my way home from school so that I could stare in through the bars of the gate. I never saw that man standing there again. Never saw anything.

When the girl went missing, they rounded up people from the neighborhood to help look for her. I had moved back to care for my father when he took sick, and when the deputy came to my door, I agreed to join the search party. How could I say no?

~~I didn't want him to come into the house~~

At first, we looked in culverts and drain pipes, in the creek where we used to play as kids, in the dark woods along the bike path. I didn't know that we were going to that house, or I would have made up some excuse. They knew that my father had been ill, after all. What if he needed me and I wasn't there to answer his insistent knocking. It would just go on and on and on and on and on and on—

When we got to the metal door the chain was already broken. It lay in two pieces on the ground, one inside the metal gate and one outside. The lock was still stuck to the chain, rusted in place.

"She might have gotten in here," one of the men said, swinging the gate to and fro, as if we couldn't tell, just by looking, that it was open. It made a sound like brakes going out. Tires screeching on wet pavement. Two bright eyes—

I'm getting ahead of things.

We didn't know that she was dead then, you see. We thought we might still find her hiding somewhere, hurt or scared or sleeping. We hadn't yet imagined all the blood.

So we went on into the grounds of that house, around the corner where, as a child, I had seen the man. It was night and we had flashlights and I shined mine at the ground to see if I could tell that the dirt was different where he had been digging, but the night before had been rainy and all the ground looked the same.

The house didn't have normal doors, like a normal house. Nothing about that house is normal. It had double-doors and they were the color of weathered statues and they opened outward so that the dark spilled down the steps. The dark inside the house was *thicker*, somehow, than the dark in other places, and our flashlights just made beams and cones that only showed exactly what they were pointing at and not anything else.

The floor inside was black and white, but not checked. The black tiles made diamond shapes to offset the larger diamond shapes of the white tiles, yet they're what drew the eye, what I mentioned first—why is that, do you think?

The first room of the house was tall, two stories, and it looked like there was a mural or fresco on the ceiling, but time and mold had obscured it and what had perhaps once been a representation of the Last Supper was now just eyes peering out of a seeping blackness.

There were stairs leading up—marble, with gilt banisters—and doors going off in other directions. Past that first room, the house became an endless series of hallways all alike. They seemed impossibly long, so that we must be walking past the limits of the house, past the dirt and the walls and into the neighborhood surrounding us.

The hallways were lined with doors all alike. Behind some doors were rooms, while others just opened onto more hallways. Most of the rooms were bare, their lack of furnishings serving to render them indistinguishable. It was impossible to tell what had been an office, a bedroom, a den. The rooms were more like cubicles in a highrise—each one a functional square, nothing more.

Only one room was different. It had padded walls, like in a mental institution, and the door locked from the outside. We all looked at one another and we said, "why is there a room like this in a normal house," though we all knew already that the house was far from normal.

We became lost in the rooms all alike, in the halls all alike, with the doors all alike, and to combat our sense of disorientation, our growing fear, we agreed that we needed to split up. We didn't yet have any *reason* to be afraid, you have to understand, and we were ashamed. We were supposed to be the grown-ups; the big, brave men, trying to find a lost girl, not afraid of some house just because it was spooky and strange.

Which is how I found myself alone at the top of the steps.

I don't know where I was in the house by then. I hadn't realized that the house even had a basement, but then again, why shouldn't it? Many of the houses in the neighborhood had basements—probably most of them did. This house seemed so huge and strange I had completely lost any bearing on where I was in those twisting halls—turn down one, then another, then another, and you should come back to where you started from, shouldn't you?

The stairs went down. They seemed damp and unfinished in comparison to the rest of the house. The smell that came up from down below wasn't one that I could immediately place, but it made me think of metal, moving slowly in the dark.

As I went down the stairs, I called the girl's name, gently, coaxingly, as we had been coached to do before setting off on our mission. At the bottom of the steps, I found another hallway, but this one looked different from the others. When I was in school there was a building on campus that connected to another building across the street through an underground tunnel. This hallway reminded me of that tunnel, complete with a metal pipe that came up from out of the floor and ran along the wall.

The pipe was rusted and damp and smelled like the drain of a shower. The hallway was damp, and water dripped down from above. I thought maybe I was going under the street but, like I said, I had lost track of where I was in the house, so I might have been going anywhere.

—Do you remember how you came here?

I ran.

I ran out of that building out of those double-doors down those rain-wet steps out that iron gate out into the street. There were eyes in the dark, big and bright, and they were coming right toward me! And then—

—You were hit by a car. They brought you here.

I don't remember an ambulance ride. I don't remember a hospital. Where did I go?

—They brought you here so we could take care of you.

All I remember is this room.

—You had blood on your hands, on your shirt.

I was hurt in the accident.

—You were, but it wasn't all your blood, was it?

No. No. No. No. No. No.

I don't want to talk about the basement. Please don't make me. I'll tell you anything else. Anything you want, just don't make me talk about that place, about what happened there.

—Tell us about your father, then.

His illness made him seem so strange and thin and small. Like when seed heads burst into downy streamers. He seemed to have burst like that. His hair was just wisps plastered to his head. The dome of his skull was like a lampshade. His lips and gums were pulled back so that his teeth seemed to be bared, always, like he was growling, and his eyes had sunk away until they were just pinpricks in a mask, and then nothing at all.

He didn't even seem to struggle when I pushed the pillow down over his face. It was hard for me to tell when he was dead, he was already so still. I wore his green raincoat when I went to bury his body by the corner of the house. When I cut the chain and let it rattle to the ground.

I kept the hood up because of the rain that night.

I didn't hurt the girl, though. I didn't want to hurt her. I didn't want to do *that* to her. Put her limbs all backwards-on like that, like doll parts. I didn't want to make her move like that, her one remaining eye peeled back and staring. It was the house that wanted to hurt her. It was the house. I can still see her, in the shadow of that *god-damned statue in the basement of that house she is waiting for me still.*

No, you're right, I'm feeling better. You didn't want to know about that, you wanted to know about the dreams, when they started. I think they started after I came here. I never remember having them before. They started after I left that house.

I fell up the stairs from the basement. I remember the bark of the steps against my shins—funny, that I remember that. Then it was hall after hall, all alike, and at every turn my brain concocting some new horror to lurch out of the shadows, spider-quick, but nothing ahead save more halls.

I ran like I had when I was a child, and every hallway felt like I was trying to squeeze myself through those bars all over again. My flashlight was still in my hand, but I was running so hard that its light bounced everywhere, and the blood just looked like a shadow until I slipped in it.

They were all dead. The men I had come into the house with. No, that's not quite true. Some of them weren't quite dead yet. I saw them in the cone of my flashlight, picked out from the thick dark inside that house. Saw them where they jutted, here and there, out of the walls, the blood-slicked floors. My beam caught the face of one, just his head and one shoulder, his eyes gone, replaced with what looked like fleshy cobwebs, his mouth stuffed with something, his lips gawping open and closed around a soundless noise that he no longer had lungs to make.

The house hadn't finished with them yet, you see, but it has by now. That's why you haven't found them. Why nobody has found them. Why nobody will. I suspect that you think I killed them, but I didn't. They're still in that house somewhere, buried in the walls somewhere, just like her.

I ran outside and there were those burning eyes and I woke up here and it was between those eyes and here that I began having the dreams, I think. In them, I'm standing outside the house and looking up at the window. It seems like it was a long time ago, maybe when I was still a child.

The windows don't look right. They're arched, like the windows of a church, even though the windows in the actual house are tall rectangles, but I know that it's the house, in that way that you know things in dreams.

I'm looking at one particular window. It's lit with a violet glow—flat, it provides no illumination beyond the pane of glass, but creates a perfect silhouette of a familiar figure on the other side. The figure raises a hand to the glass, and I raise mine in response.

I'm drifting up a set of stairs. These stairs are black and gold—they resemble the stairs in the house, but are not identical to them, like the windows—and I am drifting up them and up them and up them.

I am a little boy, sneaking down the hall to listen outside the door of my parents' room. I drift down the hallway until I reach a door that I know opens onto the room of the purple light. There is a brass knob and, beneath it, a keyhole. I bend down to look, press my eye up against the keyhole, and on the other side—

—Do you know where you are?

I can't be sure. Why won't you just tell me? Don't you know

where I am?

—We brought you here to take care of you.

Can't you tell me where I am? Tell me the name of this hospital. The name of my doctor. Tell me an address, a street, a telephone number. Let me see your faces. Step out from behind that light and let me see you.

—We brought you home.

I'm sorry. I didn't mean to. I swear I'll never do it again. Don't you hear me say I'm sorry?

—We brought you into our house.

It wasn't me. It was the house. *It was this house!*

In the basement in the attic in every room of the house there is a black statue that sweats beads of darkness. At its wide base it is like nothing at all—a shapeless geological extrusion thrust up by cooling magma or tectonic plates—but what is it that happens near the top? Are those shoulders, the arms in which they terminate still fused to the base? Is that a head, rugose as a dried bouquet of night-blooming flowers, pocked and cragged like the dark side of the moon?

At the foot of the statue something skitters and moves—then many things do.

When did you first begin having the dreams?

Author's Notes:

This is…not what I was expecting to write, when Scott Dwyer asked me to contribute something to *Pluto in Furs*, an anthology, by its own logline, of "diseased desires and seductive horrors." I can tell you what the *influences* on this one were—Junji Ito and *The Cabinet of Dr. Caligari*; *Silent Hill* and the Danny Elfman song "Sucker for Mystery"—but I'll be damned if I can tell you how they got from *there* to *here*.

MANIFEST DESTINY

I made the acquaintance of the man who called himself Vernon Sawtell in a tavern called the *Mary Queen of Scots* in Frisco, bobbing upon the tide. The gold rush had driven everyone mad. When ships docked, their crews abandoned them like rats to seek greater fortunes in mountain streams than they might ever have found upon the crashing waves.

This mass exodus had left behind a forest of masts in the harbor. Without enough men to sail them, the abandoned hulks had been converted into taverns and hostels. The *Mary* was one such, the moniker that once adorned the vessel now serving as the name of a darkened drinking establishment, where the clink of glass was accompanied by the soft groan of wood-on-wood as ships rubbed against each other with the swell of the surf.

"Welcome to the Sargasso Sea," Sawtell said when I pulled up a chair two down from him at the makeshift bar. The barkeep—a small man with bowed legs and a bristling black mustache—sat a glass before me and I indicated two fingers of whiskey.

"Pardon?"

"You're not a seaman?" Sawtell asked, and I shook my head. "Me either, but I read more than is good for me, and so I've read the sailors' tales of a graveyard of ships mired in a floating continent of seaweed. Seems we've built our own here," he said, raising his glass. "The American way."

Frisco had, of course, only become a part of America a year or so gone now, but I knew a fellow American when I met one, and Sawtell obviously did, too. He did not cut a dramatic figure and, honestly, had he not spoken, I probably wouldn't have spared him more than a glance. I was there to drink, after all, not to make friends.

He wore clothes that would probably have been fine at one time but that, even in the dim light cast by the swaying hurricane lamps, I could tell were frayed and threadbare. His hair was brown and plastered flat to the top of his head, and his face bore the evidence of having passed a few days without a proper shave, the stubble black on skin that had gone from pale to weathered by sun and wind and was now on its way back toward pale.

It was mid-afternoon and the place was abandoned save for the two of us and the taciturn bartender, so I scooted one chair closer to Sawtell and introduced myself. He did the same, giving the name that I have given here, though I later had reason to believe that he may have fabricated it. "What brings you down from the mountain?" he asked, and I shook my head.

"I'm no prospector," I said. "I don't have the blood. I'm a newspaper man."

At this he laughed, a sound filled with an admixture of genuine mirth and bitterness. "This world is a fickle bitch, isn't she?" he asked.

In lieu of answer to what seemed to me a rhetorical question, I posed a query of my own. "And yourself? Why aren't you in the mountains? You have the look of a man who has known the world well."

Sawtell (or whoever he was) shook his head, tipping the all but empty glass before him up onto one edge and rocking it in a slow circle. "I've had my fill of adventurism," he said. "If there's gold in them thar hills, it can stay there. I've seen gold enough to last a lifetime. All I want is a nice dark bar and a good stiff drink."

When he finished speaking, he picked up the glass and drained off the last drops of amber liquid from within. "Though it seems that you need gold to get that second thing, after all."

I am, as I had told him, a newspaper man, and so I had developed the newshound's nose for a story, and he seemed a man who had one. I told him as much, and offered to buy him a drink or two if he felt like telling it.

"I'll make you a deal," he said. "You keep this glass full, and I'll tell you a tale that you won't hear the like of anywhere else. Not on God's earth, anyway."

What I hadn't mentioned to him was that I was hiding out from my editor, which was why I had come down to the disreputable establishments on the docks to drink. An afternoon spent listening to a tall tale from the lips of a man who seemed so comfortable with speech felt like an appealing activity in comparison to the bawling out that awaited me back at the office.

I indicated to the barkeep that he should set us both up with another drink, and agreed to Sawtell's terms. "I was born in North Carolina," Sawtell said. "That doesn't matter much to my story, save to tell you that I was out of my element. I wanted to be a newspaper man myself, and so I worked a heap of different jobs in printer's offices and papers here and there, working my way steadily westward until I got what I thought was the opportunity of a lifetime."

Here, I will interrupt Sawtell's telling to point out why I take pains to indicate that Vernon Sawtell may not have been his real name. My curiosity piqued by what you will soon see is his very unusual tale, I later tried to track down a Vernon Sawtell from North Carolina who matched my drinking partner's background and, for my troubles, received a letter from that man's cousin, accompanied by a rubbing of his gravestone from a cemetery in Raleigh where he had been laid to rest a year before this story was ever told to me.

"America had just declared war in Mexico," Sawtell said, "and my employer at the time, a penny press out of St. Louis, saw a chance. He said he needed reporters to go down there and cover the conflict. If I was willing, he said, I would have a byline and an opportunity to report upon the most important events of the day."

Sawtell drained his glass and tapped it on the bar, indicating to the barkeep that he should fill it back up. The barkeep looked at me and I nodded.

"This was only a few years ago," Sawtell continued, "but perhaps you've been around enough to understand what I mean when I say that I was still just a lad then. Wet behind the ears and all that. I imagined hardships, certainly, but I imagined them as the kinds of hardships I had already endured—going hungry, sleeping rough. I couldn't conceive of what was ahead of me.

"When I was a boy, I went to church with my mother, and I remember the preacher's sermons about hell. Brimstone and sulfur and an exile from all those who ever loved us. As a child, the idea scared me, but by the time I was writing for the *Dispatch*, it just seemed quaint and faraway, like a ghost story at Christmas. I had never heard or seen a depiction of hell that could match what I was walking into.

"I guess this far west, most of us have seen men die, but when I headed down the Mississippi, the closest I had been to death was a wake. That changed in short order. I saw men chewed to bits by cannons and rifles. I saw boys ten years my junior with half their faces missing. Have you ever been to war?"

I shook my head. During the war he described I had been in the North. I had seen gunfights and bar fights and men breathing bubbles of blood behind buildings and I had been in hospital wards ravaged by consumption, but war, at that time, was foreign to me.

"I was there at Chapultepec," he said. "I saw the sky turn black with smoke, lit from beneath with muzzle flash and cannon fire. It was like standing on a stage, the curtains behind you, the audience in front, the only sound the thunder of gunfire and men screaming and crying and dying." He was silent for a moment, staring down into the whiskey in his glass, and I knew that, for that moment, he was there again, at Chapultepec.

"If that's not hell," he continued, "then it's only because the devil hasn't ever seen it, either."

"Barkeep," I said, tapping the wood of the bar, "another round."

Sawtell drained his glass and the bow-legged man refilled them both.

"After Chapultepec, my regiment got separated from the rest of the column. One of the last things I saw, when I still knew where I was, was a break in the clouds of smoke, revealing the walls of the castle. After so much darkness, they seemed blindingly white.

"Standing on the ramparts were these young boys. They couldn't have been more than fifteen—cadets at the military academy there—and for just a moment I couldn't figure out what they were doing. Had they come out to watch the fight? I wanted to yell for them to go back inside, that they were in danger, and then the first one jumped.

"They knew we were going to take the castle, you see, and they weren't going to be taken alive. I watched them drop, one and then another and then another. Like dolls tipping off a shelf. Thump thump thump," he struck the bar with the edge of his hand, for emphasis, and I flinched. "And then they were as still as dolls. To nationalism," he said, raising his glass. I left mine untouched on the bar in front of me.

"At any rate," he continued, after he had taken a long drink and wiped his lips, "my regiment got separated from the body of the conflict. They tell me we won there, but I wasn't around to see it. Somewhere in all the smoke and blood, we got lost, and after a little while it was just me and one other man, a negro named Olympus, my hand to God. Olympus Jackson.

"Some of the men hadn't been keen on the idea of serving alongside a negro, but we'd had free blacks in North Carolina when I was a kid, and I hadn't ever really understood the difference in a free black and a free white man, if we're being candid. I remember asking my mother once why some folks kept blacks as slaves, and she told me that it was just the way of things. I wish then that I'd had the sense to say, 'Not forever,' but I was just a child.

"All of that is just to say that I'd always gotten on with Olympus, and when it was only the two of us, I was grateful to have a familiar face nearby. He'd taken a bullet in his shin from one of our own fighters who couldn't tell us from the enemy in the billowing smoke, and he had his arm across my shoulders, limping something fierce. Neither of us had uttered the word gangrene, but it was on both our minds.

"Even then, though, I wasn't sad he was hurt, that he might die. That's how we work, after all. I was just happy not to be alone.

"If you've never been lost," Sawtell continued, "this may seem ridiculous, but I was sure we were separated from the rest of the men by nothing more than a low ridge, and as soon as we got over it we'd be back in the thick of things. But we crested that ridge and nothing looked familiar. If you've never been to Mexico City, Chapultepec is on a hill. It's right in town. It seemed impossible that we couldn't see it, yet there we were.

"I said as much to Olympus, and he replied through gritted teeth, 'We shouldn't be here.' At the time, I thought he meant that we were lost, that we needed to find the rest of our regiment, the rest of the American army, but I've since had cause to wonder.

"I think that's when I realized I couldn't hear the cannons anymore, couldn't hear any gunfire at all, any men or horses. That there was no town in any direction. We had waded through blood and gunsmoke to get here, but now I couldn't see much of either, except the blood that still stained both of our uniforms.

"The clouds were still thick, but they were normal storm clouds now, leaden and gray but as natural—or so I thought at the time—as rain or wind. All around us was just scrubland and as I walked the scrub became strange. Have you ever seen coral?" he asked, and I nodded. I'd seen sailors bring it in for sale, brittle and fading.

"Bit by bit, the plants started to look more like coral. Or maybe like a child's drawing of plants, if you see what I mean. Someone who hasn't learned how to make them look natural yet. They looked more like the *idea* of plants, and I thought about my grandmother telling me Bible stories about the time before the Flood, how the earth was different back then, when plants and animals hadn't settled into their proper shapes. There were monsters in the earth in those days. Why shouldn't there be monsters still?

"'We shouldn't be here,' Olympus said again. 'They tore us away. Talk o' the devil, but the devil is here. Not out in the trees and the fields, he lives in a city upon a hill.' I realized that he was becoming delirious, his weight getting ever heavier across my shoulders. He was going to die if I didn't do something soon.

"That's when we came upon the house. You can explain it any way you like, or not at all, so long as you keep the whiskey coming, but I'll tell you now I sure as hell can't account for it. One moment, we were walking through this impossible antediluvian field and the next there was the house.

"It should not have been there. Wherever we were, whatever direction we had been heading, we should still have been in Mexico. Hell, we should have still been in Mexico *City*. And there's no house in Mexico that looks like this, at least not as far as I know. I've never seen a house like it this far west. It was taller than any building in Frisco, I'll tell you that now, and it was a Victorian of the kind I had only ever seen back home.

"It was painted white, from stem to stern, and the paint looked so fresh that I half believed I would find it still tacky if I put my hand upon it—and yet, at the same time, that fresh coat of paint, upon closer inspection, seemed inexpertly applied, somehow. Dolloped on too heavy, like congealed cream, and I had the feeling, sourceless but inescapable, that it was covering over rot.

"What would I have done, if Olympus hadn't been raving at my side, the weight of his injury slowly bearing us both down? I wish that I could say I would have turned away but, as I said earlier, I was still young then, such a short time ago, and while seeing the war had already changed me, I had wanted to be a newspaper man for a reason, and that same curiosity might have driven me inside regardless.

"All I know for sure is that we went in. I dragged Olympus up the steps to the porch, which sagged as though the house was very old, for all that the paint looked fresh. I put my hand on the worn gold knob of the door and it opened under my touch.

"'Hello,' I said to the dim interior, but even as I did, Olympus sagged hard against me, causing us both to stumble, and I knew, instantly, that it would mean his life to wait any longer, so I dragged him across the threshold.

"In telling this story, I make my actions sound selfless, but as sure as I sit here now, I can tell you that they were not. I wasn't concerned about Olympus's well-being. That was what I told myself, even then, but it was a lie. I was terrified, and I didn't want to be alone. I was using him to prop myself up, as surely as he was leaning on me to keep off his shattered leg.

"Inside, the house was fine and well-appointed, though once again I had a sense that the gilt and lace covered something that was going to rot. The door opened onto a vast foyer with tile on the floor that looked to be marble and a staircase that swooped up into the darkness to my left. Straight ahead was a fireplace so wide you could have driven a two-oxen team through it with room to spare on both sides. Across the mantel was inscribed a short Latin phrase: *Deus in speramus.*

"Above the fireplace hung a painting. I don't have enough learning about art to tell you the style or the period, but I can tell you vividly what the painting depicted. It was a landscape, and upon each end of it was the ocean. Toward the left-hand side, the skies grew dark with clouds and mountains huddled up close to the sea; toward the right the sun was rising over a bay filled with ships. None of this was the focus, however. In the center of the painting, so tall that her head brushed the sky, was a woman dressed all in white. She dragged behind her what looked to be telegraph cable and at her feet traveled stagecoaches and trains. Before her she drove Indians and bison toward the darkness and the sea.

"This was all that I took in, aside from a general impression of disuse and disrepair behind the finery, before I deposited Olympus onto a couch at the edge of the room—beneath the inscrutable gaze of that giantess. His skin was clammy to the touch, and I reached out gingerly toward his mangled leg before drawing my hand back, unwilling to look at the wound.

"I was no doctor, I reasoned, and so there could be nothing gained by my examining his injury, which would accomplish nothing save to turn my stomach. Instead, I should work to find something that could help him.

"'You wait here,' I said, putting my hand against his chest and pressing gently, in the sort of tone you might use with a sick child. His eyes stared ahead but did not see me, I knew. Still, I hoped he would stay, and I left him there and went in search of water, spirits, and clean linens with which to bind his injuries.

"That he needed some greater intervention I had no doubt, but unless I found someone at home in that strange house who knew more of medicine than I, there was little I could think to do save try to make him comfortable.

"From the foyer, I passed into a dining room, where a table was piled high with fine foods, all of which had turned black with decay. Whoever lived there had been long gone, I reasoned, though, in thinking back, I realize now that no insects swarmed upon that mummified food."

Sawtell's story stopped there, and I realized I had been holding my breath as I listened to the last few sentences of it. I let out a puff of air that I covered by lifting my glass—which was untouched—to my lips. Sawtell tapped the edge of his with a nail, and I saw it was empty.

I gestured to the bartender, who had been keeping his distance, as though the story made him uncomfortable. He sauntered slowly over and poured another slug of whiskey into Sawtell's glass, then just left the bottle and hurried back to the other end of the bar, where he made a great show of polishing the glasses with a gray rag.

"Your generosity is appreciated," Sawtell said, taking a drink of his whiskey. "I don't remember just now whether there were windows in that dining room, or whether I had gone into another part of the house. I seem to recall a jumble of rooms—all bare of life but filled with *things*; tables and chairs, wardrobes and chests, all the accoutrements of life in such proliferation that they seemed, at times, to simply be piled in the rooms, like attic storage—yet I can't recollect which rooms I went into, or where they were located in relation to one another.

"All I know is that I was looking out a window and something else was looking in. I told you about those antediluvian plants? Well these must have been their matching fauna. Things that were not yet animals, but were on their way. Strange prehistoric creatures with beady red eyes and great, unformed jaws.

"Any bravery I had mustered up to that point evaporated, and I ran through that concertina of a house and back into the foyer. The room was dark, as if night had fallen outside, though it ought to still have been afternoon.

"In the dim light, I thought for a moment that Olympus, perhaps driven to madness by his injury, had gone berserk. I found pieces of what I took to be furniture strewn about, but all the furniture in the room was still where I had left it, and Olympus still slumped on the couch, his skin gone gray, his eyes glassy, his mouth moving, forming the same few words over and over again in his delirium.

"'They made me kill all those boys,' he kept repeating. 'an' for what?'

"It wasn't until I drew close enough to him to hear what he was saying that I realized what the shapes on the floor were. Not furniture; bodies. Not fresh ones, either. Skeletons, their skin drawn tight over their bones. They wore the uniforms of the Mexican army, but the uniforms were faded, as though the war had been years ago, instead of still raging somewhere that wasn't where we now stood—or was it?

"For all that, though, Olympus was wrong. He hadn't killed *all* these boys.

"I wasn't a soldier. While they fought and died, I cowered and scribbled on a pad of paper, telling myself I was doing something that mattered, that people back home would know what was happening here, would know what this war was about, thanks to me.

"I sent stories back by telegraph where that was possible, mailed sheets of hand-written scribblings back when it wasn't. I was no soldier, yet I worked alongside them, which meant that, after a while, one of them had given me a gun. A pistol he picked up off the ground. It was Lester Scott, who I later found dead in a ditch, face down in mud. I tucked the pistol into my pouch. Another soldier later handed me a bayonet, which I slipped into my belt.

"When the enemy broke through to my regiment, rifles cracking and shouting, I had been standing right there. Wallace Fremont pushed me down, and I rolled partway down a small hill and fell into a gulley, away from the others. There, a Mexican soldier waited. It sounds like an ambush, doesn't it? That would make a good war story. Something I could have been proud to send home.

"No, he cowered. He clutched a pistol in his trembling hands, and he raised it toward me, speaking in a cascading waterfall of Spanish that I couldn't understand. I could have done a hundred things then. Raised my hands in the air to show that I was no threat. Turned tail and ran. What I did was reach for my own pistol.

"When my hand went into the bag, the soldier pulled the trigger, and the hammer clicked on an empty chamber. Had he done it again and again, I would have had time to pull my own pistol and fire, but that isn't what happened. Instead, he dropped the pistol and made a dash for me. That's how I saw it then, anyway.

"My hand wasn't all the way into my pouch when I saw him

drop the pistol and rise. I knew he was coming at me. He had nowhere else to go. The gulley dead-ended there, at a wall of yellow earth against which he had his back. There was no way out but through me.

"Was he planning to attack me, or just run past? It's what I asked myself as I stood in that foyer and looked down at his body. But that day, on the battlefield, I didn't ask anything. I pulled my bayonet from my belt and slid it into his guts.

"That was his face on the floor at my feet, gray and drained of life, the eyes empty holes that nonetheless stared into me. I heard a sound behind me, one I had never heard before and am thankful to have never heard since, though I think I will hear it at least one more time, on the day I finally die.

"I didn't look back right away, though. I looked up. Past the staring eyes of Olympus, which were focused on something behind me now, and up at the painting above the mantel. It had changed and yet it was still the same. It was as if before there had been a veil over the painting. Now the veil was lifted, and the true painting was visible. The one that had always been there, waiting.

"The white woman still strode across the land, but now her face was a skull. Stars pulled themselves from the heavens to form a diadem around her brow and she dragged a chain from which black bodies were suspended. From where her feet touched the earth, black ribbons extended out in every direction, and on them were wheeled beetles that scuttled everywhere.

"The cities and the towns of the coast near the sun had been replaced by shining towers and great chimneys, and the sun was now a blazing eye looking out across this new world of gods and monsters.

"I heard another sound behind me. A more familiar sound; like the lid of a trunk dropping closed. I turned, and a man was standing before me, and behind him one of the black beetles from the painting.

"This one wasn't a painting, however. It was like nothing I

had ever seen before or since; like a carriage but polished until it shined. I could see my reflection in its surface. I had no idea how it had gotten into the room. It was far too big to fit through any of the doors.

"There were no horses, nor anyplace to harness them. No driver, and no place for the driver to sit. Just wheels and an enclosed compartment and the man who stood at my side, dressed in a fine black suit, the hat on his head not dissimilar to the ones our soldiers had worn. His glasses were mirrors that hid his eyes and reflected my own face back at me, and his smile was a mile wide and white as anything.

"'Who are you?' I asked, and that smile stretched wider still, though I would have said that was impossible. 'I'm an American,' he replied.

"'I'm glad,' I said, not sure what else to make of the cryptic statement. 'We're sorry to intrude on your home, but do you happen to know of a doctor nearby? We're with the army, and my friend here is badly hurt.'

"'I think you know that your friend is beyond the reach of a doctor,' the man said. 'But I'm sure I can help him, if I set my mind to the task. Here's the question, though. Do you want me to?'"

Sawtell stopped, looking down at the dregs of whiskey in his glass. I could see his knuckles whitening with his grip, and I feared that the glass might shatter before he relaxed.

"I should have said that of course I did, that the question was ridiculous," he continued after a long and pregnant pause. "Instead, I looked back at my feet, behind me, at the body of the boy I had killed with the bayonet. His eyes were empty sockets, but I saw he was rising up. They all were. They were filing, one by one, up to the black beetle which now looked less like a beetle and more like a long, shiny coffin.

"As they filed up, the man opened the door and one by one they got in. 'Your friend can go home, good as new,' the stranger said. 'He may have a bit of a limp, but he won't even lose the leg. You have my word as a gentleman. All you need to do is come with me.'

"He held the door open for me, and I could see inside a bit. The dead boys were all gone somewhere I couldn't see. Inside, everything was made of gold. The ceiling was covered in gold leaf. The seats were woven of gold thread. There was a golden tray holding golden cups and a bottle of what looked like good scotch.

"'And if I don't,' I said, though I already knew the answer.

"'You really shouldn't,' the man replied. 'Look at him,' with a jerk of his chin toward Olympus. 'He was never one of ours. Let me take him away from here, and you can head on home. Back to St. Louis—he pronounced it lew-y—or even back to Carolina. Wherever you want. The world is your oyster. After all, we're both Americans, you and I.'

"I couldn't see his eyes behind the vast mirrored spectacles, but I knew he winked at me then. And let me tell you something. If I had spit in his face, stabbed him with the same bayonet that had killed that boy—I no longer had it with me, had lost it somewhere gone and forgotten—burned down his house, I wouldn't be here today. Not because he would have taken me away, though he might have, but because I wouldn't be drinking away what remains of my life in some place that never sees the sun.

"But I didn't do any of those things. I walked around him, around the black beetle coffin, and out the front door of the house. I left it hanging open behind me.

"I heard the stranger whistling an unfamiliar tune as I walked away. Later, I tried to play it on an old piano in some wharfside tavern and the piano player told me that it was a song called 'To Anacreon in Heaven,' which came from a British gentleman's club.

"It was night outside, and I didn't look back until I saw the sun rising in what must have been the east. When I did, the house was gone.

"And that's my story," the man who called himself Vernon Sawtell concluded, tapping the bottom of his glass against the now-empty whiskey bottle. “I don’t know what to make of it any more than you do, and the last drops are gone, so I wouldn’t go trying to ask me any questions.

“If you don’t like it, just remember you’re the one who’s been paying for the drinks, so you have no one to blame but yourself.” With that, Sawtell-or-whoever stood up and walked out of the tavern, leaving his empty glass behind.

I settled up the tab and went to face my editor.

Author's Notes:

Poor Ben Thomas. He helped me get my start in this business, as much as anyone did. Back more than a decade ago, I was a regular contributor to his "classic-style" weird fiction periodical, *The Willows*. And when he hit upon the idea to re-release the entire run of that august mag in hardcover with a little help from Kickstarter, he was kind enough to invite me to be one of a handful of authors contributing a new story for the project.

How did I repay him? With one of the weirdest and most overtly-political things I've ever written—a story at once scathingly and *specifically* critical of American exceptionalism, imperialism, white allyship, and more. Fortunately, Ben has always been a stand-up guy, and he published the thing in spite of all that.

When I got the assignment, the only requirement was that I write a story set during or before the golden age of the weird tale—around the turn of the century or earlier, in other words. Which is how we ended up with this weird thing set in the immediate aftermath of the Mexican-American War of the 1840s. This is another story that I researched pretty heavily, and some of the weirdest stuff in it is true, including the "Sargasso Sea" of boats in San Francisco's harbor, some of them turned into bars and other establishments.

The anachronistic car that shows up before the end almost certainly drove in from Neil Jordan's *The Company of Wolves*, while the driver is emphatically that damned chauffeur from Dan Curtis's *Burnt Offerings*. In a career with a thousand monsters, both on the page and on the screen, he's the one I'll take with me to my grave, I'm sure.

THE DRUNKARD'S DREAM

Stage 1
La Taverne

It was the mosaic tile on the wall of the kitchenette that made me choose the apartment. It reminded me of our first place together, that long one-room loft where the kitchen walls had been tiled in slate, not mosaic, and there was an inexplicable bas-relief of a trout above the sink. Where we drew hearts in the fog that formed on the windows in winter and could walk down to the post office and the coffee shop and the Chinese buffet around the corner.

The mosaic tiles were each about the size of a postage stamp, mostly blues but streaked with gold and silver, like the art deco version of a Van Gogh painting of constellations. They hugged the wall of the kitchenette, breaking up at the edges like graphics just beginning to pixelate. Where the kitchen in our first apartment had occupied one whole end of the room, here it was just a corner, a sink and a microwave and a hot plate, with a window that provided a view of the alley and the rooftop of the building next door.

At the other end of the apartment, though, was a big bay window that looked out over Main Street and the tourist shops. How you would have loved that window, curled up there with a book and a purring cat, to watch the town fall asleep or wake up. That was where I set up my drawing table, and I reclined on the cushions in the window seats while I watched old black-and-white movies on my lunch breaks.

Between the kitchenette and the bay window was just a stretch of empty floor where I put the futon and the old TV on its rolling stand. Not much else was left. Next to the door I put a little shelf that I had salvaged from a dumpster, and on top of it an old cigar box with a picture of a devil on the lid. Every time I got a check, I cashed some of it into rolls of quarters and dropped them into the cigar box, pulling one or two out and sticking them in my pocket whenever I left the apartment.

I had visited Basin Springs once when I was a kid. Nothing more than a stopover on some trip my parents were dragging me along on, to visit relatives I didn't know in some place I didn't want to be. We had stayed only for part of one day, but I fell in love with the little town, nestled in its valley and bisected by two clear streams crossed by dozens of footbridges.

Basin Springs was full of strange stores that sold old bones and Native American trinkets, antique swords and armor, cheap plastic do-dads that were made in China but designed to look rustic. It was a town of meandering alleys and half-hidden shop fronts, of parks where ducks puddled around in the cool streams and trees hid sculptures in shaded grottos.

More than anything, though, my young affection had been won over by the old arcade. Not like the ones that we had in the malls back home, but an arcade in the original sense of the word, a roofed space open to the elements, with arched doorways leading into the shadowed interior.

The arcade was situated between two streets running north and south, and in the middle of the two streams running east and west. It made up the whole middle part of a building, like a hive that had been hollowed out and filled with amusements. The doorways all bore gates with wrought iron bars that could be closed over them, but in all the time I've spent here since getting the apartment, I've never seen them shut.

In order to reach the arcade, I have to walk only three blocks from the apartment and cross a footbridge over the stream. It's an easy walk, rain or shine, day or night. When I first visited it as a kid, the arcade had seemed infinite, insurmountable. The way that used bookstores always feel, like I could literally browse there forever and still find something new.

It was a working arcade, but it was also a museum. Older games were at one end, with the newest arcade cabinets—rhythm games and shooting games and race car games—at the other. Pinball machines lined one entire wall, their backs emblazoned with the pop culture icons of the moment in which they were manufactured, so that walking along in front of them was like walking through the history of Americana: Elvira and KISS, Indiana Jones and Freddy Krueger.

In the deepest, darkest recesses of the arcade, at the end furthest from the main street, were old penny arcade machines that still worked, and still only cost a penny. Not even games, as we think of them now, but simple automata and motorized dioramas. A sinister-looking clown who covered a ball with a cup only to have it appear again from his mouth, a re-creation of the hanging of Dr. Crippen, mechanical fortune tellers and an animatronic devil holding a hand of playing cards.

Somewhere in between, nearer the dark end of the arcade than the lighter, newer end, was a game that I had never heard of. Called *The Drunkard's Dream*, it seemed to have been inspired by one of the old coin-operated dioramas. Not one that was located in the Basin Springs arcade, but one that I had heard of, in the House on the Rock up in Wisconsin. At a glance, *The Drunkard's Dream* resembled *Ghosts 'n Goblins*, but when it came to the actual contents of the game, it was something else entirely.

I don't remember seeing it when I was here as a kid, but my memories of that trip are all golden-shaded blurs, like looking backward through one of those tubes that turns all the light into an exploding kaleidoscope of color. Since coming back, though, it is the one game in the arcade that I've played the most.

What first drew me to it was probably the artwork on the cabinet. In shape it was like any other arcade cabinet, with a joystick and a couple of big colored buttons that pushed in with a satisfying, smooth click. The sides of the cabinet were partially obscured by the games next to it—*Tapper* on one side, *Dragon's Lair* on the other—but they seemed to boast a garishly-colored painting of a dungeon tableaux, one that I would eventually come to partly recognize from the later levels of the game, with the titular drunkard center stage, leaping over rolling barrels while skeletons reached out from nooks in the walls and chains were frozen in mid-clank. In the upper-right-hand corner a woman in a red dress has her face turned away from the scene, her hair falling in a golden cascade down her back.

Each time I played the game it asked me to enter my name, and every time I did I always gave it the same one. Not my real name, but the one you always called me. It seemed right, and I thought that maybe, if I managed a high enough score, then it would be left behind somewhere, at least. A memento, even if no one else would ever understand.

The opening scene is a fancy dress ball at an old-fashioned English manor house. The only sound is a glitchy midi track playing a waltz. No text scrolls beneath the picture to explain what is going on, only the graphics—still highly pixelated, but slightly better than what the actual gameplay will present, like a cutscene in *Ninja Gaiden*, though the art style here is more storybook in quality, the animation only ever a frame or two that repeats, to lend the illusion of motion.

It opens with a bunch of people, frozen in tableaux, dancing in their glittering gowns, their coats-and-tails. In the foreground, our protagonist stands against the wall holding an empty glass, a whole bunch of others stacked on the table next to him. His gaze is directed out at the floor, his back to the player, so we can't see his face, only where he is looking. At a blond woman in a red dress, dancing with a tall, dashing man.

In the next scene our protagonist is outside in the hall, kicking at the rug, his head down, his face still hidden. He grabs the helmet off an empty suit of armor and plunks it down over his head, and that's how he will appear for the rest of the game: a short little man in a tuxedo and bowtie with a knight's helmet stuck on top. He only opens the visor to pour in more booze, and even then, what lies beyond is always hidden in shadow (so that we, the player, can better empathize with him, one can only assume).

He is standing outside, the knight's helmet turned to look over his shoulder at the lights of the manor house where they are cast on the lawn. Beyond the windows, we can still see the shadows of the dancers twirling and twirling in a never-ending waltz of just two frames, repeated again and again. Our protagonist turns from the house and gradually, one frame at a time, the tavern down the road edges into view. Then the game truly begins.

As we transition from the opening scene to the actual first level, the graphics drop in resolution considerably. What was already a storybook aesthetic becomes the simple, two-dimensional layout of a *Ghosts 'n Goblins*-alike, with commensurate gameplay style and difficulty. The status bar stretched across the top of the screen tells us the name of the level in a florid banner held aloft by pixelated cherubim, and has a picture of the drunkard's helmet with an X beside it and, beside that, the number of additional lives that we currently have stored up. The maximum appears to be three.

The status bar has no indicator of our drunkard's health, which seems to be determined not by his amount of armor, as in *Ghosts 'n Goblins*, but by his level of intoxication. At full health he slumps a bit, and animated stars swirl round his head. As he sobers up, he straightens and his tuxedo becomes less rumpled. If he ever sobers up completely, there is an ominous tone, followed by a sinking, three-note tune that sounds almost like mocking laughter. The screen seems to melt and run, the pixels all falling down into one another, and then the screen goes dark, replaced with an image of a broken bottle and the drunkard's discarded helmet along with the simple words, "You lose."

Thematically enough, our hero attacks by hurling empty bottles at his foes.

The only power-ups in the game come in the form of bottles of hooch, marked with one, two, or three Xs to indicate their potency. Grabbing one can refill your "health," but they also have a negative effect. As the drunkard gets more and more inebriated, the levels become stranger and more difficult. Backgrounds begin to swim and change, and the controls grow ever more sluggish and unresponsive. So there comes a point, when our drunkard is at maximum health, where dodging bottles becomes just as important as dodging enemies.

The first level is pretty straightforward. A tavern about two screens wide, split into three tiers. The drunkard can stand on the floor, jump up onto the surface of the bar, or up even higher onto a sort of shelf that runs around the top of the screen. The bartender seems to want him to leave, or maybe to tell him that he's had enough, and he paces back and forth behind the bar throughout the level, making noises that are probably supposed to be shouting but that sound like laughter as interpreted by the adults from old Charlie Brown cartoons.

The drunkard can't hurt the bartender, but the bartender is constantly hurling things at the drunkard. Sometimes power-up bottles, other times empty mugs and bar rags and things that might be pots and pans. Besides this detritus from the bartender, the main threats in the first level are little purple devils who fly in from off the sides of the screen carrying big spoons, possibly filled with liquor. The devils seem to be in opposition to the bartender, trying to convince our drunkard to drink ever more, and whenever one of them is destroyed it usually leaves behind a power-up bottle. Drink too many, and the walls of the tavern seem to run, the colors switching to garish purples and greens, the bartender taking on a more terrible aspect, his face pale and skeletal, his eyes glaring purple, a mouth in his stomach.

The level is easiest if our drunkard can get through it without grabbing too many bottles, but regardless of how much he drinks, the bartender ultimately takes on that same distorted form at the end of the level, when he leaps up onto the bar himself and becomes the first boss, pacing back and forth, kicking bottles and mugs at the drunkard and occasionally stopping to belch a cloud of green smoke from the mouth in his stomach. Chuck enough empty bottles at him and he tumbles from his perch and disappears behind the bar, leaving it unguarded and allowing our drunkard free rein to very literally crawl inside a bottle for level two.

Stage 2
Une Bouteille

I sold the house after you were gone, along with most of our stuff. I was still working full time as a freelance illustrator, and without your income I couldn't pay the mortgage. Which was just as well. Had I stayed, I would have paced the rooms like a ghost, and I know it, and you know it.

I had always intended to take you to Basin Springs, you remember me talking about it. For our first anniversary, for our fifth. But we never got around to it. Maybe that's why I came back.

When I moved to the little one-room apartment with the mosaic tile kitchenette, I had one big client, the only one that had stuck with me through the bad months. I drew pretty much all the covers for Otranto Books' reissues of old Gothic romances, those books whose original covers always had some woman in her nightdress running away from a big, dark house. On a good day, I could turn out two or three in an eight-hour period. It paid enough to cover my rent and for me to buy groceries once a week from the farmer's market and the grocery store out on the edge of town. If I had any cash left over, or if I caught another gig somewhere, I turned it into quarters for *The Drunkard's Dream* and other games, or bought food from the stands and food trucks that were set up all up and down the main drag.

If I opened the windows of the apartment, the smell of fair food was always carried on the air. Corn dogs and funnel cakes and pretzels and cotton candy. When the wind was right, I could even hear the noise of the arcade from my apartment. A susurrus of blips and bloops and the unmistakable ringing of pinball machines. In the evenings, the shadow of the mountain cast the tourist shops below in purple shadow.

In the center of the arcade was a booth where its only visible employee worked, an ancient matriarch named Janice who sat behind the partitioned glass in an old conductor's cap and changed dollar bills into quarters, or handed out cheap plastic novelty items in exchange for tickets won in the skee ball machines. Up near the newer end of the arcade there were soda machines and a little shop attached to the building that sold slices of pizza and deep-fried Twinkies out of a little window during the day.

For the first few weeks that I was in Basin Springs, I did other things besides play *The Drunkard's Dream*. I walked around town, tried going to the movies at the little two-screen Gem Theatre. I haunted the tourist shops, walked through the public library looking for books that I had drawn the covers for.

I even hiked part of the way up the side of the mountain, explored the grounds of the Castle Inn up there, an old stone house that was now a bed and breakfast that overlooked the rest of town. Its garden paths were lighted with pale yellow lamps designed to mimic gaslamps—all the way down to the flickering—and were full of quiet cul-de-sacs for lovers young or old to have their trysts. There was a time when I would have loved it, the romance and atmosphere of it. Now it served only to remind me of your absence, and I didn't stay long.

Within a month, I was going to the arcade every day. When I finished my work, I would grab a roll or two of quarters from the old cigar box and head down the stairs to the alley. From there I'd walk over onto River Street, past the park where two swans lived and to the footbridge that led to the arcade. Sometimes, I would finish work early in the afternoon and play until dinner, when I would go back to the apartment and eat SpaghettiOs or ramen that I cooked on the hot plate. Other times I wouldn't finish drawing until night had already fallen, and I would go to the arcade anyway and play 'til midnight or later, waking up when the dawn cut through the bay windows to go back to work.

I started with the penny arcades, the old moving dioramas. Some of them were stained with dust and age. Those I stayed away from, but I "played" a few of the ones that were in better repair, dropping in my penny and watching them act out their scenarios, like those old-fashioned clocks that you see in murder mystery movies from the '30s and '40s. I arm-wrestled a scary-looking mechanical clown, and tried out a love-tester machine that told me I was "naughty, but nice," which was just above "mild" but just below "wild." Maybe you would have agreed; certainly, "wild" was something I never could have been accused of, even at my wildest. At least I wasn't a "cold fish."

I paced the length and breadth of the arcade. I tried my hand at pinball, something I had never been very good at, and spent an entire afternoon and a whole roll of quarters playing *House of the Dead* until my trigger finger went numb. I sampled every title available in the multi-game Neo Geo cabinets. Most of my time was spent among the older machines, the *Jousts* and the *Galagas* and the *Pac-Mans*.

I kept coming back to *The Drunkard's Dream*. The games around it were never very popular with kids or out-of-town tourists, so there was never really anyone around to interrupt me. I played for hours, usually until I ran out of quarters.

The second level opens with our drunkard quite literally falling down inside the neck of a giant bottle. For the first part of the level he is in free fall, with the only real gameplay amounting to moving the joystick from side to side to dodge bubbles that rise up from below. Some of the bubbles contain power-up bottles, which our drunkard can get by attacking, while others have strange little round homunculi riding on top who poke at him with what look like giant dinner forks. (The demons who haunt our drunkard seem to have a penchant for cutlery.)

At the bottom, the drunkard drops onto what looks like a big cork floating in a sea of black liquid. The cork fortunately stays underneath him for the rest of the level regardless of what he does, and moves back and forth when I move the joystick, even when the drunkard is also jumping. Once he's on the cork, the level of the black liquid begins to slowly fall, revealing ledges in the sides of the bottle that sometimes hold power-ups and other times harbor skulls that spit blue fire.

Serpents rise up from out of the liquid, coming in two varieties. The purple ones have fins on their backs and one orange eye, and they pop up just long enough to breathe a chain of fire at the drunkard. The green ones are segmented and jump up and out of the liquid in an arc before splashing down again. Meanwhile, more of the same purple demons from the first level gradually descend from above, making the screen a madhouse of pattern-based danger.

Eventually, the liquid drains down to the bottom of the bottle, where creepy maggot-like worms with pincer mouths wriggle around. Once they're all dead, the boss shows up. I call the boss the Green Fairy—I'm guessing that this is a bottle of absinthe we've been in all this time, which really makes a kind of sense—though it looks more like a locust, with a fan of lacy wings that appear from its back each time it moves or attacks. It carries a staff or wand from which it shoots bubbles that can trap our drunkard, making him easy prey for it to crash into him, or for more of the maggoty worms that it occasionally shakes loose from the top of the screen.

When the Green Fairy is finally destroyed, the screen begins to blink and rumble as the bottle breaks apart and finally shatters, plunging our drunkard into an inky black void through which he falls until he finally tumbles into the third stage, a rainy cemetery.

Stage 3
Le Cimetiere

Movies had taught me that funerals were slow pans across black umbrellas in the rain. I wasn't prepared for yours to be on a sunny April day, without a black umbrella to be found. Tempting as it is to say that I can't remember much about that day, it isn't true, not really. I can remember so many things, in such vivid detail, but they're all out of order, all jumbled up. None of them are connected to anything else. They just float there behind my eyes, like snapshots scattered on a black pool.

It's like that whole day and all the months that followed are a bunch of Polaroids that I had spread out on a table, and my mind couldn't bear to look at them all at once—so it just scooped them up and dumped them into a box, with no regard for order or clarity. When I try to remember back, I just pick one from the box at random—one image, one moment, one fragment of speech—and hold it up for a while before dropping it back in.

The sheen of your casket—the one that your mother had insisted on, though you had wanted to be cremated; the one that I paid for half the price of, while she paid for the other.

The white butterfly that landed on your headstone midway through the service.

The sound of the crank turning as they lowered you into the ground, after most everyone had already left.

The way that even the light in the house seemed different afterward, as though you were a crystal through which it had refracted, and with you gone, it now fell lifelessly on everything it touched.

Hands touching my shoulders, arms wrapping around me. Tears

on the faces of people who, it seemed to me, had no particular reason to cry, while my cheeks remained dry until everyone had gone and I cried in the dark until I felt sick, until eventually I slept.

Days of drifting in and out, forgetting to eat, forgetting to do anything else. At first my clients were understanding, but that lasted a few days, a few weeks, a few months. Only Otranto Books stuck with me the whole way through, being patient when I blew deadlines, handing me more work when I eventually came back up for air and realized how dire my situation had become.

I think your family was scandalized when I sold everything and moved. I know that mine was. They had wanted some of what you had, what *we* had, but I couldn't bear to parcel it out, to decide what went where, and to whom. I couldn't even bear to sell it myself; I hired a local woman who ran estate sales. Before the sale began, I walked through all the stuff, let my fingertips rest on the scarred surface of the old kitchen table, the first piece of furniture we bought together after we were married.

Everything that I kept could fit into two small boxes. I put them in the storage space of the new apartment in Basin Springs, a crawlspace in the wall next to the kitchenette. I take them out sometimes, when it is late at night and I can't sleep. Letters you wrote to me. A rock that you found on a walk once, with a perfect hole through it, that I had carried in my coat pocket during all the years that I still went into work as a graphic designer at a big office downtown. Your copy of *Demian*, your favorite book in college, where you had underlined all your favorite passages. *"The bird fights its way out of the egg. The egg is the world."*

I still wear my wedding ring. I probably always will.

Sometimes, when I'm in the arcade, I can feel it tap against the joystick in my left hand. A different feeling than the stick against my finger, the quietest little click. Sometimes it makes me feel better, sometimes it makes me feel worse. That's life, I guess. Like the power-up bottles in the game. Each new thing you grab always has a chance of making everything harder.

***

As the third level opens, the drunkard drops out of the black void and onto the loamy earth of a pixelated cemetery. Rain is falling in the background, and an occasional flash of lightning splits the sky, showing swollen clouds and distant, skeletal trees. Tombstones line the level, and other markers like leaning crosses and a skeletal statue are occasionally illuminated by the errant flashes of lightning.

Groping hands reach up from the dirt as he passes, and every now and then a coffin will burst out of the soil, the lid opening on its hinges to discharge a shambling corpse, more bone than flesh. Some have only one arm, which juts out ahead of them as they shuffle forward like Karloff in an old *Frankenstein* movie. Other times the coffins contain weird skeletal bat-like creatures—gargoyles, perhaps, or demons—that spread their bony wings and then fly up, spitting fireballs. Regular bats fly down from the stormy sky, dropping bombs and power-up bottles before flying off again.

At about the midway point there is a dead tree with a hangman's noose dangling from one limb. When the lightning flashes, a body is visible hanging from the noose. As the drunkard approaches, a bolt of lightning strikes the tree, splitting it down the middle. In its wake, the corpse that was previously hanging there remains visible, on the ground now and pacing back and forth with the branch dragging behind him, noose still tied round his neck. It takes several hits from empty bottles to destroy him, so call him a mid-boss, I suppose.

From there it's more tombstones, more groping hands, more bursting coffins. Strange cemetery weeds add themselves to the mix, sprouting vivid flowers that spit thorns at the drunkard, and near the end of the level the headstones themselves begin to attack, floating up from the ground and hovering in the air before smashing down at him and shattering on the earth when they miss.

Finally, the drunkard reaches a grave set apart from the others, past a gap in the iron fence that marks the border of the cemetery. A grave for a sinner, a witch, or a suicide, dug away from consecrated ground. The grave is fresh, open, and from its depths rises the boss of the level, which is, of course, Death.

He looks like a pretty classic Grim Reaper, skeletal and hooded, but He terminates at the ribcage, with only a few vertebrae and the tattered edges of His cloak hanging down any farther. Death flies around the screen, hurling His enormous scythe like a boomerang, and smaller versions of Himself appear from within the shadows of His cloak to spread out and attack on their own.

Perhaps fittingly enough, Death is maybe the most difficult boss in the entire game, and I get to that spot only to perish and run out of quarters time and time again. It isn't until I've done it easily a dozen times that I come back with *three* rolls of quarters and set myself the task of finally getting past Death. (Where else but in a video game could such an endeavor be accomplished at all?)

Once the drunkard has finally hurled enough empty bottles, Death's scythe disappears and He raises His bony arms up toward the moon—which is just appearing from behind the bank of clouds—and then slowly dissolves from the top down, the individual pixels that make him up breaking apart and sliding down the screen only to blink and then vanish. Were that it was so simple in real life.

Stage 4
Catacombes

After Death is destroyed, there's a brief cinematic as the drunkard looks at the tombstone and sees the name that I entered when I started the game. The name that you always called me. It's an unwittingly chilling moment, maybe for just that reason, but it doesn't last long. In the open grave there are stairs leading down, because of course there are, and so the drunkard has to take them, because of course he does.

At the bottom, the drunkard finds himself in some sort of underground crypt or dungeon—the very one depicted on the side of the arcade cabinet itself. The walls are lined with skulls and bones, and here and there mummies have been jammed into narrow fissures. When the drunkard approaches, they tear themselves free and shuffle toward him, their arms bound to their sides, their feet pigeon-toed. Some of the skulls in the walls light up and spit balls of fire, while others tumble from their perches and roll along the ground.

Here and there throughout the level are huge blue ogres or maybe golems who roll barrels at the drunkard. The barrels seem an odd touch in the otherwise crypt-themed level, but they also show up in piles that our protagonist has to jump over.

I wonder if they are meant to be casks of wine or spirits. I've spent some time contemplating the themes of this game, by now. The drunkard's travel from jilted lover to, well, drunkard, to the depths of the bottle, to the grave, to this purgatorial tomb. Mayhap the barrels aren't so thematically off after all. They make me think of Poe and Amontillado and that's a very short run from the crypt, indeed.

This level is tough. Every so often the whole place rumbles, and skulls and bones fall from the ceiling. There are these creatures that show up from time to time—wheels of fire with lion-like faces in the center, and five horse-legs that radiate out. I don't know what the hell they're supposed to be, what they mean. And I've got to keep the drunkard's health relatively low, because when he starts to get too inebriated, the level becomes damned near impossible. The ground shifts and breaks apart, jutting out at odd angles. The walls come to life more and more, the skulls lighting up to spit their little round orange pellets of fire, skeletal arms reaching out to grab at the drunkard as he passes by.

In the end, the drunkard reaches what I guess you would call a crypt. If the rest of the level has been an ossuary, this looks more like what I consider a tomb. In the center is a sarcophagus with a carven lid, the kind where they used to inter knights that came back from the Crusades, or didn't. I expect the lid to slide open, the boss to come out of there, maybe a ghostly knight in a suit of black armor, carrying his head in his hands. Instead the screen shakes again, and there's a crack that splits the sarcophagus.

Torches burst to life on the back wall of the room, illuminating two columns, and behind them the statue of a giant skull. Then the skull's eyes begin to glow, not as bright as the torches, but more fitfully, humming in and out of existence. The skull rolls forward into the room, and I realize that this is the boss the drunkard will be facing.

Initially, the skull just rolls back and forth across the floor of the crypt, which is bad enough. It's huge, taller than the drunkard can jump over, so he has to leap up onto one of the broken pieces of the sarcophagus to make it over the rolling skull. I also quickly learn that its eyes are its only weak point, and only then when they're glowing, which is sporadic, with no pattern that I can discern.

After rolling back and forth a few times, the skull suddenly takes another tack. What look to be legs sprout from its mouth—its bottom jaw is missing—and carry it up the wall and across the ceiling, where it then drops back to the crypt floor with a crash that shakes the screen and immobilizes the drunkard temporarily if he is unlucky enough to be standing on the ground at the time.

On closer examination, the things that looked like legs are actually mummified arms.

Throughout all of this, the skull occasionally discharges smaller skulls that roll around the room until the drunkard destroys them. It's pandemonium, and I don't know how many quarters I pump into the game before the skull finally gives up the ghost—quite literally, this time, the stone skull cracking open and a snake-like wisp of smoke with two pinprick eyes escaping up into the air and then dissipating in the shadows of the crypt.

After that, the torches go out and the screen plunges once more into darkness until, one by one, fires begin to sprout up around the drunkard, urging him on through a passage that has now appeared in the wall of the crypt.

I had never been a drinker myself, but I became one after you were gone. I became anything and everything that I needed to be in order to insulate myself, to keep myself numb. Like Arthur in *Ghosts 'n Goblins*, I put on suit after suit of armor to keep that pain at bay, because I knew that if it reached me it would skewer me, pierce right through me, burn me down, and there would be nothing left. And that wasn't even the part that scared me. It was the time it would take. How long could I endure that agony before it destroyed me? Maybe it was better if I just destroyed myself first.

I abused the drugs that the doctor gave me, mixed them with booze, which was a big no-no. For the first time in my life, I slept deep, black, dreamless sleep. Like sackcloth. And I wondered, "Is this what death is like?"

And if it was, I longed for it.

How many nights did I sit on the edge of our bed, rolling that bottle back and forth in my hand, wondering if there were enough pills to do the job, if I downed them all with every drop of liquor that I had left.

What kept me from it? I think it was fear. Fear that what waited for me on the other side of that big GAME OVER screen wasn't sackcloth oblivion, but rather all that pain I had been pushing away, with no barriers left between me and it. Truly, that would have been hell.

And living wasn't far removed. What I could never explain to anyone was what I lost when you were gone. Not just you, not just your laugh and your touch and your advice and your companionship. Not just the way that I could always count on you, when I couldn't count on myself. I lost a part of myself. I know that everyone always says that, but maybe that's because it's always true.

We had been together so long that I no longer knew what parts of me were really me, and what parts were you. In your absence, I had to begin to sort those out, and I couldn't do that in the old house. It had become a dungeon, one in which I imprisoned myself, and to which only I had the key.

Did anyone understand that? Does it matter if they did? I had to sell it, though, at the same time, I regret it every day. But it was killing me, and some part of me welcomed that. The slow rituals that I went through every day, doing, each time, what I would have done had you been there. Did I expect that you would suddenly appear? No, not even once. The cold knife of grief, even held back by drugs and drink, was still lodged too deeply to allow me even that false hope. No, I just did them because they were what I had always done, and what else could I do?

I became a ghost, clanking about the house in chains that I had forged, not in life, but instantaneously in the white-hot moment of your death. Every day they weighed on me more and more heavily, and every day I knew that I must succumb to them eventually, or make a change. That sooner or later the pain I was feeling would become greater than my fear of the pain that might wait for me on the other side, and I would go to that bottle of pills, or something else.

When I remembered to drive to the store, every tree along the side of the road was a siren, calling to me. Saying that if I just steered a little to the right, then there would be a loud crash and silence and darkness and I would no longer have to feel anything at all. Not even this muted pain, bracketed by pills and booze.

That's why I left, why I kept so little of the life we had built. You have to believe me. I had wanted to stay, to rebuild something in the ruin that you left behind. But that place was contaminated now with the knowledge of what I could never have again, and every surface was radioactive, not with memories, but with the memories that would never be made.

Did I run away to Basin Springs? Maybe, but I prefer to think that I did something else. That I brought your memory with me here, since I never got around to bringing you while you were alive. I had an unhappy childhood, filled, you always told me, with more worry and pain than was my lot. This was a place where I had been happy, for just an afternoon. Happy the way that I always was when you came home to me, when I kissed the back of your neck while you were making spaghetti, when you fell asleep against my chest and I could feel your heartbeat, your breath. I wanted to bring what was left of you here, to share it with you, and to share you with it. And I had to do it while there was something left of me.

At least, that's what I like to think.

Stage 5
L'enfer

You killed yourself. There, I said it.

You had struggled with it before, when you were younger. Pallid scars on your thighs from cutting, on your wrists from a previous attempt, when you had held ice cubes to the spot to numb the pain. By the time I met you there was medication, and you were better.

You still thought about it sometimes, talked about it, but we were getting by. And then insurance changed, and one medication was suddenly no longer covered, so you were on a different one and it was supposed to work the same way, and yet one day I came home to poppy-bright drops of blood on the kitchen floor.

Not that there weren't warning signs. We knew you were getting worse; I even took you to the emergency room one night. Ten hours of you huddled under a blanket on a bench in the corner of a sterile white room, me sitting on the floor beside you, holding your hand.

They took away the bags that we had brought in with us, locked them in a cabinet there in the room, wouldn't let us have anything out of them. For hours we sat there alone. From time to time a nurse came in, asked questions, took vitals, drew blood. Eventually a social worker arrived, asked some more questions, gave you some platitudes. Then they just let you go.

It isn't that they didn't care. Help was on its way. We had the number of people to call, we had discontinued the bad medicine, were trying to refill a script of the stuff that had worked before. But these things take time, and sometimes time runs out. Sometimes you're just running along through a level, running and running and running, and then suddenly the little clock in the upper right-hand corner hits zero and then everything freezes and drops out from under you and you're just gone.

Your therapist said that it wasn't anything I had done, that it wasn't anything you had wanted. You didn't want to die because you were miserable, unhappy, hurting. It was just the medications, an unfortunate interaction that exacerbated a condition that had always been there. An imp in your brain, just waiting for the opportunity to whisper in your ear when your defenses were down. A stark reminder that our minds are controlled, not by us, but by chemicals that we desperately try to balance, like ancient alchemists attempting to strain base metals into gold.

That should have helped. I talked to the therapist myself—the same one that you had gone to, thinking maybe she could help me to understand—but all that I learned was the brute indifference of the universe. There was no grand story here, no drama. Nothing to overcome, nothing to slay. Just banality that could still reach up and snuff you out, no matter how precious you were to me, nor I to you.

I blamed myself because it was easier than accepting the truth, that there was no one *to* blame. But more than that, I just missed you. I couldn't imagine a world without you, and I didn't want to live to see one. I said before that I didn't kill myself because I was afraid that there was only more pain waiting for me on the other side of death, but that's only part of the truth, if any of it. Let me be honest now, with myself at least, and with you, whatever part of you is still here, whatever part I'm talking to. What stayed my hand, more than anything, was the thought that taking my own life because I couldn't live without you would cheapen the tragedy of your death, somehow.

So instead I drowned myself in drugs and booze and repetition, until the day I realized that I was still killing myself, just a lot more slowly. That's when I came here, to Basin Springs, where I tried to lose myself, for a few hours a day, in the games in the arcade, in food that was bad for me, in this place that I found myself still able to love, even after all my love seemed to have abandoned me.

Like the drunkard in the game, I saw you waltzing away, in the embrace of oblivion, and I turned to drown my sorrows. In drink and pills and solitude, then in games and simplicity. In a strangely soothing new routine, one that required little of me.

"Was there anything I could have done?" I asked the therapist at my second-to-last visit, and she shook her head.

"There never is," she said. "Not really. We do our best, but sometimes, in spite of all of our efforts, love and will are not enough."

Friends and family encouraged me to pursue some legal recourse. After all, the change in your prescription had been what drove the blade, surely I could sue someone for malpractice. But I knew then that it wouldn't bring you back, that I couldn't stand there in front of a lawyer, in front of a judge, and see you picked apart, see you taken to trial.

"She had tried it before," they would point out, and I couldn't disagree. I could never make them understand how special you were, and no settlement, no money, nothing but you could ever be a replacement. So I walked away, and I hid in my own version of the bottle, the grave, the flames.

The beginning of the final level is obviously modeled on the French Cabaret of the Inferno, with its angry demonic visage framing the door as our drunkard enters through the mouth, which then promptly closes behind him, sharp teeth coming together with a crunch that shakes the floor. Inside it is initially dark, and then flames spring up to illuminate the goings-on within.

How to describe them? They are a Bosch painting come to life, an animated version of the stereoscopic clay sculptures of hell that were popular in France in the 1860s. The floors and pillars that hold up the level are wreathed in flame, and in the background, emaciated devils torment sinners with hot pokers, with bellows which they jam into their mouths or anuses and pump furiously, with other implements of torture that I cannot begin to understand or explain.

The enemies in this level are sometimes these devils themselves—striding forth on legs that are far too long, their beaked faces peering down as they jab at the drunkard with pitchforks; bouncing forth on round bodies with no discernable legs at all, the faces in their stomachs burping out balls of blue flame that hover in the air and don't dissipate, turning every inch of the level into an infernal obstacle course—and sometimes their animated devices of torture. An iron maiden bursting up from the floor, spilling open to reveal a bloody skeleton which stumbles several paces forward before collapsing into a pile of red bones. As the drunkard approaches a body being broken on the wheel, suddenly the wheel itself separates from the rest of its apparatus and comes bouncing toward him through the flames.

Everywhere in this level there are perils, and power-up bottles are few and far between. Not much comfort in Hell, I suppose, not even for the very wicked. Giant devils stomp back and forth in great iron boots and swing gigantic hammers. Helmets cover their heads, which must be knocked off before they can be destroyed, and once they *are*, the demons' movements become much faster.

Enormous worms tipped with gigantic pincers—larger versions of the maggots from the second level, perhaps—burst up from the flaming ground. When they're destroyed they disgorge a mass of zombie-like sinners who stumble forward, half-melted. At other times, balls of sinners bound together come rolling through the halls of Hell. When they're struck, sinners go flying off and the ball decreases gradually in size until it is gone completely, and only a skull remains, coming to rest on the ground and standing still.

At the end of the level, the drunkard enters a room and the doorway behind him is shut by a curtain of fire. At first, the background of the room is darkness, but then a throne is illuminated. On it sits a skeleton, a crown perched crookedly on its head. It has partly collapsed into dust, and I wonder, for a moment, if this is the monarch of Hell.

But no, the room is illuminated further, and I see the power behind the throne, the devil that the drunkard has come here to vanquish. It is huge, literally filling the room, so that there is virtually no space left to maneuver, and even then it is hunched, bent almost in half, so that its overlarge head both brushes the ceiling and nearly rests on the floor. It looks like a skeleton, the skin desiccated and stretched taut across the bones, but also like a puppet, somehow carved, its joints not quite right. On its head is a crown, perched against malformed horns, and in its hand it holds a long, crooked sword, the blade stained red with blood.

This is the final boss, and it moves back forth in the room something like an ape. At times it brings down that enormous sword in a blow that, as near as I can tell, is impossible to avoid. At other times it simply works its jaws soundlessly, as though chewing something invisible—a traitor, perhaps, for that would fit with Dante's account—and reaches out its long arm, its empty fist, to strike at the drunkard or at the air, if he has managed to vacate the premises.

I only defeat this final boss once, and even now I can't quite say how. By the skin of my teeth, I know that. With nothing left in the tank, all of my "health" depleted, no more quarters in my pocket or stacked on the machine, and only one more blow left between me and GAME OVER. And yet, I strike that final blow, and the huge skeleton devil puppet begins to shake, and the whole room begins to shake, until it shakes itself apart.

A strange wind comes up, and the dust and bones on the throne are blown away, one pixel at a time. The drunkard approaches the throne, and lifts the only item that remains, the crown, up onto his head, placing it atop that ridiculous knight's helmet. The screen fades to black, and a message appears:

Is it better to rule in Hell than to serve in Heaven?

Bonus Stage
Les Amoureux

That is not quite the end of the game. The credits roll, but I feel, somehow, like I need to watch all of them, and at the end, I am rewarded with a final cinematic. Or, no, not a cinematic, because it doesn't move. Just a single image, of the same gravestone from the end of level three, with that name carved into it, the one you always called me.

The grave is no longer open, no stairs descend into the underground. Now there is a mound of earth, and a battered knight's helmet, and someone has left a single white flower. I wonder if it was the blond-haired girl who was dancing with the dashing gent, or if, perhaps, the drunkard had someone else in his life who cared more for him, someone he didn't think of as he descended into oblivion.

It is pouring rain outside when I beat the game, and I stand in the archway of the arcade, considering the walk back to the apartment. The rain is hammering on the concrete roof of the arcade, and I think about staying, but I'm out of quarters, and have no cash that I could change for them, even if Janice were still in the booth, which she isn't. According to my watch it's after midnight. The place is pretty much deserted, except for a few young townies who are messing around with the skee ball machines. The food vendors up and down the street are all closed and dark. Everything is closed. There's nothing for me to do but walk home in the rain.

Home, is that where I'm headed? The tiny apartment that reminds me of ours, where I keep the handful of things that I still have to remind me of you? Is that home now?

Difficult as it is to believe, I haven't had a drop to drink since I came to Basin Springs. In our house I was well on my way to drinking myself into the grave, just like in the game, but here, something else replaced that addiction. Still, tonight I think about it. There's an all-night liquor store near the highway. It's a long walk in the rain, but I can see the gleam of the neon, and I've made longer.

By the time I come up the steps to the apartment, I'm soaked through, and still haven't completely talked myself out of turning around and heading for that neon sign. I drip water onto the hall carpet as I fish for the keys in my pocket, and then push open the door.

Inside, you're waiting for me, as I somehow knew you would be. Moth-pale and dressed all in white, you are radiant, and I think, as you must have wanted me to think, of our wedding day. You're smiling now, as you were smiling then, and I remember watching you walk up the aisle. How you glowed.

You were so happy in that moment, the happiest that I had ever seen you, and the best feeling that I ever had in my life was knowing that I had helped to make you that happy. Your smile was so wide, and I could tell that you were trying to tame it, to break it down so that you would look dignified for the wedding photos. I could see you fighting the desire to cover your face with your bouquet. I could never explain to you—then or later—that it was not the whiteness of your dress or the light streaming in through the stained glass windows that made you shine so brightly that day. It was that smile; the happiness so great that you couldn't hold it in.

Your smile tonight is the same, but different. Your hair is uncut, your bangs have fallen over your eyes, hiding your face in shadows save for that smile, and it is growing *too* big, stretching too far, creeping past the edges of your face. Your dress is white, white as a scar, white as the edges of your wounds when I found you that day, and you are dripping wet, as though you, too, have just stumbled in from out of the rain.

My first instinct is to run to you, no matter what. Angel, ghost, devil, death. Whatever you are, it's you, and that's all I care about, all I want. But I don't run. I walk, slowly. Your hands are cupped together, and you extend them out toward me, holding something in your palms.

They are full of water, and beneath the water are two eyes, closed now. The eyes that should be in your face, but up close I see that they aren't. Maybe the water isn't water at all but tears, leaking out from around their edges.

Floating atop the water is something I recognize. It's a straight razor, one that you got me for our second anniversary. As a joke, more than anything, because I always cut myself shaving even with regular razors, and I'd always said that with a straight razor I would inevitably slit my throat. It had a handle made of horn, matching a comb that you had inherited from your grandmother. You bought it for me from an antique shop. I sold it in the auction, along with everything else, and yet here it is.

Gingerly, I pick it up. The water in your palms is cold, and when the straight razor is gone, the eyes there open, and they are bright yellow, like molten gold. You hold your hands up to the side of your face, your smile growing ever wider.

Slowly, I open the straight razor.

I know what you want me to do. I remember the puckered skin around your wounds, how strangely bloodless it looked, given how much blood there was everywhere else. The doctor said that it was quick, that you'd taken pills to numb the pain, that it hadn't lasted long. This won't last long either, I know. I'm cold already, so very cold, but you're even colder. It comes off you like the air from inside a freezer.

You reach out a hand to take my wrist, to guide me, to show me where to cut, and how, but I step back, outside of your reach. You make a sound, a gasp that's also a screech. You know that something is wrong. I raise up the straight razor so it's between us, held up like a talisman, and then I snap the handle from the blade, and let both clatter to the floor.

The reaction is immediate. You expand, your dress suddenly flying up on either side of you as if in a gale, and then it's a dress no longer but long, diaphanous wings. And your smile is no longer a smile, it's a maw, filled with shining teeth. And what's more, I know that it isn't you, that it never was. And it makes a sound like weeping as it collapses in upon itself, all the fabric of the dress disappearing into a black hole the size of a half-dollar in the middle of the room, and then into nothing.

In its absence, the room seems warm and close and strangely silent. I can hear the water drip off my clothes and onto the carpet. I pick up the two pieces of the straight razor, which are still there on the floor, and carry them over and drop them into the trash.

I'm sorry that I ever thought it was you, there for me in my apartment tonight. Maybe it was the same thing that drove the razor along your skin, come looking now for another victim. But I know that is something that you would never have asked of me.

I once feared what was waiting for me on the other side of death, but not anymore. I can't say what it will be any more now than I could then. I hope that it will be you, but I have my doubts. I think maybe that death is a vast ocean that drags us down and drowns us, and that whatever emerges on the other shore probably won't even know who I ever was, and that's fine. Maybe that's for the best.

There was a time when my fear was the only thing that kept me from welcoming death, but that's gone now, too. On the off chance that you *are* waiting for me there, beyond the veil, I know that you will still be there if I'm a little late in following. In the meantime, there are rolls of quarters in the old cigar box by the door, and plenty of games still left to play.

Author's Notes:

When Jonathan Raab—one of my very favorite contemporary writers—asked me to contribute a story to *Terror in 16-Bits*, his anthology of video game horror, he also asked me to write an author's note to go with my tale. This is what I wrote there:

Like the narrator of this story, I am married to someone who has struggled with suicidal ideation for most of her life. Many of the details of the narrator's history are drawn from the events of my own marriage, including the catastrophic near-misses that can come when something goes wrong with medication.

In the wake of one of those near-misses, I felt like I needed to write something that not only confronted what it means to live in that shadow, but that attempted to imagine a way forward if that unthinkable eventuality ever came to pass. Leave it to me to turn a story for a video game anthology into one of the most personal and difficult things I've ever tried to write.

Basin Springs is based on the real-life town of Manitou Springs, Colorado. Like my narrator, I visited it once as a kid, and it left a big mark, though I've never actually gone back. It was fun to return for a while, even if only in my imagination.

The titular video game is inspired by *Ghosts 'n Goblins* and its assorted permutations, but even more by the various *Ghosts 'n Goblins* imitators that have cropped up over the years. Specifically, I was inspired by a game that I've never played and that may not even exist. I saw a few sprites for it years ago on some website or another, and my memory tells me that it involved a hunchbacked cemetery caretaker battling monsters, but I can't remember a title and have never been able to find it again. Chances are it was some kind of homebrew thing, or I just made it up whole cloth.

The "Drunkard's Dream" penny arcade diorama is a real thing, and you can find video of it online, but I wrote the story based on my memory of a description of it in, I think, Neil Gaiman's

American Gods. Sometimes inaccurate memories make for better inspiration than immediate reference. The knight-helmeted drunkard owes a more than minor debt to the swashbuckling protagonist of Gary Gianni's delightful *MonsterMen* comics. Jumble all that together for a few thousand words and, as Mike Mignola says, there you go.

THE ROBOT APEMAN WAITS FOR THE NIGHTMARE BLOOD TO STOP

So, I just talk into this thing? I guess we're making this documentary for fans of the park, right, so I don't have to get too much into what OmniPark was all about—who Dalton Teague was, any of that? What's that? Oh, right, introduce myself. That makes sense …

My name is Paul Kirby—no relation to Jack—and I was, am, a concept artist. I've worked on a few big movies and a lot of small ones, especially back during the '80s, when I did concepts for stuff like *Seeds of Change* and *Out of Space*. Lately, I've mostly done work for cartoon shows on Netflix that are currently under NDAs.

One of my very first gigs, though, was working at OmniPark. I wasn't a Technosopher. Nothing so exalted as that. Cary Egger, one of the original Technosophers that Teague hired to design the park, hired me to do artwork for his concept. Its working title was just "Primal."

That's … will the viewer know what a Technosopher is already? Should I get into that?

***

Technosopher was a word that, as far as I know, Dalton Teague made up. To him, it was kind of like an engineer and kind of like a philosopher and kind of like a wizard. They were the people responsible for designing the rides and attractions at OmniPark, but they were more than just contractors. They were … what's the word … practically revered. Teague believed, or claimed to believe, that they were doing something truly special. *Meaningful.*

It was a nice environment to work in, but it was also high pressure, especially for a kid who had dropped out of design school. This couldn't have been later than, what, '74, '75? To say that I was still a damn sight wet behind the ears is an understatement and a half. I was probably twenty-one, twenty-two years old, if that. I was a baby.

And I was working for Cary fucking Egger—can I say fucking on here? You can edit it out later? Okay.

Egger was the Technosopher for my project. He had been a rocket engineer before he came to work for Teague. He claimed to have worked on the Apollo program, though I never saw any proof one way or another, but when he was in his cups or high as a kite—which was often—he would sometimes make these … claims about how "we didn't know the half of it," whatever that's supposed to mean.

Working for an actual rocket scientist would probably have been intimidating enough, but that wasn't the weirdest—or hardest—part. Egger was a Thelemite. He had known Jack Parsons before he was killed in an explosion—"assassinated," Egger said, "by the corporate jaybirds." I don't know what he meant by "jaybirds." He often used these weird words that sounded made up.

What? Oh, Thelema … I don't actually know a lot about it. It's some, like, cult religion that Aleister Crowley came up with, I guess. A bunch of people were into it, back then, but it was before my time. It was, like, counter-culture back in the '50s, I guess.

Before Manson and all that.

Parsons was a rocket scientist, too. Early days stuff. He and his wife were big into Thelema, and Egger was apparently one of their protégés. Egger even had this kid with him who was around my age. Long, stringy hair and the palest skin I had ever seen. It seemed almost translucent. Egger called the kid Theophrastus—the rest of us called her Theo.

Her, yeah. Egger claimed that she was a hermaphrodite, and I guess she was one of Cameron's "moon children."

Shit, I'm getting way out on a limb here, huh? So … Cameron was Parsons' wife. Marjorie Cameron Parsons, something like that. Later on, she was in some Curtis Harrington films. *Night Tide*, maybe some others. She was an occultist and an artist and who knows what else. Parsons called her "the elemental woman" and thought he had summoned her with a ritual he did with L. Ron Hubbard—I shit you not.

Anyway, after Parsons died or was assassinated or *whatever* you believe, Cameron—that's the name she went by—moved out to some ranch in SoCal and started this group that did sex magic to try to create a new race of "moon children" who would be devoted to the god Horus or something. Theo was, I guess, one of the kids that came out of all that.

Where was I? Oh, right, working for Egger. So, Teague hired Egger, who brought along Theo, and Egger hired me and a whole team of other people to work on "Primal," which almost certainly would have gotten renamed if it had ever gone public, which, I suppose this is the part where I say that it didn't, though you already know that if you know that park, because it's not in any of the literature, and it certainly wasn't ever on the park map.

We were working in parallel with the folks who made the "Time Tunnel" ride that eventually went in. Like them, we were supposed to tackle the notion of time in ride form. I gathered that Egger was hired because of his Thelemic background, as much as his engineering prowess.

"I want every avenue explored," Teague was saying to one of his assistants the one time I met him, when he came down to see how we were doing. There was some bean counter with him who was apparently trying to convince him not to develop multiple attractions at once.

"It's my money," Teague had said, "I'll spend it how I see fit." That was before he said that he wanted every avenue to be explored. Teague seemed like a nice guy. Like somebody's grandfather. He shook my hand, even though I was just one of the grunts crouched over a drawing table.

Egger, by comparison, was a force of nature. Egger didn't enter a room—he *blew* into it, *sailed* into it. He never passed anything without completely rearranging it. If you were three-quarters of the way through a sketch, you'd suddenly be back at the start. But, at the same time, he never breezed in without making whatever he touched better, either. It was frustrating, but inspiring, and when you're that young and that hungry, inspiration is more important than respect.

Back then, I probably would have followed Egger off a cliff. The only thing I didn't like about him was how he treated Theo.

Describe him? I mean, there are photos of him floating around, but they don't do him justice. He had ginger hair and this impossibly curly, flyaway beard that always reminded me of pubic hair, if I have to be honest. He wore silk bathrobes over whatever street clothes he was wearing. Just, like, the picture of eccentricity, you know? And I never knew how much of it was a put-on and how much was really him.

Do I think he was a genius? I mean, yeah. What do we mean by genius? Someone who thinks differently than everyone else, right? And he was on another level. I got to ride the "Time Tunnel" ride when they launched it, and I got to see the kind of "big bang, big crunch" thing that was sort of its raison d'etre. It was pretty amazing, especially for back then. Nobody normal designed those things, right? They were all made by geniuses.

But just because someone is a genius doesn't mean they're stable. Far from it. Often the opposite. Like, Einstein was a genius, but they tell me that he couldn't tie his own shoes. I never looked that up to see if it's true, but it's the right idea, y'know?

Egger was a genius, but he was also crazy. Maybe that's why his ride never got off the ground.

Oh, don't get me wrong. We *built* "Primal." Shit, my friend Ronnie, who worked on it—he died in the Boston Marathon bombing a few years ago, he was in the crowd—hand-painted the sign above the entrance. Big, red claw-slash letters. Not fit for kids. This ride was *never* going to be fit for kids.

I keep calling it a ride, but Egger never did. Teague called them "attractions," but Egger called it a "thaumatrope." I looked it up later. It was the name of a toy from more than a hundred years ago. You've probably seen them. A disk on a string with a picture on either side. Spin the disk, and the two pictures seem to merge. It's the same principle as the movies, just on a much smaller scale.

"Primal," it wasn't a dark ride like the "Time Tunnel." You walked through it, like a series of museum exhibitions. Which is honestly what it really was, all things considered. An animatronic wax museum, though we didn't use wax.

"People need to be able to spend as much time with each tableaux as they need to," Egger used to say. That was the word he used. "Need."

This was back when the park hadn't fully been planned out yet. The various "realms" weren't entirely set, so we weren't sure whether our attraction was going to go into what became the Realm of Man—"humanity" would probably have been better, but this was the '70s—or the Realm of Time.

It was focused on evolution, absolutely, but on specifically *human* evolution. And not just that, the evolution of our *emotions*, which, according to Egger, were the only things about us that were real.

"There is the Will," he said, and somehow, the way he said it, you could tell that it was capitalized. "And there is the spirit—our emotions—and everything else is just chemistry and geology, ghosts and shadows."

According to him, emotions were what set humans apart not just from animals but from the rest of the universe, and it was only through the development of emotions—"a cosmic accident," he called it—that we developed Will. "Animals do not have it," he said. "They do what they must because they must. They do not choose. Only we choose."

So, the idea was to take the person attending the attraction through the development of every human emotion in order, at least as Egger perceived them. We started in the dark, with Fear. "The oldest and strongest emotion of mankind is fear," it said in gold letters above the arched door to the black chamber, a quote attributed to H.P. Lovecraft who, you have to remember, was a more esoteric name back then.

That first room. It was my favorite. I always liked designing monsters, and we designed some doozies for that place. So, you went in through the door of the attraction and passed down this short hallway. Then you walked under those gilded words through a doorway covered with thick black curtains. The room on the other side was pitch dark; deep-in-a-cave dark. It had to be.

Then, there was a spark. Most of the rooms were shaped the same way; a circle, with a wide causeway running down the center, blocked off from the rest of the room by heavy bars. The causeway was metal, with a metal grid beneath your feet, so you could see down, as well as to either side. In this way, you were surrounded by the visions we had created.

In that first room, though, there was no way you could yet know that. The spark appeared off to your left, and then it grew, slowly, into a fire, which was really just a rotating bulb inside an amber-colored lamp that was designed to make it look like it was flickering.

Crouched around the fire were three hominids. One of the things that was made very clear to us from the start was that we were *not* to design classic movie cavemen. No John Richardson in *One Million Years B.C.* These should be accurate—as much as was possible—depictions of early hominids, our ancestors stuck somewhere between primate and modern humanity.

So, these hairy, unclothed things that, nonetheless, had the unmistakable marks of proto-humanity about their faces—at least, if we did our jobs right—were crouched there in the dark, huddled close to that one source of light, just as we expected the audience to do, gathering up against the railing on that side, peering at the tiny fragment of illumination we had provided, so that they weren't expecting it when the monsters came from the other side.

I remember that our first pitches for the monsters were far too tame for Egger. We made what were essentially Pleistocene predators. Saber-toothed cats and huge, shaggy bears and even a mammoth. "No," Egger said, when we brought him the sketches. "No, no, no. I don't want you to show me a field guide. I want you to show me *fear*."

The things that came out of that darkness on the right-hand side of the path would never have passed muster from the bean counters. I know that the big mantis shrimp thing in the "Time Tunnel" was everyone's favorite, even while it also caused plenty of kids to get off the ride crying, but these would have made it seem like chump change.

They walked on impossible stick legs, like a Dali painting of an elephant. Their skin was wasted away, clinging to unlikely bones and rags that hung from them to make them seem a bit like ghosts, but made of all-too-real flesh. Their faces were like horse skulls, their eyes pinpricks of light. When they raised limbs, they were praying mantis sickles of hardened bone.

The apparitions didn't come slowly. They appeared out of the dark in a rushing, breathing mass, swarming over and under and around the walkway, toward the fire. For a moment, they hovered over the hominids, who raised their fearful eyes toward the dark, and then the light went out.

So it went, throughout the development of the spectrum of human feeling. Egger had identified what he believed were the eight essential human emotions. Disgust, Exhilaration, Angst, Affection, and so on. I had helped design the monsters for the Fear display, but my baby was one called "Wrath & Regret."

It was *very* simple, compared to the Fear diorama, but I put a lot of work into it. The tableaux was nothing but two hominids, comparatively more advanced than the ones who had been gathered around the campfire. They appeared to be engaged in some sort of quarrel, with one pushing the other, then snatching up a rock and striking his fellow in the head.

As the blow fell, the lights in the room changed from naturalistic tones to red. The backdrop had been coated with a special paint so that, when the red light shined on it, the image of a skyline disappeared, replaced with an expressionist crash of red and black, like a comic book panel.

The injured hominid fell, and his companion stood above him, the rock still gripped in his hand. Then, the attacker dropped to his haunches, looking more closely at the wound that he had inflicted and, here's the part we were really proud of, the expression on his face changed as the blood began to pour out onto the ground. Anger to regret, all with one animatronic apeman.

"Nightmare blood," Egger called it. "It has to be the worst thing he has ever seen. Because, for the first time, he knows what it means, and he knows that *he* caused it. That it will never stop."

It helped that the blood was able to pour out and pool on what looked like just more sand, but was actually a porous substance, designed not to stain, that let the blood slowly sieve through and back into the apparatus under the floor, so it would be ready to pour out again when the next group arrived and the scenario repeated itself.

Do you need me to say what's happening? Okay, we are back from lunch and I guess we're going to talk a little bit about me and Theo now. Back then we didn't talk a lot about preferred pronouns and that sort of thing, but it was still striking the way Egger talked about Theo. He never used pronouns to describe her. Not ever. It was always Theophrastus.

"He says that I don't have a sex," Theo told me once, at a time where the double entendre possibilities of that phrase made us both giggle a little. "That I'm made up of 'equal parts masculine and feminine energy.' But I don't want to be. I just want to be a girl. I want to wear skirts and put on makeup and fall in love with a boy," here she put her hand against my cheek.

"How do you feel when we're together?" I asked her—it might have been part of that same conversation, it might have been another time—and she said that I made her feel, "Like it doesn't matter. Like I can be whatever I want to be, whoever I *am*, and you won't make me change."

I'm not going to say we were in love. We were both so young, I'm not sure either of us knew what we were doing, but we were certainly in *something*.

When Egger was awake and working, he kept Theo by his side at every moment. When I first hired on, I thought that she was his assistant, but she hardly ever did anything. He just made her stand there. She wore this weird thing, sort of like a poncho. You could see her blood pumping in her neck, her skin was so translucent.

She had long black hair, which really stuck out against her skin, and her eyes were so pale they looked like they didn't have any color at all. You had to get as close as she and I got later to see that they were blue.

After we'd been working together for a while, I realized that Egger didn't keep her around for anything that made any sense to anyone but him. "The presence of Theophrastus helps me to stay in touch," he would say.

"He doesn't treat me like a person," she told me. "He treats me like … not a *thing*, exactly, but more like a medium. If a person is nothing but emotion and will, like he says, then they're like a movie, being shown out of a projector. He treats me like the movie *screen*."

"Why don't you leave?" I asked her once.

"And go where? Do what? My parents didn't want me. They said that I 'wasn't what they expected.' Now my mom has abandoned the whole Thelema thing; she's a lawyer in Boston, I don't think she'd appreciate a reminder of her past. My dad was in Costa Rica the last I knew. They literally *gave* me to Cary. They signed papers. He's my legal guardian."

"But you're an adult now," I told her. "You can do anything you want."

"Can you?" she asked. It's why I remember this conversation so well, after all these years. I replay it in my head, still, to this day. I've had lots of other relationships since Theo. Two ex-wives. I've even got a daughter who's fourteen that I see every summer. But I still replay this one conversation, because I don't think I got it back then, and every year it seems like it makes more and more sense.

"What do you mean?" I asked her.

"Can you do anything you want?" she replied.

"Of course," I said, and kissed her. "And I want to be here."

"Then so do I."

Here's the thing. Back then, I was a kid who was in love, or lust, or just in the midst of a crush, or something. I was at my first real job as a concept artist. The world was simultaneously opening up around me at this heady pace and, at the same time, still so claustrophobically small in ways that I didn't even understand because I hadn't ever experienced anything else.

In that moment, I thought I was telling her the truth and, what's more, that I understood what she was asking. And, I'll admit it, I thought she was … sheltered, I guess. Naïve. She'd never had a normal life, like I had. Never gone to school. Her parents were part of this weird sex magic commune, and she'd been raised by Egger, a brilliant eccentric. I figured she just didn't understand anything else.

Now, I think she understood a lot more than I did, back then. Because the real answer to that question was that of course I *couldn't* do anything I wanted. I was a prisoner of everything that had come before that moment. Every prior moment slapping inexorable bonds of cause and effect on the moment that would come next.

Did I *want* to be working on an ultimately doomed attraction at an ambitious theme park? I certainly thought so then, but only because it was better than what I saw as my other options. I couldn't design my own stuff, because no one was willing to pay those bills. But it went far beyond that. I couldn't change my body by will alone. I was stuck being a person, stuck being Paul Kirby.

Sure, I could change my appearance with plastic surgery, though that was still a comparatively clumsy thing back in the '70s. I could change my name. But I couldn't be a dinosaur, if that's what I wanted. I couldn't stand on the surface of the sun.

I was trapped by circumstances, and by time. Just like Theo was. I was just arrogant enough not to realize it yet.

"I'm sorry that your parents didn't want you," I told her, or something to that effect.

"It already happened," she replied. "It's always happening." At the time, I thought she meant that people often rejected her. Now, I think I know better.

"I want you," I told her, trying to make her feel better, showing my ignorance. "I'll always want you."

"You do," she said, giving me a kiss. "And so you always will."

Let's talk about the word that Egger used to describe the ride we were building. "Thaumatrope." A disc, like I said, with two pictures, one on each side. Let's imagine a picture of flowers and a picture of a vase. Spin the disc, and the flowers are inside the vase. Leave it static, though, and you can see the flowers *or* the vase.

So, which is real? You can't see both at once except when they're together. The flowers are always separate from the vase. The vase is always empty. But, at the same time, the flowers are always in the vase.

The ride was doomed before it even began, if I haven't already made that clear. I don't think I realized it at the time. It was just work, and I did it every day, and I didn't think much beyond the next challenge, and then the next, and then the next. But there was no way anyone was ever going to sign off on it, not as a part of a theme park for kids.

It's easy to say that it's because the ride was "too scary" or "too violent," but in reality it's because it was too abstract. The history of the development of human emotions, as filtered through one weirdo's understanding of what that meant? That is way too fuzzy a concept to make a good ride.

When you're doing concept work, you need to be able to convey the concept as quickly and directly as possible. You should be able to identify a character from just a silhouette. People need to be able to take in information at a glance. Not because they're stupid or even lazy. Just because there is a *lot* of information out there, and if you get too esoteric, you're going to need people who are willing to come meet you at that point. It's not a crowd-pleaser.

So, I guess none of us should have been too surprised when they shut us down. I think we had finished five of the eight emotions. They weren't being built out in order. We all kinda worked together on Fear, but then different teams worked on the others, and we finished at different speeds.

I know we had completed Wrath & Regret, and I know that we were done with Affection—the blush-pink tinge of sunset and tangerine silhouetting a slow, tentative embrace that shrunk, gradually, to suggestive darkness. It was where Theo and I had snuck off to be together, when no one was working.

I think Disgust might have been the other one that was completed. An animatronic apeman shrinking away from this swampy muck that seemed to be rising up to meet him, maybe? I didn't spend as much time in it; it isn't as clear in my memory.

The others were all in various stages of partial-completion when the shutdown order came. "It doesn't matter," Egger said, when they handed him the proverbial pink slip. They tried to do it quietly, but he never did anything quietly. He flounced. Made sure we all knew it. "It's already done," he said. "It will always be done."

That night, he brought bottles and bottles of accelerant—paint stripper and stuff that they used in the animatronics—and poured it all over the inside of the ride. Then he struck a match.

Not really. He didn't really strike a match, I mean. He used a lighter that they had given him when he left NASA.

He had Theo with him. As always.

Egger died in the blaze. Theo died in a hospital bed two days later. If this was a movie, I would have rushed into the burning pavilion to save her. Or at least I would have tried to. But this was real life, and I didn't even know it happened until the next morning.

We had all been given rooms in a motel down the highway for the duration of the work, and I was on my motel bed, sketching out my own designs for my own projects while giant atomic ants menaced a desert town on the TV.

I guess someone on the crew had told Teague about Theo and I being together, because he got them to let me into the hospital to see her. She looked like a mummy, all head-to-toe in bandages. I thought about those old mummy movies with their reincarnated loves, and if I had been a poet instead of an artist, I might have tried to write something suitably melodramatic and saccharine on that theme.

Instead, I held the hand they'd let me hold and told her that I loved her. "You did," she replied, her voice barely a whisper. "So you always will."

That's the thing, you see. That's what I didn't get, all those years ago. When Theo and I were making love, when I was working on the ride. Once you make something, it's made. You can't unring that bell.

Oh, you can tear it down, burn the storyboards, destroy the pavilion, scrap the animatronics. I never set foot back inside what had been the building. I went down to the site, saw the burned remains—the rib-like supports that had held up the domes that encased each exhibition, each emotion, and I saw then, maybe for the first time, how much like a human body our ride had been. Each exhibition contained inside an organ, each piece needing the next piece to survive.

But no matter what you do to the physical structure, in that moment, it still exists, if only as a memory. No, that's not right, not even a memory, because a memory requires a host, someone to remember it, and this is more solid than that—more real.

Time isn't an arrow fired relentlessly forward, after all. That's what Theo was trying to tell me, over and over again. Matter can be neither created nor destroyed. Every crystallized moment of time still exists, trapped there forever in an endless loop, like a .gif forgotten on someone's Twitter feed, repeating itself over and over again in the dark, with no one to observe it. Every moment is infinite, and no moment can ever be completely eradicated. Because it *has* happened, it is *always* happening, over and over again. Big bang, big crunch.

So, someplace out there, our ride is still sitting, waiting for us to finish it up. Waiting for the first kids to clamber aboard. Somewhere, Theo and I are still together in the shadows of the Affection pavilion. The hominids are gathered close to their fire, the monsters are emerging from the dark, that first tentative embrace is underway, and the robot apeman waits for the nightmare blood to stop.

But it never will.

Author's Notes:

I guess Ben didn't learn from the *last* time he had asked me for a new story—"Manifest Destiny," earlier in this collection—because he approached me again to contribute something to *Tales from OmniPark*. Like "The House of Mars," this required me to do something I never do, except for hire: write a story in a shared universe.

In this case, the universe was our own—or one directly adjacent to our own. One in which the amusement park of the title had been a tourist destination for decades. I opted to write about the creation of the park—or, rather, the botched creation of a ride that never made the final cut.

Like "How to See Ghosts," which opens this collection, there's less of a fantastical element to this story than most of what I write—and, as with the other story I wrote for Ben, much of the *most* fantastical stuff is true, including pretty much all of that business about Jack Parsons and Thelema, Curtis Harrington and Marjorie Cameron Parsons, L. Ron Hubbard and sex magic and moon children.

My degree is in philosophy as well as English, and ever since I first studied it, any variation on Nietzsche's "Eternal Return of the Same" has always struck me as having the potential to be a unique kind of hell—or heaven. An eternal frozen moment, repeated over and over again like a .gif, like a stuck record. It's something I've brought out in a lot of stories, including ones earlier in this book. A version of it is in "Doctor Pitt's Menagerie," and in an earlier book you can find it in "Walpurgisnacht."

Here I just leaned into it a little harder. The title is, believe it or not, a near-quote from a line Ray Bradbury wrote about Disneyland, of all places, in a 1965 issue of the magazine *Holiday*. The essay was called "The Machine-Tooled Happyland," and the original quote actually went like this, "Robot animals feasting and being feasted upon as robot apeman waits in the wings for the nightmare blood to cease flowing."

The title was my attempt to pull the quote together from memory. Even after I had looked it up and knew the right one, I kept it as it was because I think it serves the story better.

AFTERWORD & ACKNOWLEDGMENTS

Obsession.

It's one of my favorite tropes, and it's a concept that has haunted my writing since the earliest days. Maybe my favorite thing in a story (besides a monster or two) is when a character wants something *so much* that the longing for it becomes its own thing, larger than the object of that longing ever was. Until the obsession becomes not the means to an end, but the end in itself. Until it hollows them out, consumes them, drives them to terrible, sometimes superhuman acts in their desperation to reach something that has become so monolithic in their own hearts that, were they to finally achieve it, now it would probably mean nothing. The goal is no longer the thing; the obsession has taken its place.

Not every story in this collection deals in those themes, but many do, just as many in my previous collections have. What keeps me coming back to writing these kinds of stories, as much as anything, is one impossible-to-name drive, one that I mentioned in the notes to the title story all the way back at the beginning of this volume. The desire for the magic to be real, even—and maybe especially—if it kills you.

Maybe more so than any other book I've published thus far,

the stories in this collection span an enormous gulf of my writing life. The oldest publication dates back all the way to 2009, though there are stories here that I wrote the first drafts of even before that. At the same time, there are stories here that I wrote *and* published as recently as 2021. What ties them together, I hope, besides that they were all written by me, is that shared sense of longing, of obsession, of reaching for something beyond all of *this*.

There's a movie I really like, *The Prestige* from 2006. And one of the reasons I really like it is because it gets that longing, that drive. There's a scene where Hugh Jackman's dying magician explains the reason for his obsession, and it's a scene that has influenced my own fiction ever since. "The audience knows the truth," he says. "The world is simple, miserable, solid all the way through. But if you can fool them, even for a second…then you can make them wonder. And you get to see something very special."

That's why I come back to these kinds of stories, over and over again. I want to fool you, just for a second. And, while I'm at it, I want to be fooled, too.

As always, a book like this—any book, really—is the work of diverse hands. I may have written and rewritten (and revised and rewritten ad nauseum) all of these words, but plenty of other people had to come together to make this volume happen. Ross Lockhart, my publisher, and my cover artist Nick Gucker, who have helped to bring my last three collections to life, are at the top of that heap, along with Scott R. Jones who designed the cover and everyone else at Word Horde.

Everyone who originally published one of these stories did their part in getting us to this point, too, and they are too numerous to name. Then there are all the people who have read my stuff, given me advice and counsel, lent an ear or a shoulder over the years. There are all of my peers who have said kind words about my work, and Silvia Moreno-Garcia who wrote the introduction. There are my friends and family, who have stood by me, supported me, put up with me, and encouraged me. And then, of course, there's you, dear reader, who (hopefully) bought this collection, or got it from the library, or received it as a gift, or found it in an abandoned railway station next to a mysterious skeleton key.

For all those people and so many others, my sincerest thanks, and I hope that, just for a moment, I made you wonder, if only a little…

ABOUT THE AUTHOR

Orrin Grey is a skeleton who likes monsters, as well as a writer, editor, and amateur film scholar who was born on the night before Halloween. *How to See Ghosts* is his fourth collection of weird stories. You can find him online at orringrey.com.

Lightning Source UK Ltd.
Milton Keynes UK
UKHW011105151122
412237UK00005B/54

9 781956 252057